LOVE HAPPENS
Eventually

FEYI AINA

First Published in Great Britain in 2020 by
LOVE AFRICA PRESS
103 Reaver House, 12 East Street, Epsom KT17 1HX
www.loveafricapress.com

Text copyright © Olufunmilola Adeniran, 2020

ISBN: 978-1-914226-03-8
Also available as ebook

Acknowledgments

I want to express my gratitude to God for his grace in my life and for his words of wisdom. He gave me the talent, and sent people my way to help translate this beautiful story from just an idea in my head, to a book I can share with the world.

I'm grateful to my family and friends who have in one way or the other supported me and encouraged me to be the author I have become.

Akinpelumi, you are more than my confidant, you're my best friend and the father of my children. You are my rock. You encourage me to go for what I want every day that we share together and you don't complain too much when at 2am I'm up in bed disturbing your sleep with the light from my laptop. I'm more than eternally grateful to have you in my life and I can't stress it enough, I love being married to you.

Special thanks go to Kitan, my number one beta reader for this particular work; to Zee, for her invaluable advice in the editorial process and for pushing to get the best out of me. Also, Kiru my hero, coming across your books opened my eyes in ways I cannot begin to explain. I'm grateful to you. Thank you for taking a chance on me.

Seun, Goke, Olayemi, Bro Dan, you believed in me when I was still writing in the closet. I appreciate you because you gave me courage to share my work with the world.

To every Nigerian who reads this book and laughs with understanding at our little quirks as a nation, thank you. It was what I observed in our society that helped make this dream of mine a reality.

Thank you, all.

Chapter One

I hate babies!

Okay, I know that doesn't sound right, or maternal, or like something a woman should say out loud or even think about. And I'm an African woman, for that matter. But I don't care, and I don't apologize for it.

My mother says I'm supposed to love babies. I'm supposed to know how to calm them, burp them, back them, sing, and do all that fancy stuff women like to do when they hold babies. But I don't. Apparently, something went wrong somehow and somewhere with me, sometime between my childhood when I loved playing with dolls and my adulthood. Something that never got fixed, that I don't know how to fix … nor do I want to fix, to be perfectly honest.

I never know what to do with babies. So you can't blame me when Aunty Norma hands me her fifth child and I hold him—or her, or it? Whatever! —at arm's length and stare like it's an alien from outer space.

The squirmy thing curves into a huge C-shape, and I am anything but awed.

"Aunty Norma." I clear my throat to hide uneasiness. "How much time are you going to take doing what you're doing?"

I have my uses, and they are plenty, and they are great … but they don't involve handling babies, or pretending to like them.

"Abeg hold pikin, I dey come," she says.

My heart, instead of melting, begins to throttle. My palms sweat, my arms ache, and I grimace. I really don't know what to do with the baby.

Everyone I know loves to carry them, feed them, and kiss their soft baby cheeks while murmuring a lot of gibberish that adults love to mutter when they hold babies. I'm sorry. I'm just not made that way.

There are babies all around me. Friends, family, heck, two of my sisters have babies. But my interaction ends on the naming day when I drop off a gift, peek in the crib, and wave at the little tots. I usually do not carry them, and no, I never want to.

The baby gurgles, and I bite my lower lip. It has curly black hair slathered in copious amounts of fragrant oil, and a little pink bow by the side. It's a girl. I still keep her at arm's length as we both examine each other and admit one salient truth: we don't like each other.

While I am good at hiding my feelings, my rival is not. She turns down the corners of her mouth, and her eyes glaze over.

"*No!*" I murmur as the face crumples into descending protest. *Don't even … don't cry.*

She opens her mouth, whimpers for a moment, and the sound fades into oblivion. I'm not deceived; there is more where that came from.

"Aunty Norma," I yell and look at her. "Come and take your baby!"

Aunty Norma, who is winding a tough-looking piece of damask *gele* with all the strength she can muster around my sister's head, ignores me.

My younger sister, Olamide, squeezes her eyes shut and mutters under her breath at the same time. "Ewo ooooooooo …"

I hear it, but Aunty Norma can't, or chooses not to. She places a foot on the wooden frame of the bed right beside Olamide's thighs and pulls both ends of the papery fabric hard. I wince right along with my sister and hunch my shoulders. She has a brand-new head of braids underneath that *gele*, and I can feel the hurt all over my own scalp.

"Aunty Norma! *Ye pa!* Yeeee!"

Olamide's cry coincides with the baby's next sound.

It's loud. I am embarrassed to say that as sophisticated as Olamide can sometimes be, pain brings out the villager in her.

"*Wetin?* Abeg, no fall my hand. Make your *gele* collapse in front of our in-laws hen?" Aunty Norma says as she winds one arm of the *gele* towards the back of Olamide's head.

The baby is howling, Olamide is yelling, and I am panicking.

"Haba, it's too tight nau!"

"Olamide, hold still o."

"Aunty Norma, it's paining me nau!"

"*Iyawo*, endure. *You think say na only teeth dem dey use do oge?*"

Enitan, my youngest sister, giggles from the other end of the bedroom where Aramide—Olamide's twin—is busy fixing her own *gele*. Interestingly, it's a much quieter affair.

The baby is screaming, and I'm lowering and raising my hands with her still in them while looking around the room for possible help.

Kenny, a cousin from my dad's side of the family, is painting brows into her brow-less face in front of a mirror. Imisi, another cousin, is stuffing herself into her lace skirt and blouse, wondering where all the space in it went to. Aramide is now helping Enitan. No one is taking this baby from me.

"It's like this dress has shrunk!" Imisi announces.

"When I tell you that you are getting rounder, you tell me the scales have not shifted ground since the last time you stood on them," Aunty Norma says with a hiss.

"But they haven't!" Imisi wails. "I still wore this dress last month with no issues."

"Be asking me how the washing machine shrunk your dress," Aunty Norma says, tone unkind.

Kenny snorts. "I've been telling you to join the keto diet since, and you keep posting me."

"Go away." Imisi eyes her above Enitan's head. "I don't know what you're doing keto for."

"I'm doing it to be healthy."

"You are thin and healthy enough."

"Health is not measured in the size of one's body!" Kenny says. "My new ketofied body is blazing!"

Imisi clicks her tongue. "Health is not measured in the size of one's body! So leave me, madam keto."

The baby decides to take her scream a notch higher, and so does my panic. "Aunty Norma!"

"Femi, find a way to keep that baby quiet *nau*," Aramide snaps from the other end of the room. "Everyone else is busy."

I toss her a venomous look and swing the baby from side to side. I'm two years older. A ringed finger and a pair of cute children don't give her the right to talk to me anyhow. These days, Aramide seems to think they do.

Aunty Norma turns to me. "Femi, *na like that dem they hold pikin?*"

"*Oya*, come and carry your baby," I say in my defence.

"*Yee!* Aunty Norma, this thing is giving me headache already!"

"To do *oge* requires pain and sacrifice. You look nice. Wait, let me show you mirror."

"Aunty Norma!" I call out as she dashes to the corner of the room, yanks the mirror out from in front of Kenny, and hurries back to Olamide.

Kenny turns around, angry.

"*Wetin? Na you dey wan come see? Your name na iyawo?*" She hisses. "*Abegi!*"

The baby's eyes are squeezed shut, and its mouth has formed a round O. She is howling in cycles of high and low sounds so I swing faster, feeling a bit like Alice in Wonderland. *"Don't turn into a Cheshire cat, don't turn into a Cheshire cat,"* I murmur.

There is mucus all over her nostrils and tears all over her face. I'm thinking of dropping her on the bed.

"Femi, put Jolomi on your shoulder *nau!*" Aramide shouts.

I toss her another venomous stare that doesn't sink past the skin of her face. "With all this mucus?"

"Yes." Aramide doesn't care much about the looks I give her. "So she can stop crying."

"Dance and sing for her," Enitan advises. "Turn her onto her back and hold her close."

"But she's all sticky!" I moan.

"*Sisi Eko, as if you no go born pikin one day. Wait jo, I dey come.*" Aunty Norma displays the mirror to Olamide who checks out her head from all angles. The *gele* is actually beautiful.

My mum, God bless her soul, barges in at that moment.

"Olamide, your husband's people are here already." She takes one look at me and her mouth drops open. "Femi! What are you doing?"

"It won't stop yelling!" I say while swinging Jolomi.

She runs to me and scoops Jolomi out of my hands.

"Is that how to carry a baby, *ehen*? Jolomi darling, Jolomi sweetie, don't mind Aunty Femi." Cradling the baby, she dances from one foot to the other and rocks her. I watch, totally divorced from the actions. "Femi, pass me the wipes, please. Let me clean her face."

Wipes? I can do that. I can handle non-living things.

I reach across the bed for a 'Winnie-the-pooh' rubber envelope and pull a piece out. The baby has quietened now and is cooing in my mother's arms. My mother's face is full of love and delight, emotions that never fail to run from me when I hold a baby. I shudder, because she looks like she doesn't mind having another one at sixty-three.

She collects the wipe from me with a brief glance and reserves her comment. I can hear it however. I know she will say it when time and opportunity bring us both together alone.

"Let's hurry up!" she says out loud. "Daddy and Aunty Ladepe are the only ones out there welcoming guests. They need to feel like we have family."

I smile. I like Aunty Ladepe. She is my grandfather's youngest wife, and she doesn't act like the world needs to respect her because she married the great Chief Awotunde of Ibadan land.

Aunty Norma steps back, looks at Olamide, and starts shaking her shoulders from side to side. "*Iyawo olele, Iyawo asiko, Iyawo tuntun, Omidan, Omogee, Arewa titi lai lai.* Aramide, *oya* come and finish her makeup."

Olamide turns to us, wincing. "What do you think? Is it fine?"

Aramide smiles at her twin. "It's perfect."

"Is this *gele* not too tight, Norma?" my mum asks. The baby is clinging to her chest, looks content and is—annoyingly—quiet.

"No *naaau*, mummy." Aunty Norma steps up to adjust it. "It has to grip well so it doesn't fall off."

"It's tight!" Olamide allows a frown to cross her face. "I'm going to remove it as soon as possible."

"Not before you welcome your in-laws," my mother replies.

"Not before I collect my money from them," Aunty Norma shouts in her naturally loud voice. "*Dem go see today, today.*"

She bends down and proceeds to shake her huge, round buttocks in my direction in one of the famed Ibo dance styles. I roll my eyes. I have not told anyone in the family that I do not plan to wear *gele* at my own wedding engagement, if ever I have any.

My wedding will be at night, on a beach, with just twenty people. I will be in a white Grecian dress, with my hair down one side of my face and a flower clip holding the other side above my ear. This idea is one my mum will fight, and I'm ready.

That brief moment of thought makes me realise that I want a wedding. My three younger sisters are in various stages of marriage, and I'm nowhere near starting the journey.

Despite complaints, Olamide looks pretty in the well-made, burnt orange head gear. The champagne coloured lace skirt and blouse is *Aso Ebi* from Enitan's wedding two years ago, but it doesn't matter because this is just the family introduction. All we need is for her to look pretty for show today. Besides, no one else is wearing theirs.

"*Oya, oya o!*" my mother cajoles. "Our guests are waiting."

I hear Imisi fussing harder than ever over her clothes and Enitan pointing her to me.

"Femi may have one of her numerous Ankara dresses from when she was a size up."

Yep, I was a size or two up about a year ago. My sisters had hounded me about looking young and *'snaggable'* so it wouldn't hurt my chances at marriage. So I did everything I could to drop the extra weight.

"Let's go ooo! Ara, stay with Ola. It's not time for her to come out yet," my mother shouts.

"Femi, won't you tie *gele*?" Aunty Norma asks from behind her.

I'm the first one out of the room. Tie *gele* ke, and have Aunty Norma cutting off the blood supply to my head 'til I faint?

I run smack into one of Aramide's four-year-old twins in the corridor. The boy slams me in the shin with the toe of his boot, and I howl in pain. '*Terrible,*' as I call him, runs into the bedroom, excited about being chased by his twin sister and the younger two of the rest of Aunty Norma's children.

"No running in the house!" I hear Aramide caution from inside the room.

"Leave them. When I remove one slipper from my feet now," Aunty Norma says. "*If I catch una—*"

The children scream and run back outside, shoving past my mother and me. They're ecstatic. There is food, and music, and all the cousins they don't see often to play with. I've been at that age before, where the worries of the adults meant nothing, and family gatherings were just opportunities to run round and play to my heart's content. Now I'm older, there's a lot to stress me out at parties and less time to play around.

A robust figure bursts into the carpeted hallway decked in Gupion lace and lots of gold jewellery.

"*Iyawo* mi," she rushes at me, and all of a sudden I'm swathed in scratchy lace, thick perfume, and hard as nails bangles. "*Oba ni fe e, nitoto.* Finally, the Lord be praised."

It's Mama Bimpe, my father's older stepsister. She holds me at arm's length and examines me. "*Arewa,* all our prayers have been answered! Someone has come to take you away from this household. *Oluwa modupe!* The devil will know shame all the days of his life. Only sounds of praise and rejoicing shall be known in this household. Forward ever, backward never. The crowning beauty of ..."

I'm more than mortified as my mother tries to get a word in.

"I've been saying it. Such a beautiful girl, and not married yet," she continues, loud enough for everyone to hear. "Eh, I've been wondering if the men were all blind, or if it was you hiding from them. Thank God one of them has decided to show face and hide all our nakedness. Where is your *gele*?"

"Welcome, Mama Bimpe," my mother butts in from behind me. "Your *iyawo* is inside the room."

"*Ehen* ..." she frowns. "Is it not Nifemi that is getting married?"

"No, it's Olamide."

"Ah, sorry my child, the Lord will provide the big bone of your own bones in time." She pushes me aside and rushes into the room past my mother. "*Iyawo mi* ..." she starts the tirade all over again.

I lean against the wall and put my leg down. I'm not sure if it's pain from the shin slam or the sting of her well-meaning prayer. I'm hurting, however, and I can't exactly tell where from. So when Imisi asks to get something else to wear, I'm more than happy to take her to my room and lose myself in something I have some form of actual control over.

Everything is a blur from then on as events unfold rapidly. Korede, the groom, sits in our living room with his family. His father, Chief Okanlanwon, is a mild-mannered man in a simple beige lace outfit. His mother, the more extroverted parent, is dressed in a dark brown and gold Ankara. She has a domineering personality that keeps every member of the groom's party of ten somewhat in check.

The ceremony begins with an opening prayer. Mama Bimpe stands to speak for our family as the '*Alaga Ijoko*.' We introduce one another, and there is a little joke about coming back for me when I stand to introduce myself. The joke is thanks to my mother. She can't resist mentioning that I'm single and searching. I see the groom's uncle checking me out after then, and I avoid all eye contact with him.

We serve them *amala* with *ewedu* as well as white rice with fish, goat meat, and peppered snails. They would like to see their bride come out before they touch any part of the meal. Imisi comes out first, and the spokeswoman for the groom's family refuses her.

"This is not our wife." She waves both hands at Aunty Norma. "Our wife is the most beautiful girl in the compound today."

Imisi goes in, and Jumoke replaces her, covered in a lace headscarf. Thirteen years old and already as tall as a lamp post, Aunty Norma's first daughter is a budding beauty. She is not the one the visiting family has spoken for, however.

"Our wife has a slim shape and wide hips, good for birthing sons. She is not too tall, not too short, not too dark, and not too fair. She is Agbani Darego."

There is laughter. I laugh, as well, a hollow sound that's in between being happy and being upset. I'm wondering which other young girl aside Jumoke will be brought in my stead if I decide to get married since my sisters had decided to skip to the next stage of life before me. Imisi is in a relationship. Perhaps Jumoke will marry before me.

Jumoke married. It is a thought, brief and scary.

Olamide comes out covered in bridal lace. She holds the lace with both hands and steps gingerly towards her in-laws who all give a shout of delight when she arrives. Her smile is enchanting, and Korede is all smiles at the sight of her. I'm happy he loves her. It's the most important thing. The mood in the house thereafter is light and easy, an atmosphere that comes with acceptance. Our family has agreed to give my sister away to the visitors.

I sit with our grandpa in the balcony later. We listen to the sounds of cars zooming around in the streets below us. We hear Aunty Norma and Mama Bimpe scouring leftover food in plastic packs while my mother goes round, thanking everybody for coming.

Grandpa tells me his take on marital life from the perspective of a guy who has had three wives. "Don't ever lose yourself in the children and home-making. Don't take your husband for granted, and don't expect too much from him. Look the other way. Not everything that displeases you should be brought to the limelight."

"I'm not the one getting married," I say.

"But you will one day."

I rub the back of his hand. There goes the subtle reference to my unmarried state again. When everyone says it, I don't bother to hide my irritation. When it comes from Grandpa, it's different. It sounds caring and genuine, like he wants me taken care of.

"You should come and visit me in Ibadan," he continues. "I don't see you as often anymore, and it's not like it's a man that has kept you this busy."

I stare out through the balcony railings. "My job keeps me busy. Marriage is not all a woman is made for, but I guess it would be nice to have someone."

"So why haven't you decided? You are an enchanting girl. I know the men are flocking."

I shrug and think about the last jerk I had dated. The first time he slapped me, the shock of it broke my heart. It wasn't so much that it was unexpected—and painful. It was more that he had done it. The second time landed me an appointment with an eye specialist—I knew then I had to end it.

"You're too focused on career to let a man tie you down." He says this to me in Yoruba, and I know what he means. "You cannot go at life on your own."

"I know, but I want to be able to have both marriage and a career. Not sure it will ever happen."

"It will." He sighs out the words. "I'm just not going to be there to see it. I know my time is up. I hear angels singing every day now. It is beautiful music."

I am alarmed. My grandfather is ninety, but I don't want to lose him. "You still have ten years."

"My dear, I've spent a long time on this Earth."

"Wait a while longer, please. Maybe I'll find someone within the next one year. Then you can be at my wedding and give me away."

His response is a smile. "Your father will give you away, and I will watch with pride, wherever I am. I can't displace your father, not while he's alive."

"You can both give me away. I know Daddy won't mind."

He doesn't say anything, so I lay my head on his frail shoulder. It's a little game we often play, of speeches and love, of wishes and dreams. I pray for him to live a little longer, and we listen to the night sounds of the city that never sleeps.

My grandpa will return to Ibadan in the morning. He has always believed the air is better there than here in Lagos and he never stays a day longer than he has to. He's probably right. He has ninety years to show for it.

Chapter Two

The day I turned thirty-five, I woke up in bed with an epiphany.

'Love is elusive, and only a few find it.'

I had accepted the idea that marriage was maybe not written in my future. And so I stopped searching—consciously, that is.

The guy on the supermarket aisle across from me was not trying to catch my eye; he was looking for something on the upper stands behind me. The guy I bumped into at the pharmacy store entrance had a nice smile, but only to communicate his apologies, not because he was hoping to obtain my number. The boring blind date from Aramide's office had been more interested in the sound of his voice than in mine. So I'd sipped my drink and studied the fancy restaurant he'd brought me to, while he droned on and on about accounting principles.

In truth, my eagerness to be hitched has faded into a comfortable understanding of myself and the fact that there is more to me than being married. So I'm rarely bothered.

"When are you getting married sef?"

Pariola—our cousin on my dad's side—throws my least favourite question in my face as we sit around the table at my cousin Solape's noisy, crowded wedding reception. That question has been asked of me more times this year than I can count, and I give my usual answer: silence.

In that moment, I spot a fair-skinned guy at a table by himself. He's nodding to the music around us and sipping from a bottle of Smirnoff Ice.

Dear God. I look away. *I have said no guys!*

"Marriage starts with a relationship," Olamide replies. "She's not in a relationship."

"Does she even want to get married?" Kenny throws in. "I don't think so. When last did you go on a date, Femi?"

Olamide laughs. "Femi's idea of a good time is binge-watching *Pointless.*"

"*Pointless*?" Pariola looks confused. "What's that?"

Aramide hisses, "One boring British TV game show, where you have to give obscure answers to weird questions to win."

I move a dessertspoon of strawberry ice-cream into my mouth and ignore them. It's none of their business, really.

Kenny looks even more confused. "Obscure answers?"

"Say for example, the things you can find in a first aid box. The popular answers would be bandages, plaster, and antiseptic solutions. Tweezers, however, that would be a pointless answer, because no one would think of it."

Pariola casts a bewildered look at me. "So is she finding it hard to get dates, or is she just that 'not into dating'? 'Cause I can get her dates."

"Ask her," Aramide snaps, turning angry eyes in my direction. "I got her one with Paul from my office. Guy said she was as mute as a wooden pole."

"Perhaps Paul is not her type," Olamide offers.

"I don't see her having a type," Aramide says. "She was asking the guy what he does with his money, like has he heard of financial instruments and money markets? That type of thing."

Everyone looks at me.

"It was an ice breaker," I say in my defence.

I'm amazed at how they're able to have this conversation with loud music and the MC's voice butting from the speakers every now and then.

"It was pointless." Aramide sounds cross.

"What is wrong in trying to scope out a guy's future before you commit to something long-term?" I can't believe these girls.

"On a first date, Femi," Pariola moans. "You should be concentrating on getting him to even want a second date."

"He called her boring and too intense for his liking."

I roll my eyes at Aramide. "Don't you guys have something better to do?"

"I've a good mind to add you to Sexy-Naija." Aramide pops a piece of puff into her mouth.

"Sexy what?" Olamide's eyes widen. "What is that?"

"An online dating website." Pariola scrunches up her mouth and nose. "Been there, done that, rubbish!"

"My friend found her boyfriend there o." Aramide nods to convince us. "They've been dating for six to seven months."

Pariola points a finger at her. "Not enough time for a guy to show his true colours."

"At least my friend is in a relationship." Aramide points her own finger at me. "She clearly needs help."

"Let her answer for herself. Femi, do you need help with guys?"

I don't answer. I'm busy studying Mr. Cool Fine Guy who looks like he's not with the other people at his table.

I notice everyone looking at me again. "Must I have a guy in my life?"

"You do realize that everyone is getting hitched!" Olamide says. "We don't want you to be alone. It's been a year."

"Six months." I frown at her and stick a toothpick in a piece of puff puff on her plate. "And what makes you think I'm not in a relationship?"

"You're not. I know that for a fact," Aramide butts in.

"What happened with this guy, Michael abi Muyiwa?" Pariola snaps her fingers several times as she tries to recall the name. "That one that was busy going up and down like he has paid bride price during your wedding, Ara."

I twist in my seat so I can have a fairly good view of Mr. Cool. He is well-dressed, very attractive, and happens to be looking my way just then. Our eyes meet, and I look away. I can't believe I'm doing it again, allowing myself to hope that he might be Mr. Right.

"Matthew," Kenny hisses. "That one that was busy dating all the girls in her office."

"She found a note-book," Olamide says, "with a list of girls who had seen the insides of his bedroom. Needless to say, he wasn't looking to settle."

Aramide nudges me. "Not like you're looking to, anyway."

I'm caught halfway towards glancing at Mr. Cool Fine Guy again.

"Yeah, well done, you guys can keep having discussions about my love life like I'm not even here."

I roll my eyes and turn to find Mr. Cool actually looking at me.

He lifts his eyebrows in two quick successive moves, and I don't know whether to be flattered or irritated.

When guys are too forward, they turn me off. When they are too laidback, I turn them off. When they are too fine, I think they'll never be able to keep a monogamous relationship. When they are not fine, I'm not even interested. When they are too quiet, I give up and get tired of doing the chasing. When they are too talkative, I want them to shut up and never call me again.

So there you have it. It's a no-brainer why I'm still on the shelf and inching towards my sell-by date.

"Okay, how can we help?" Olamide says. "What kind of men are you looking for?"

Pariola gives a faraway look.

"Hmmmn, rich, handsome, handy around the house, and fair-skinned," she nods at the table behind us. "Like that guy in the light brown Atiku."

I frown and turn towards Mr. Cool Fine Guy. He is wearing light brown Atiku. I hadn't even noticed. Pariola has had her back to him, talking in all this while. How in the world did she spot him?

"Which guy?" Kenny twists backwards in order to see.

Pariola glares at her. "Stop it, you'll spook him!"

Aramide stretches upwards in her seat opposite them and squeals. "Oh, I see him. How do you know he's not married?"

"Ring finger," she says and taps hers. "No mark tells me he's never worn one."

"How do you know he is rich?" Olamide asks.

She gives us all a coy look. "Car keys on the table beside his drink, ninety per cent positive it's a Range."

My eyes swing to Mr. Cool Fine Guy. I hadn't even noticed anything beyond the fact that he is alone. His key is one of those transponder devices that start cars without an ignition. They usually don't come cheap.

"It might not be his," I say, quite positive he'd borrowed the car from a friend or parent.

"He has an iPhone 11, and he is not making an effort to flaunt it. That's how you separate the haves from the wanna-haves." Pariola sips her drink and winks at me.

I am taken aback. How had she managed to spot his phone?

"Impressive," Aramide says. "What you just did is an art! Can you teach Femi how?"

"Excuse me," I interject. "I know how to get dates just fine. Like that guy Pariola was just analysing, I actually saw him first."

"And you are still here, trying to prove to us that you don't need help." Pariola grabs her purse off the table and stands to her feet. "Let me get to working him then, before you get any ideas. Wish me luck."

With that, she turns around and heads over to take a seat by the guy.

I let out a growl of frustration. Pariola is slim with an hourglass shape, an interesting face, and a great fashion sense. She's more likely to keep Mr. Cool Fine Guy interested than I am.

Okay, I'm not putting myself down, but Pariola has mastered flirtatious moves down to a tee. The bell-like laughter, pouty lips, gentle touch on the target's shoulder—thigh if you are bold enough. The rapt attention, fluttering eyelids, and the lean-in towards the guy to let him know you are interested.

She tried to teach them to me once, and I'd ended up looking like an idiot in front of the guy I was trying them on. He was quite rude, though I was just using him as target practice.

"You are supposed to do them without him noticing," she'd corrected.

"Thank you," I had replied. "I'll just do it my own way next time."

"Oh, really, and what way is that?" she'd asked. "Put your nose in a book, and pretend like the guy is bothering you?"

I marvel at how natural she is at tossing her hair and laughing out loud. She places a casual hand on his shoulder, and Mr. Cool Fine Guy seems impressed.

"Okay, Femi." Aramide scoots closer to me. "What is your problem?"

I'm short of words as I try to convince myself that Pariola could have the guy and I didn't care.

"Femi." Aramide shakes me by the elbow. "What kind of guy?"

"What, a cerebral guy. Okay, can you guys just leave me alone?"

"What's that?" Kenny grunts and looks at me, "A disease condition?"

"Right," Aramide says with a frown. "Talk to me like I didn't go to secondary school."

I sigh. "Someone I can carry on a conversation with without getting bored. Someone smart, and funny who doesn't think that the only things that make me beautiful are my external physical features."

"Oh, so you want someone who loves you for your liver?" Kenny sounds sarcastic in spite of her feigned ignorance.

I pick up my half-empty bottle of water. "Yes, and why not?"

"And Lord knows she has loads of that!" Aramide murmurs out of the side of her lips.

I know what they mean by me having loads of liver, and the pun is intended. I can do and say the kind of things people often back down from. Especially if I know I'm right, even if my opponent is older. Sometimes, I think it's the reason why Akpan hit me.

Kenny gives me this look like she can't believe what I'm saying. "So intelligence is what blows your bubble."

"Hush, Kenny," Aramide replies. "At least we are getting somewhere with her."

"Authenticity is what blows my bubble. Being real, and comfortable enough to be yourself and talk about the things that matter. Not shoes or houses or cars or how rich you are. Plus, I do want someone who loves me for the mental, intellectual me, liver included."

Just then, Pariola returns to her seat and sinks into it.

"What happened?" Olamide asks.

"He has a girlfriend." She reaches out to pick up her drink and take a sip out of it. "You bet I'm going to get an earful from Sola about making a move on her best friend's boyfriend."

We all turn. There is a well-dressed lady standing over Mr. Cool Fine Guy with her hands on her hips. She's giving him a scolding loud enough that we—I'm thinking Pariola— can hear. I feel sorry for her. Mr. Cool had in fact been putting it out there that he was available.

"She can't be the best friend if she isn't the maid of honour," Kenny murmurs.

"And she's not even fine," Olamide adds.

"Hey, don't look at them." Pariola widens her eyes and stands up. "I'm going to dance. Who's with me?"

Dancing—the act of looking like a fool while feeling like a pro, with people cheering you on as you make a colossal fool of yourself. I hate dancing, but the music is intoxicating. I know she wants to get away from the angry girlfriend behind us.

"I'm in." Olamide stands up. "It's the only way we're ever going to get into the wedding video at this rate. The camera man just keeps following the couple, no one else."

Aramide hisses, "Before nko?"

Olamide and Pariola dance to the centre stage. A lot of our family is there, bitten by the dancing bug. They are loose, loud, and inebriated, from all appearances. Naira notes explode into the air from time to time and drift downwards like cotton candy. Aramide's twins weave in between the crowd, picking up the pieces wherever they can.

I am not amazed at how happy everyone is. Parties bring us together—weddings, house-warming ceremonies, naming ceremonies, birthdays, funerals, or general get-togethers. Then we all scatter into our different lives and don't see each other again. Until another occasion pops up and we all come to catch up with what's new, and who's where, and what additions we have in the family by birth and marriage. It's great to belong to a Nigerian family. Home or abroad, we know how to rock life and squeeze the essence from within it.

"See how these children are embarrassing me like their father doesn't have any money!"

Aramide stands up to go join the fun. Her twins are fighting over money one of them had picked up from the ground. I laugh. It's a ploy to go and partake in the dancing. Aramide can't sit around and let music go to waste. She, like most of my family members, is not made that way.

I see the wedding favours and cringe. That's another thing that is not going to happen at my wedding. Goody bags with my spouse's and my faces plastered all over it, filled with toothpaste and sachets of detergent thrown in by well-intending family members looking to give something away as a sign of their contribution to your wedding.

I catch myself thinking about weddings again and hate the girls for asking me questions.

As Aunty Norma hurries towards us, Kenny stands up.

"You know," she says, raising a finger in the air. "My husband did want me to meet his buddies. That's him over there signalling." She points in the direction of the hall where the in-laws have formed an association around a table. "Honey-boo—"

She runs off before Aunty Norma skids to a stop beside me. "Femi love!"

"No! Aunty Norma, hire a nanny. I—" The baby is deposited in my arms before I can complete my statement. She hurries to join the others on the dance floor.

I panic and look down at my charge. With hands clenched into fists and a frown between her brows, she looks ready for a fight, and I'm just not in the mood. She is calm, however, full too, judging by her tummy size.

Someone pulls out a chair beside me, and I look up to see Korede plop into it.

"Hi," he says.

The baby's eyes flutter open and then slowly slide to a close. "Ssshhh! Can't you see she's trying to sleep?"

"Ah, sorry, I just saw you sitting alone and decided to come and keep you company."

"Go keep your fiancée company. She is over there, dancing."

"In a group of your ever-boisterous family?" He wrinkles his nose at me. "I doubt she needs me. You, on the other hand, might be interested in meeting—"

"Your uncle?" I give him an incredulous look. "No."

"Come on, the guys want to meet you. But of course, priority goes to my uncle. Loosen up, come and sit with us."

I look over at the table he is coming from. "Those noise-clattering, wine-babbling, high as a kite twits? No, thank you."

"Wow, Olamide did say you liked using big words."

"I'm carrying a baby and she just fell asleep. I'm sorry, I'm declining."

Imisi pats my shoulder as she passes by. "Sister Femi, Sola is about to throw her bouquet. Let's go."

I eye Imisi. *Catch what?* That little tradition of catching flowers and hoping to be the next person to get hitched is kind of lost on me. It reeks of desperation. "Have fun."

Korede notices my eye movements. "So you don't want to sit with us, you don't want to meet any guys, you don't want to catch the bouquet, and you don't look like you really want to hold that baby. I get it.

You want to be alone, grow old alone, and die in your bed alone with no one to tell anyone that you are gone."

I make a face at him. "That is not going to make me meet your uncle!"

"Fine, but don't call me when you are looking for someone to go to Aunty Ladepe's birthday with." So saying, he gets to his feet.

Twerp! I really don't have to go with anyone. I will be up to my ears in arrangements with no time to moan about my dateless status.

Just then, the music slows to a stop, the dancing ceases, and the MC announces the bride's intention to throw her bouquet.

My mum signals for me to join the chorus of girls forming a cluster by the one-man band stand. I raise a finger upwards and then point it sharply down at the sleeping baby. I don't think she gets me, however; she keeps right on signalling.

For once, I'm glad Aunty Norma chose me to watch over her little tot. I'm not joining that 'bouquet catching' charade.

I fix my eyes on Solape. Her chief bridesmaid adjusts her train on the podium. She's been excited all day. Her husband looks a little too stern for my liking, but Solape is a sweet girl. She will make him a good wife.

My eyes mist over as I realise that I might never get to wear a wedding gown. Or throw a bouquet, as silly as I think the tradition is.

I'm still moping when Solape's flowers sail above the chorus of hopefuls gathered below the podium. A few girls jump. I remember wondering what Olamide is doing in the midst of them. Does she not remember we gave her to Korede already?

Pariola's left hand reaches for the flowers amidst others. Her right elbow buries itself into Olamide's face, and the latter tumbles into another girl who pushes her forward. Unknowingly, her shoe heel is caught in between the musical instrument cables, and the sequence of events bring her and a few others crashing down.

I stand in alarm with the baby in my arms. Most of the guests stand, too, as the girls all scramble to their feet. All, except one. Olamide has a cluster of bouquet catchers right on top of her.

Pariola, who has been busy jumping around with the bouquet, stops and turns around. Solape stands still on the stage, and everyone watches to see if Olamide will get up. When she doesn't, Korede runs towards his fallen fiancée. I stand on tiptoes trying to figure out if she is okay.

"OMG, I think she broke something," I hear someone scream.

Chapter Three

As far back as I can remember I've never been at home at hospitals. My earliest memory involves a rather large needle and a very frightened me, running bare-bottomed from the injection room with a host of nurses and hospital attendants behind me.

Of course I was caught, but it took two strong nurses and one doctor to administer the lethal jab. Needless to say, I wasn't friends with my mother and any other doctor for a very long time afterwards. Today, I still don't enjoy visiting hospitals for a bunch of different reasons.

I've discovered that doctors don't hold a candle to Google—my estimation, though. Before I sit down with any doctor I Google the five most likely causes of my symptoms, and I'm most often right. Or right within the vicinity of whatever could possibly be the issue. It's not like I don't think Nigerian doctors are dope, but I've grown vexed with their tendency to postulate every little incidence of fever as either one or both of the two most common illnesses prevalent to the Nigerian diaspora: Malaria, and Typhoid.

Ever since a doctor misdiagnosed my cousin Lanre with them three times over when it had been in fact a serious, life-threatening, infection, I've been more wary of Nigerian doctors. So you can't blame me when on the way to the nearest hospital with Olamide's swollen ankle cradled on a towel in my lap, I'm Googling up her symptoms.

There is an ice pack around her foot. Olamide is wailing, Korede is speeding, and Aramide is fretting from the front passenger seat. I, am shouting out all the possible causes of a swollen ankle after such a huge fall.

"It might be a tendon or ligament tear." I squint at my phone and scroll up and down the page. "She will need to see an orthopaedic surgeon, and have X-rays or an MRI done."

"It's so painful," Olamide says in tears. "I'm not sure I'll be able to walk again."

"Don't say that," Aramide cautions. "You are going to walk down that aisle in that beautiful gown we bought you, and on your own two feet."

"On the other hand, with swelling this much, it might be a fracture." I turn to her. "You might need surgery and pins and metal implants to fix your leg."

Olamide bursts into more tears with my pronouncement, and Aramide starts trying to calm her down.

"Femi, you've started again. Will you quit scaring her?"

Aramide looks cross with me, but I'm busy just reading more bad news from off the Internet. "Or they'll put your leg in a cast and you'll have to hobble down the aisle with a pair of crutches. I told you all you shouldn't have gone leaping after that bouquet."

"Okay, Femi, zip it!" Aramide replies.

Korede looks into the rear-view mirror and gives his fiancée a reassuring smile. "Don't worry, sweetheart. Don't mind, Femi. You are going to be okay."

"Ankle fractures take about three months to heal," I add. "We are looking at her being off her feet for the next three months!"

"Femi, get your nose out of that Google page and quit putting fear in her!" Aramide snaps.

"We need to prepare her for whatever it could be—"

"Yeah, get a medical degree and maybe I'll listen to you!"

We get to the Samaritan's Lodge, the private hospital Korede's company is registered at, and the nurses bring out a wheelchair and help us move Olamide in. We follow, worried.

We are informed by the nurse that only one of us can accompany her into the attending doctor's office. Olamide grabs my hand. For some reason that I can't fathom—because according to Aramide, I'm scaring her—she wants me in the room with her.

Perhaps she is thinking I can hold my own against a doctor blabbing medical jargon with all the reading I've been doing.

"Hi." The doctor swings his chair around to face us, and my heart explodes right in the middle of my chest. "Dr. Esosa Aghomo, at your service, I heard one of you had a fall."

My face flames up. I have met my share of really fine guys, and I have dated one or two, but nothing prepared me for Dr. Esosa.

He has this baby face with dimples burrowing into his cheeks. His expressive eyes have long lashes, and he is on the tall, slim side. I see it when he gets up to help Olamide onto the couch. My heart starts throttling at an alarming, embarrassing pace.

"I can see you beautiful ladies are coming from a wedding," he says as he examines her ankle with me hovering over him by the couch. "What do we have here?"

"I was trying to catch a bouquet but I twisted my ankle and fell," Olamide explains.

"Seems broken," he looks up at me, and I hold his gaze and pretend like my heart is not fluttering. "Tell me the truth. How high were those heels?"

"Not that high," I say in our defence. "She just tripped over some wires and fell."

The doctor looks down at the ankle and shakes his head. "Tore a few ligaments, likely broke a bone, too, but we won't know for sure until we do an investigation. I'd like to take an X-ray of your ankle."

"Will it hurt?" Olamide looks worried.

"Hardly, it's like taking a picture." He winks at me as he walks over to a hanging hand sanitizer dispenser, depresses the cover, and rubs the alcohol rub that squirts out all over his hands.

I hide my blush. I don't like men knowing when I like them, and I run from men who wink at me. But Dr. Esosa is several shades of fine, and his wink is kind of cute.

Olamide thrusts her hand in mine.

"Will you stay while I do the X-ray?" she asks.

She is once again my baby sister and I want to protect her.

"Of course," I give her hand a reassuring squeeze. "You are going to be fine."

"I'm going to give some pain meds. We are going to do an X-ray, and then we will know for sure, but I might be putting that ankle in a cast, from the looks of it."

He says all this to Olamide while looking at me. I stare back and pretend I'm not sure what that look means.

"If you put her leg in a cast," I ask. "How long is it going to be in a cast?"

"Six to ten weeks, depending on the type of break."

I nod. He smiles.

An hour and a half later, the X-ray is done, Olamide is sedated, and the ankle is reduced and casted. Dr. Esosa washes his hands in the sink in the treatment room, and Aramide helps her twin into the wheelchair.

"You are going to get her a pair of axillary crutches," he says, to me and not Olamide. Again! I'm rolling my eyes in my mind at this point. "And I'll see her in eight weeks for a follow up X-ray to see how much the bone has healed. So we can determine if we need to take the cast off or leave it on."

"Leave it on?" I poke my head forward. "She is getting married! Can't the cast come off any earlier?"

Aramide and Korede cast anxious looks at Dr. Esosa, but I must certainly be wearing a charm bracelet. His eyes are on mine.

"Unless you want her hobbling down the aisle and tripping over her wedding gown, you might wanna move it. The wedding, that is."

I turn to look at Olamide. She turns to look at Korede.

"It's okay, sweetie," he says. "We'll move it as the good doctor suggests. I'm prepared to wait to marry you. I waited this long in any case."

"Great, all sorted," the doctor comments, and we all laugh with relief.

"Thank you," Aramide and I say to him in unison.

"Thank God," he replies with a chuckle. "Yeah, so—" he nods in my direction. "I'll see you tomorrow, won't I?"

I am confused. "You want me to bring her in again tomorrow?"

"No," he says with a small smile. "Not her, you."

"You want me to come in tomorrow?" I ask, more perplexed. "Whatever for?"

"He is asking you out, dumdum." Aramide turns Olamide's chair around and wheels her out of the room. Korede follows. I am left alone with Dr. Esosa.

We stare at each other.

"I'm sorry if I made you uncomfortable," he says. "But two months seemed like a long time to wait to see you again. So will it be alright if we both go and catch a movie on the island somewhere tomorrow evening? It's a Sunday, and I'm not on call."

It's been long since I've been asked out, and I don't even know what to say. I open my mouth, and it takes me a really long time to say anything.

"I know we've never met, and I'm a total stranger—"

"Yeah," I say. "Sure. A movie would be nice."

"Great." He smiles at me again. I see the dimples and melt inside.

***

"I am going to work."

I grab my handbag off the dressing table, and Olamide looks up from scribbling into a big white binder.

Her three minions are hurdled in a corner of the room exchanging notes on their plans for her upcoming wedding and Aunty Ladepe's birthday party. Her leg has been in a cast for the past three weeks, and she's loved the drama of everyone waiting on her.

"Where are you going?" She stares at my navy-blue evening attire, a cold shoulder knee-length gown clinched at the waist with a wide-width black belt. "You just came back from work. I need you to look at the party plans so you can be my eyes and feet on Saturday."

"I told you about the recital and book reading."

Olamide looks delighted as she stares at my bare shoulders, "Oh, the date with Dr. Esosa!"

I hang my head at her excitement. "It's a work event."

"With pearly drop earrings and cream, kissable shoulders?"

I do not want to get my hopes up with the handsome doctor, but we have had two dates, and this recital makes our third. It technically is not exactly a date.

"Oh, go, go, go," Olamide shoos me away. "You shouldn't keep him waiting."

"Just jot everything you need to happen on that day in the binder, and I will have a playbook to run things by, okay?"

She nods. I blow her a kiss.

"Enjoy your date!" she yells as I shut the door to the room.

"It's not a date!" I yell back.

***

The Recital is packed. I stand by the registration desk and look out for Esosa, a little worried he's missed his way.

"Miss Ajayi," Gbemi, the office assistant, accosts me. "The refreshment guys are already set up, but you know we told them we'd handle the drinks."

"I know," I mumble and mindlessly dial Esosa's number. As co-editor at Drift Publishers, I'm somewhat in charge, hence why Gbemi came to me with those concerns.

"They didn't provide us with ice. Do we get ice for the drinks?"

"Sure."

I am worried. Despite all my protests and Olamide's teasing, today is kind of a huge deal. I haven't clicked with anyone I like in a long while, and I am hoping we work out. We like the same movies, read the same type of magazines, play Scrabble on our mobile phones, and he's watched *Pointless* at least a couple times.

"Miss Ajayi, I need money to buy ice."

I bring out my purse and give Gbemi two thousand naira.

"Write it down," I say to her as his phone starts ringing. "I'm collecting all my money back from you."

"Yes ma." Gbemi leaves.

Behind us, my friend and co-editor Lilian, is seated at the registration desk. She and the rented ushers are sorting the crowd one person at a time.

"Nifemi."

Esosa's pleasant voice comes online, and I see someone waving at me from the back of the room.

"Hey." I wave back and cut the call as he weaves through the crowds. My heart leaps in response, and I can't believe I have butterflies in my stomach.

He's got a trim, fit frame, and shoulders that carry his light grey Oxford button-down shirt with dignified elegance. It's tucked into a pair of black jeans, with breathable black sneakers on his feet. I can't help feeling lucky. Esosa is handsome, especially with those intelligent-looking spectacles and those 'guaranteed to make me swoon' dimples.

"Hi." He plants a quick kiss on my cheek. "You look great."

"Thanks. This is Lilian, my colleague." I turn to introduce her.

"Hello," Lilian replies in her cool, low-toned voice, "nice to meet you."

"Likewise," Esosa says.

"How was work?" I can't stop smiling, I'm really glad he came.

"Exhausting, but good," he replies.

"Thanks for making time out to come. I will be a bit busy, but I'll catch you afterwards."

"I totally understand. Dinner?"

"Yes." I'm breathless.

"Great, I'll be waiting." He touches my elbow, gives another smile, and heads inside with the crowd trooping into the auditorium.

"Nice." Lilian raises her eyebrows at me. "Where did you pick him up from?"

"The hospital, when Olamide broke her leg."

"Ahhh, you've been hiding things from me." She hands out more program booklets. "Where are you guys going afterwards?"

"I don't know yet. I'm just going with the flow!"

"Did you even register him, or were you just busy gazing into his eyes?"

"I was not gazing into his eyes." I pick up a biro from the desk. "I'll register his name myself. I know his details."

I hurry in my heels around the desk and score a registration sheet from one of the ushers.

"You already know his email address. How long have you guys been dating?"

Lilian's teasing reminds me that I don't have the actual information I need to collate data for future events.

"I'll just text him for the info."

I lean over the desk to start composing the text, but as I punch in a bunch of letters, I feel a hand on my lower back. It's so warm and unexpected that I jump and turn around to see who it is.

"Cousin Toba!" My heart leaps and scatters all over the place at the sight of him. "Oh my goodness, you scared me!"

He gives me a broad grin. "Sorry, I didn't mean to."

"It's okay, I was just—" I put a hand to my heart and start laughing out loud. "Hi." I reach out to hug him. "I had no idea you were back home."

Lilian sort of straightens up at the table with her mouth parted. I can see the wheels in her eyes turning, as well. Toba's build is formidable.

My head barely reaches his chin on block heels, and my face gets squashed into his soft chest—which smells ridiculously good, by the way; Ralph Lauren or something along the lines.

"Been back a while." He hugs me for a minute and steps back to give me room to recover. Toba's voice is several levels of deep and is one of the first things you notice about him, after you ask yourself how tall he is.

"When? Why?"

"Your mother's birthday!" we say simultaneously as I laugh some more and his smile widens.

Cousin Toba is my grandpa's seventh and last child, my mother's younger half-brother from Aunty Ladepe, my grandfather's youngest wife. We call him Cousin Toba because he is three years older than I am, and it's hard to qualify him as an uncle. But he's our favourite uncle, my sisters and me, my personal favourite in truth. It's why I'm laughing frenziedly like a tickled child, and staring at him like I struck gold.

"How you been?"

"Good." I see his slow drawl hasn't changed. "I haven't seen you in what, two, three years?"

"Two years, Uncle Sesan's birthday."

He nods. It's weird, us meeting at a musical recital and not at a wedding or a burial or at any other family event like we often do.

"I'm fully back, working with Exon Mobil."

"Oh! Aunty Ladepe didn't say. I bet she's happy."

"You know my mum," he says with a nonchalant shrug. "You're coming for her birthday on Saturday, aren't you?"

"Of course, Olamide is planning the whole thing. She will literarily hang me up by my ankles if I don't show."

He laughs out loud. It's a boisterous sound, deep, warm, and endearing all at once. It makes me smile, and think of crashing ocean waves and a sunny beach.

"My mum mentioned, I think I missed her wedding. How is she, by the way?"

"Doing okay, and no, you did not miss her wedding. She had the unfortunate luck of breaking her leg at Solape's wedding."

"Ooooh," he makes a pained expression.

"Hairline fracture of the tibia, clean break in the fibular, with swelling huge enough to make us all worry."

"Wow. So how is she now?"

"Leg's in a cast, should be out before the wedding."

"Oh good," he looks relieved. "I'll be able to attend."

We grin at each other. It's good to see he hasn't forgotten the family rule of everybody being at every family event.

"What about Aramide and Enitan?"

"Both fine. You'll see them on Saturday."

My eyes lower to his huge shoulders and wide chest. His frame is still bulky within the collared Ankara shirt he has on, but it doesn't mask his allure.

Lilian taps my wrist just then, hinting at the fact that I haven't introduced them both.

"Oh, this is my colleague, Lilian." I turn to her, "my cousin, Toba Awotunde."

"Hi." Toba holds out an extra-large hand and pumps her dainty one with a little enthusiasm. Lilian blushes and stands to her feet. Toba's six-foot-and-above height makes him a little intimidating when you're seated. Plus, there's that thing with his baritone voice. "Nice meeting you," he says to her.

"Same here," Lilian replies.

I can tell my friend is interested. Toba is not bad to look at.

He's a smart, friendly guy with a first-class degree in Geology from the University of Ibadan and a Geotechnical Engineering Masters from the University of Birmingham. The pride and joy of my grandfather and his last wife, he'd worked with a multinational oil company in the US for several years and had made a ton of foreign money.

Growing up, however, he wasn't always this guy Lilian is giving second looks to. He was reserved, tongue-tied, and took his sweet time getting anything done. Back then, I remember him as a tedious, overweight cousin who lived with us for some years, till my sisters and I discovered that he was my grandfather's last child and therefore our uncle and not our cousin.

Observing him now, I see no trace of the past. Despite still being a little on the big side, he's blossomed into this very confident hunk who is not my cousin.

Toba turns from Lilian to me. His forearms are thick beneath the sleeves of his shirt, and he has a black Samsung wristwatch clasping a strong-looking left wrist. It's one of those smart step-counting things I've been seeing around.

"So how's she planning the birthday, Olamide, that is, with her leg in a cast?"

I give an exaggerated shrug. "She has an events management crew, tons of staff. Ola will not let a broken leg keep her from bossing people around."

He chuckles. "She won't."

"I'm curious. How did you hear about the recital?"

"My—" he turns around as if searching for someone, "— friend."

I look around like I can spot the friend when I see her.

"She's friends with one of the authors reading here today, and she made me promise to bring her. I wouldn't have come on my own, but— oh, here she comes."

I'm not prepared for the lady that saunters towards us hips swinging, hair bouncing, and body rocking the gorgeous outfit she's got on.

"Toba darling, there you are," she says in perfect Queen's English and has every eye cratering in her direction. Her voice is loud, the accent British.

I am wondering how Toba knows this African goddess. I glance at him, but he is busy smiling as she strides over to us.

I can't resist widening my own smile, because his *'friend'* is 'mouth hanging open' gorgeous.

She is of average height, ultra-thin at the waist, and blessed with wide hips, a small bust, naturally pouty lips, and long, slender arms and legs. With an oval face and symmetrical cat-like eyes, her wavy, mid-back length weave looks like it literarily grew from her scalp. In the figure-hugging silk jumpsuit she is in, she looks like a model—will probably be successful at an MBGN contest if she ever ventures into one.

"Where ever did you wander off to?" she says.

"I bumped into family. Meet my cousin," Toba says and suddenly frowns as if contemplating how best to introduce me. "My niece, relative," he turns the frown over to me, and our eyes meet. "Femi, Nifemi Ajayi."

"Hi." She slides her arm into the crook of Cousin Toba's right elbow and leans—Excuse me, squeezes— her chest into his upper arm while smiling at Lilian and me. "So lovely to meet family."

"Hi," I say. The sound almost doesn't come out. Toba has had a few girlfriends accompany him to family events over the years, but I have to admit that this one takes the crown.

"Femi, meet Yinka, a friend from London Business School."

London Business School, I had no idea he had even gone there.

Toba looks embarrassed as she leans further into him and tiptoes to graze his cheek with her lips. She laughs out loud, a hearty, bell-like tinkle that grates on my confused nerves.

"Yinka," she says, still giggling as she turns her face from Toba's to mine, "with a 'C'."

"Yinka," I say and force a chuckle, "with a C. Nice meeting you, I see what you did there, a 'C' instead of a 'K,' Yinca, very nice. You guys should register and pick up programme pamphlets. I'm sure we are about to start."

"Yes, do let's hurry, sugar." She pulls on Toba's arm. "I want to get a good front seat."

That ship already sailed, I'm thinking.

"Sure." Toba watches Yinka 'with a C' register both their names with Lilian.

I spend that time staring at him. I know my cousin-slash-uncle-slash-relative is a shade away from being red in the face. He doesn't need to be—he's the envy of every guy present.

"Femi, it's nice seeing you again," he says to me. "I'll see you Saturday, won't I?"

"Yeah," I say and smile at Yinca. "You, too, I hope."

"Definitely, ta-ta." She throws a beauty queen wave at me and walks into the auditorium with her arm linked in Cousin Toba's elbow.

"*Na wa o*," Lilian can't resist saying once they're out of earshot. "I should just cancel all my plans for your uncle. Where did he find that girl?"

"Ah, *na so I see am o*."

"But that your uncle is fine," Lilian says.

"Who, Toba?" I cringe and think of him as a child. "Don't lose hope yet. He changes his girlfriends like he changes clothes. This one, I doubt she will last. There should be hope for you. Just come to my aunt's birthday on Saturday. As for me, I'm going to check on Esosa."

Lilian looks at her wrist watch and glances at me. "Love *nwantiti*, he left you like fifteen minutes ago!"

I shrug as I walk away from her. "Has it been that long?"

Chapter Four

A marriage, by the Merriam-Webster dictionary definition, is the state of being united to a person of the opposite sex. It's a consensual, contractual relationship recognized by law, now being expanded to include same-sex relationships. It is also a word that describes the blending of lives and the forging of friendships, the idea that a group of two or more people can grow together to become one.

Marriage is—or should be but usually is not—the beginning of a family. And family is family, regardless of the steps, halves and non-blood-related adoptions that bring people together. Marriage most of the time is hard work and raising a blended family even more.

My extended family is a close-knit, blended one, and we celebrate everything together. So whether you were born into the family, fostered by the family, married into the family, or related to a person married into the family, or even a long-time friend of any member of the family, you were considered family. And so, any party involving any member of the family is a huge deal, and everybody needs to be there.

Olamide's worry, as we approach the day of Aunty Ladepe's sixtieth birthday, is not her painful ankle or the cast wrapped tightly around it. It is the fact that everyone needs to be at that party, and she is not sure that everyone will.

With the ever-busy Lagos life and the daily grind of chasing individual dreams, it's a little tough to make time out for social events that aren't cash cows. So Olamide is on the phone twenty-four-seven, calling every family member she can lay her hands on. No one says no. Ola has such a way with words, but when all fails, she pitches them her perfectly worded threatening speech.

"*Show up or forever remain in Grandpa's book of unblessed descendants!*"

It works, but then, I think we all love Grandpa and hate to disappoint him.

So on Saturday morning, everyone lands in Bodija. The older women are in Aunty Ladepe's room, getting her ready for the day. My dad is with my grandfather having his version of catch-up, not having had the chance to do it at Olamide's introduction. The children are running around in the back of the house, and the men of the family—my uncles and the in-laws—are in the living room watching football.

The rest of us are following Olamide's playbook, arranging the food and decorating the garden for the event. We hired ushers and bouncers, and prepared invitation cards and guest lists. Yes, Olamide insisted, or the party would be overrun by the local inhabitants of the area and street urchins.

"This is not Lagos!" she says on repeat. "Grandpa is over-generous. We have to gate the place, or we'll have a stampede."

And she is right. Everything is accounted for in her big white binder. I'm hoping we can be done in the next hour or so before the guests begin to arrive.

"Food has arrived. Where are we putting them?" Imisi heads in my direction with a big cooler.

"Over there." I point to my right-hand side without looking up. "The music is way on the other side. And we need room in the middle for dancing."

I lower the binder and order Olamide's guys around.

"Okay, guys, semi-circular table and chair arrangement. Move these tables from here to there.

Where is Enitan?" I look around and find Jumoke instead. "Jummy baby, come over here and help set the tables with plates and cutlery. Let's go people. Move it, move it!"

"Why do we have to set up forks and knives? Ibadan people don't use them!"

I hear her grumbling but ignore it while marching around the garden ordering affairs with Olamide's perfect playbook. Pity she is stuck in the living room with her casted leg raised high on a stool.

"Aunty Femi," one of Olamide's work boys calls from above the stairway leading into the garden. "There is a lady here, says she's looking for Mr. Toba."

I look up just as Aramide gets to me.

"I'm supposed to pick up the cake, and I don't have anybody to drive me," she is saying but I'm not listening.

It's Yinca, the lady from recital waving in my direction. She is in this above-knee black and white Lycra dress that accentuates her hourglass shape. Her face is a perfect blend of foundation, concealer, and powder with false lashes, well-drawn brows, and nude lipstick.

Deji, Imisi's younger brother, takes a look at her and freezes on the spot.

"I'll take her," he says and drops the plastic table he is carrying, grinning like a man who has just been called with a charm.

"Deji," I call, determined to keep him away from trouble. "I'll take her to Toba. You drive Aramide to pick up the cake."

Deji looks disappointed. I snap the binder shut and motion for work to continue as I run up the stairway towards Yinca, I don't want Deji anywhere near her.

She beams the moment our eyes meet. "Femi, right?"

"What a pleasant surprise!" I reach out to give her a hug, but she grants me air kisses on each side. Her cheek doesn't even touch mine.

"The pleasant surprise is Ibadan," she replies, "such a gorgeous ancient city. I was told it was half dead. Imagine my astonishment."

To find roads? I ask drily in my mind, but beam back as Aramide grabs Deji by the neck and hurls him out of the garden area.

"Well—" I add to my bright smile. "We try."

"Golly, that's a wicked flower arrangement. The garden looks absolutely stunning," she continues. "I daresay, when Toba told me the party was not taking place in Lagos, I wondered what Ibadan could possibly have to offer that Lagos couldn't? But so far, I'm delightfully impressed."

I look down at the garden where work is still on-going. There are green and pale-yellow flowers in vases on the tables, and their contrast with the white table cloths brings a certain classy look. The flowery arch over the cake table is enchanting and the carpet grass cements it all. She is right. It all looks good.

"So where is Toba? I don't see him anywhere."

"He is in the house," I say to her. "Let's go."

"Brilliant!"

As we go, Yinka starts to complain out loud. "I've got my stuff in the car that brought me. I was wondering if anybody could go fetch them for me."

I glance at her. *Does she not have hands?*

"We are all kind of busy now, but perhaps Cousin Toba or any of the guys inside could help you out."

I hurry into the house with her following close.

"What a delightful house—" she exclaims as we get through the front door, "—with charming décor and vintage furniture. Splendid."

I turn towards the big living room with an eye-roll and open the door. Olamide sees me first.

"Oh, Femi, thank God. Please get me out of heeeere ..." She trails off when she sees Yinca.

Just then, the match takes an exciting turn and the men in the living room yell and jump from their seats. Then they discover that the ball has landed behind the goal post and not inside it. There is a long, drawn-out chorus of 'Awww' and they start chastising the striker from all the way inside Grandpa's living room about what he did wrong and what he could have done better.

"Cousin Toba," I call. "You have a visitor."

"Surprise!" Yinka 'with a C' yells.

Toba turns. He is standing behind the long settee with his arms folded and feet wide apart, dressed down in an old pair of jeans and T-shirt. The clothes look hastily thrown together, but there's just something sexy about that lazy stance that makes me take another look at him. Yinka is staring, too, like he's some exotic dish she is about to devour.

Now Toba doesn't act like he was bred with lots of silver spoons in his mouth, but you just get a sense of it from being with him. You smell his scent, and you know it's classy. You look at his clothes, and though they are not loud, you know they are quality. You hear him speak without an accent and you know he's spent significant time abroad. He's usually very well-groomed, so I can understand Yinka's fascination.

I've known him all my life, so I don't understand mine. I haven't seen him all morning, and I'm tongue-tied. His shoulders pop through the shirt and his chest muscles are well-defined beneath his hulking, folded forearms. I can't believe I'm gawking at him.

He looks as shocked to see her as she looks relieved to see him.

"Yinca," he says as she runs to him and flings her arms around him. "You came."

Above the top of her head, he stares at me like I'm responsible for her presence in the house. I shrug and hold out my hands.

"Did you think I'd pass up the chance to meet your mum?"

He stares down at her and chuckles. "At all," he says.

Her head is nestled in his huge chest, and his thick right arm is cradling her bare back where the dress dips. I can almost sense its feel against her skin and for a second I long for someone to hold me like that.

One by one, the men in the room begin to turn around and notice her. The TV is forgotten, replaced by the ogling of perfect hourglass shape, perfect skin and hair, and beautiful Queen's English. Nigerians trip over British English because there is this sense that the person is smarter, which of course they aren't.

I go over and squat beside Olamide. "What are you so worried about? Everything is going as you ordered it downstairs."

"Who is that?" Olamide's voice is a whisper.

I laugh and look up. Toba is introducing his girlfriend to all the men in the room, and she is enjoying all the attention. "Cousin Toba's new side attraction."

"Don't tell me you are not dying to discuss that?" Olamide asks through the side of her mouth, pointing her chin in Yinca's direction. "I am looking forward to discussing that."

***

Three hours later, the celebration is rocking, and everyone has changed into their party attire. I let Kenny put some makeup on me because I usually just do stuff to my face before events and the stuff manages to wipe itself off by the time we are ready for pictures. This time, I want something a little more permanent. So Kenny hooks me up with stay foundation and matte lipstick. She blends in a tricolour purple eye-shadow and convinces me to try on midi false lashes and kajal.

The overall effect is a dramatic makeover that gets me noticed by all and sundry. I can't escape the *gele*, but I convince Aunty Norma to make it small and manageable. I can't deny that Yinka 'with a C,' showing up, and Esosa planning to be around, have something to do with it.

There is *Aso Ebi*, a purple lace that everyone has sown into various styles of which the celebrant is wearing a lilac version of. She looks lovely as she dances in with my mum and the female members and friends of the family. All except me, under the guise of directing the affairs—I know how to escape these things.

I wonder for a second what my husband will say on our wedding day if I refuse to dance with him. Then I frown as I catch myself thinking about marriage again.

Solape's nose and abdomen seem bigger than normal. Safe to say she is expecting, a little too soon to be showing, though. Pariola had chunked her lace into a gown that's a replica of Yinka 'with a C's black and white dress except this is not Lycra, it's lace, and not her finest sense of style. It has a few redeeming qualities, so she can wear it and not look like a skanky queen of the night. She points a finger at Aunty Norma when the later quizzes her about it and says she's looking for Mr. Perfect and it's none of her business.

Guests arrive in droves, family members, too. At this time, I think I should introduce you all to Enitan's quiet, unassuming husband, David Bright. Dave is British, and a good ten years older than my thirty-year-old sister. His extended family live in London, but he works as a pilot with British Airways. It means we rarely ever see him, and so it's an honour to have him around. It also means Enitan spends half of every year in the UK.

"Hey, Fem," he says as he walks in carrying their twenty-month-old son, Aiden. "You look gorgeous."

"Thank you." Praise from Dave is rare and always honest, so I know I'm looking good. He's never quite gotten the hang of pronouncing everyone's names, and Obanifemi is a tad tough for him. So he calls me Fem, and I don't let anyone else get away with doing that. "It's great to see you around, too."

Aiden is sitting still in his father's arms. He looks cute, with his fair skin and 'Mohawk' curly brown hair. Dave has him forward-facing with his arms underneath the boy's buttocks.

"Hey Aiden," I reach out and roughen his hair. He gurgles and blows up spit bubbles so I snatch back my hand. Enitan's been complaining about him doing that a lot lately. It's my first experience, and it's gross.

"Sorry," Dave says. "We haven't the slightest clue how to make him stop."

"Oh, it's okay," I say with a careless wave of my hand as Aiden blows up more spit bubbles, and I fantasize briefly about sticking him in a cupboard with a masking tape over his mouth. "Kids do stuff all the time. I'm used to it."

No, I'm not! Children and chaos is one reason why my subconscious probably repels marriage. I hate soiled clothes and messy environments and like babies, I never know what to do with them. My nephew is a rave at our parties, but no matter how cute I agree he is, I don't attempt to carry him. I have had babies spit up on me, kids spill drinks on me, and Aramide's twins test the limit of my patience with crayon on my bedroom walls. So no, I don't think I want to be a mother, nor do I know any guys who won't want kids in their future.

I can't say this out loud, though, because in Nigeria, it is tantamount to needing a psych evaluation. Marriage without children is an abomination, and husbands who don't want kids are virtually non-existent.

Dave tosses me a sheepish grin. "I suppose I should go say hi to Mum and Dad, shouldn't I?"

I look down at the kid and see the spit bubbles foam around his mouth. "Yeah, you do that!"

"Thirty-two, twenty-four, thirty-six," I hear as I hurry away from Dave and stop at the table where my cousins are seated.

"That waist is a twenty-three, I'm telling you," Kenny says.

Pariola shuts one eye and holds up an index finger. "It's a twenty-four. I know the average sizes, and she's a size two on top, eight at the bottom."

"That waist-hip ratio, though, and those curvy hips," Kenny responds.

"Do you want me to ask her?" Aramide says. "Because me I'm not shy. I can do it if you guys are going to keep arguing!"

I follow the trail of their gazes to the top of the garden staircase where Cousin Toba is adjusting his *Aso Ebi fila*, and Yinka 'with a C' has a leg angled backwards, adjusting her stiletto heel and holding onto the stairway railing. "Oh my god, you guys!"

They are a beautiful couple, I think as they stand for a moment on the staircase, poised to start heading down. Everyone gawks. Her dress is a magnificent purple lace whose name I do not know as I'm not into fashion and Nigerian fabrics, but dare say is beautiful. With cap sleeves and a deep vee neckline, it has a loose 'wrap' look, with a tail that makes it lower in length behind than in the front. It's moulded onto her amazing shape and exposes the skin between her breasts, of which she has next to none.

The catch of the day, however, are her hips. They look admirably rounded in the whole ensemble. Toba offers her his hand and helps her descend.

"Those hips definitely don't lie," Pariola says. "They are bigger than the bust by so much."

"She has no bust!" Imisi adds with a wail.

I look at my sisters and cousins and clear my throat. "You people, really?"

"Korede has been staring at her all day," Olamide moans. "How can someone be carved like that? It's not normal."

"Exercise," Kenny says. "and Keto. I'm sure she spends an inordinate amount of time in the gym doing squats and side lifts. It grows the bum."

"Ohhh," Aramide and Olamide moan at the same time.

Compared to them, I have more hips. I can boast of that.

"And her tailor is super," Imisi says. "Super, super good, and probably expensive."

Aunty Norma hisses. *"Girl wey no get flesh! How person go like that one?"*

"Her makeup is on point!" Pariola adds.

"Why Toba come bring that eye-candy come here nau?"

"He always brings eye-candy. It's his signature MO," Olamide moans. "And Korede won't stop looking at her!"

"Korede loves you." Aramide pats her arm. "That girl might look like she's a ten on ten on the outside, but I bet she's got nothing compared to you on the inside."

I'm not getting into the conversation. Who Toba likes is not for us to judge.

Toba and his girlfriend are downstairs now, trying to scour a seat on Uncle Juwon's table. There is only one chair available, so Toba sits. Yinca perches her bum on his right thigh and flings an arm around his neck. His head is bent, typing away on his phone, oblivious to the eyes on them. She, however, is soaking up the attention, and the men at the table don't hide the fact that they are staring.

"Like my chemistry teacher will say—" Kenny goes ahead to carve out the shape of Yinka's butt in the air with her hands. "Round bottom flask."

There is a general burst of laughter. I can't believe how childish my cousins are.

"If Papa Jumoke make mistake use even one eye to look at that akata girl, I go remove the eye myself!" Aunty Norma announces.

We all laugh again. She looks quite capable of doing so.

"That Atiku just fits Toba's statue," Pariola says. "If he wasn't our cousin, I would have locked that girl sitting on his lap inside one toilet and thrown away the key."

Toba stores his phone. He has one hand in the middle of Yinka's back and is scrutinizing her face, listening to her endless chatter. I know Pariola will walk over to him sometime during this party and challenge him about where he picked her up from.

"*Wetin bi her name sef?*" Aunty Norma asks.

"Yinca," I say to everyone. "As in Y, I, N, C, A."

"C *ke,* does the Yoruba alphabet even contain that consonant?" Aramide says in disgust.

"It's the British version of her name," I say, spotting Esosa. "I gotta go, I see my date."

"*Come oh, that girl na half Toba's size, when dey wan, you know—*" Aunty Norma shakes her head and gives us all a knowing look.

"Aunty Norma!" Aramide hits her shoulder before she completes her question.

"*Na true talk nau,*" she says, laughing. "*Toba go squash that girl!*"

I shake my head as I leave the group. It's appalling what they are discussing.

"Dr. Esosa," I call and wave. He's found his way down to the garden.

"Femi, thank goodness." He gives me a quick hug and a peck on the cheek. "I was beginning to think I had walked into the wrong party. You look beautiful, absolutely."

"Thank you." I'm grateful I took the time to make my face up. "Come, come and meet my sister, your patient."

When Esosa and I arrive at the table, the girls are all ecstatic. He is thoughtful and well-mannered. He greets the girls one after the other and accords Aunty

Norma with the right amount of respect. She takes an immediate liking to him.

Aramide is grateful for his help at the hospital—and for taking me off the Singles' corner. Olamide can't wait to level all her complaints at him, chief being the itchiness in her ankle and her inability to reach her skin below the cast. Pariola wants to know if he has other doctor friends, and me, I'm just sitting there wondering what I ever saw in Akpan, my previous boyfriend.

Pariola raises her eyebrow at me, turns her face sideways, and lifts a shoulder. The look means *'well done, great catch.'* Esosa is courteous, bold, and funny, and seems to have everyone eating out of the palms of his hands. Adenrele had been sweet but a tad timid. Akpan had been handsome with a huge dose of arrogance. Esosa is a breath of fresh air.

Guests give their tributes to Aunty Ladepe, and she is toasted by none other than my Grandpa's long-time friend, Engineer—Nigerians like titles—Oladimeji. When the family all go out and celebrate this, I decide it's time for Esosa to meet my parents. I'm not eager for introductions so early in the relationship, but I need everyone off my back.

My father is delighted. My mother heaves a sigh of relief underneath her apparent surprise. There is just something about dating a qualified medical doctor that rubs Nigerian parents the right way. That's when you hear a father saying quite loudly to his friends.

"That's my daughter's boyfriend, Esosa." (Normal loud voice)

"And, he's a *doctor* o!" (Voice goes an octave higher)

Then you see the friends all nod and grin and murmur their approval. "Aaaahhh," they will go, "Doctor, very good, very good. What hospital?"

The guy has passed the first test. He is a doctor, qualified to even visit her at home, let alone ask for her hand in marriage. Now mention that he is a senior doctor at a Teaching Hospital and you will have them all salivating. Esosa works at a private hospital, but we don't have time to get into that with my parents.

As we return to our seats, we run into Cousin Toba and his girlfriend.

"I hope you are enjoying the party," I say to her.

"Yes, darling, it's been fabulous, the highlight of my first week here in Africa."

Africa? I widen my eyes and keep a smile on my face. She can't tell me she doesn't know her own country is part of a larger continent. I'm irritated. I hide it though as I turn my smile over to Toba. I am once again struck by how dapper he looks, how spruce in his black native wear.

"Enjoying yourself?"

He nods and gives Esosa an inquiring glance. "My mum is happy, can't thank you enough."

"Don't," I say. "She is like my mum, too, so it was nothing."

"Oh, yes, I'm about to meet Toba's mum officially, such a delightful looking lady. I can't believe she is sixty. She hardly looks a day over forty."

Yinka gushes on, but Toba is quiet, his countenance in between bored and expectant. I deduce that he is waiting for me to introduce Esosa.

"This is my friend, Esosa," I say when Yinka finally stops talking. I turn to find Esosa smiling at her. "My uncle Toba, and his friend Yinka. With a C," I add with emphasis.

"Hello, sir." Esosa's eyes dart from Yinka to Toba and back as he holds out a hand.

Toba's right eyebrow lifts somewhat, and he reaches out a huge hand to shake him. The grip—I suspect—is hard because Esosa grimaces. It's brief, but I catch it before he masks it. *Toba is being territorial,* I think to myself. *This is new.* He is most often always gentle. This girl must mean something to him.

"Nice meeting you," he says to Esosa with a smile that doesn't quite reach his eyes.

Esosa pumps his hand. "Nice meeting you too, and congratulations on your mum's birthday. I wish her many more years with good health."

"Thank you." Toba's smile is stiff.

"Esosa is a doctor," I add smiling at the man beside me, "Medical, not PhD."

"Oh, you're a doctor," Yinka purrs. I see the gleam in her eyes at the sound of that. "Where do you work?"

"The Samaritan's Lodge, it's a private hospital in Victoria Island, Lagos."

"Oh, the Island is where all the rich folks live, right?" Yinka replies. "So you must be having a blast being a doctor making all that quid."

"We are open to everyone. As long as you're covered under a health insurance scheme, we can see you."

"Health Insurance in Africa, Toba you didn't tell me that." She hits his arm playfully. "That's fabulous news. So if I need you while I'm here, I'd best get one."

"I'm taking Yinka over to meet my mum," Toba says, cutting off all the chit-chat. He looks at me before glancing again at Esosa and lowering his head to whisper in Yinka's ear. "We should head over."

"Yes sugar, we should. Have fun guys, and see you later." Yinca throws her beauty queen wave and clings once more to Toba's upper arm.

I drag Esosa away. I honestly hadn't liked the way he'd been looking at her.

"You say that guy is your uncle?" Esosa rubs his right hand.

"Yes. Did he break your fingers?" I take his hand and rub it myself. "You were kind of like staring at his girlfriend." I give him a pointed look.

Esosa laughs. "I didn't mean to offend him."

"Nah, everyone has been staring at her all day. She is kind of impossible not to notice."

"So your uncle, who doesn't look old enough to be your uncle," Esosa continues. "What's the deal?"

"Cousin Toba? He is my grandpa's last child, only son of the celebrant."

Esosa is still rubbing his hand. "He seems very protective."

"Of his girlfriend, I guess. Would you want someone to swoop in and take your girlfriend away from you?"

"But I don't have designs on his girlfriend." He leans into me. "I have designs on you."

I blush for a second at the gleam in his eye.

"Would you like me to get you something to eat?" I ask. I really don't want to spend any more time discussing Toba and Yinca.

"I think at this point, I would."

"Great. Let's find a place to settle down, and I'll prepare you a plate."

Somewhere along the night, I yank off the *gele* on my head and let my braids down so my scalp can breathe. It's a huge relief to shake them out and run my fingers through to get them to stay away from my face. I catch Esosa watching and smile. It's been long since I've been admired, and the first time we share an intimate look. I realize I want Esosa, and I'm not even thinking about marriage.

The party starts winding down with the cake-cutting. My grandpa poses with his arm around Aunty Ladepe. He stands up straight and tall, and pauses to give her a kiss on the lips after their picture is taken. Everyone gives a whoop of delight and clap. We can't believe he is ninety.

The MC announces a couple's dance, and *'the lady in red'* comes up over the speakers. We all clear the dance area for them, and there is a hush as they dance. Aunty Ladepe is radiant and shy. I am shy with her. It's obvious my grandfather is delighted with her, and it's surreal that at sixty and ninety, they are showing us this romantic side to them.

I catch my dad with his mouth to my mother's ear. He might be asking her to dance, and she might be refusing. I shudder at the idea and turn to find Yinca dragging Cousin Toba onto the dance floor. He doesn't look like he really wants to but eventually caves. Even with her stilts, the top of her head just brushes his shoulder, and she is like a tiny mop stick in his arms.

The younger couples take the floor after them and dance under the party lights in the garden of Grandpa's compound. Uncle Deola twirls Aunty Norma around. They look like a clumsy old couple from a century away. Dave and Enitan do the British waltz. Aramide and Diran are not left out, and even

Korede has managed to wangle Olamide with her casted left ankle onto the floor. They are not moving much, just oscillating. I can bet that's Olamide's doing, her not wanting to be left out.

The youngsters all give a whoop of delight when Ed Sheeran's *'Thinking out loud'* comes on. It's apt! It's a lovely, magical end to a beautiful birthday party, and I am awed just watching it all.

I feel a tug at my elbow.

"May I have this dance?" Esosa asks.

I look up at him. "I don't know how to dance."

"Come on, I'll do all the work. All you have to do is hang onto me."

Dancing embarrasses me, but I do want to hold Esosa close. "Please don't be offended if I step on your toes."

With a laugh, he twirls me into his arms. I'm blushing as my hands find his neck and his arms cradle my back. I'm thirty-five and blushing like an adolescent.

"I love your family," he whispers. "I think I'd like to be a part of it."

"Really?"

It's a promise of a future for us, and I am thrilled.

"Sure. You guys know how to party."

I reward him with a big grin. "Yeah, we do."

When he leans forward and places a tiny kiss near the corner of my mouth, I lay my head against his cheek, scared. We're moving too fast, and I'm scared I will lose him like I did the others. But his arms are snug around my waist, keeping me secure.

Just before the party ends, I wander to the back of the house in search of my grandfather. He's seated next to Toba, holding his hand in a tight grip. They stop talking when I arrive.

"I am sorry to interrupt." I walk over to my grandfather, squat before him.

"I hope nothing?" Grandpa says.

I eye Toba. His irises are obsidian in that dark corner of the compound, and his face is a hard mask. "You haven't eaten anything all day, and I was wondering if I could bring you something."

"I'm fine, my dear."

"We still have moin-moin, and crème caramel."

"I'm alright," he says.

"I'm bringing it!" I say and get up.

Toba doesn't say a word throughout our exchange. He just looks from me to Granddad and back again. I leave the two of them alone but can't help wondering what it is they were discussing. Toba seems detached, and Grandpa seems cryptic.

I will later remember this moment, because after that wonderful party, things begin to fall apart.

Chapter Five

There are a lot of steps in my family on both sides of the tree, a happy consequence of the Yoruba men of old and their affinity for marrying numerous wives.

My father's father had five wives and twenty-two children. My mother's father had three wives and seven children. Between them, there are seventy-seven grandchildren, and with all the drama that went on in both households, it's easy to see why my parents decided to make their marriage work.

I am Pa Awotunde's first grandchild, the first female child of his first female child. Somehow, I'm special to him. In Nigerian culture, the male children are important because they carry on the family name and are progenitors of subsequent generations. They're treated like gold, and in some cases, like gods. So it's weird that my grandfather would choose me, a female child of a female child, to fall in love with. I later found out that the fondness he has for me stems from the fact that I am the one most like his mother in looks and character. I remind him of her.

The older he got, the more his fondness for me grew. The more forgetful he became in everyday life, the more he remembered the past, and his mother with it. So when my mother got the call from Ibadan, I decided to go with her. I just knew that he would want to see me, too. He wants to see all his children, his doctor told us, because he thinks he might be dying.

My mother calls Aramide and Enitan to ask if any of them would want to come along. They show up with fruits and nutritional shakes for Granddad, but cite work as the reason they can't accompany us. I have called my Chief Editor. She understands that my grandfather is like my father, so she allowed a casual leave.

Aramide stops by my bedroom and looks in. "I saw you and Esosa the other day."

"Aren't you heading off to work?" I ask, looking up from my laptop and glancing at the clock.

"Don't change the subject," she says.

"Yeah, don't. Things looked cosy between you two last Saturday." Enitan follows her into my room.

"Everyone on that lawn looked cosy," I know where they are headed with the conversation. "Didn't I see you waltzing with Dave?"

Enitan grins. "Femi, you introduced Esosa to Daddy. That's cosier than cosy. Just be careful, don't ruin this one! Chill out with your elitist behaviour and need to show off your vast intellect—"

I give them both pointed looks. "Meaning?"

Aramide jumps in. "I could say that this chair is red, and you would immediately tell me why it isn't red but ruby, or crimson, or cherry, which are really just fancy words for the colour red."

"And there is this thing you do where you just keep quiet when people are talking and eye them with disdain, and make them feel like they're talking trash …" Enitan says.

"Or plain just talking like idiots," Aramide finishes.

I keep my frown trained on both of them. "Is there a point to this?"

"Yes. Men don't like women who think they are more intelligent than they are."

I'm annoyed. "If a guy feels inferior to me because I suggest a more interesting word for the colour red, then it's his problem, not mine."

"There," Aramide mutters, pointing a finger at me. "That's what I'm talking about, that hyper-flaunting pride. That is what made Akpan slap you."

I open my mouth. "Ara!"

"Not that I agree with that douchebag," she says. "But that subtle passive-aggressive tone you sometimes have brings out the need for a guy to show his dominance."

"What does this have to do with visiting Grandpa?"

"Nothing," Enitan says. "We just thought that Esosa is a nice guy, and we all like him—"

"Back off my relationship," I say to both of them.

"Femi." Aramide refuses to budge. "You made Adenrele feel like he didn't know enough. You didn't think he was good enough for you, and he knew it."

"That's ridiculous. It was a mutual decision to end the whole thing, and Akpan hit me for no good cause! Nothing I could have said necessitated those slaps. If he didn't like what I said or how I said it, he simply could have said so."

"We know. That's why Cousin Toba gave him a piece of our collective minds. We are just—"

"Just what—" I snap before realising what Aramide just said. "Cousin Toba did what?"

"Nothing serious. We just got talking about you and it slipped out." Aramide looks into my eyes and realizes I'm about to explode. "Okay, someone needed to go straighten that guy out. He put you in the hospital, for crying out loud."

"For a day," I screech. "To get my eye checked out."

"A slap should not result in a hospital visit! He had no right to beat you up, and just as well that someone told him so."

I glare at Aramide. "I already gave Akpan a piece of my mind. You guys didn't need to blare my business to Toba. Besides, he isn't the type to threaten anyone."

"I was there." Enitan nods at me. "Akpan looked pretty scared."

"You were there!" I can't believe my own sisters. "Oh my god, you guys! When was this?"

"Last week—"

"Last week. Akpan and I broke up almost a year ago."

"Six months ago." Aramide picks up her bag. "Look, Femi, just take it easy with Esosa, okay? Relax and have some fun, and for goodness sake, don't ask him about his money matters."

"I don't want to talk to either of you for the next one year." I frown into my laptop and clatter away on the keyboard for a few seconds before looking up. "Did Olamide know about this?"

Aramide's guilty look answers the question. I'm suddenly itching to meet up with Cousin Toba and harass him for talking to Akpan.

***

My grandfather's huge eight-bedroom mansion is filled with family members. It's serious. Whatever anger or grudges I harbour against my sisters and my uncle disappear at the sight of everyone in a sombre mood.

Aunty Ladepe is in the room with him, but Grandma Kike, his second wife, is seated in the living room with a friend she brought for company. My grandfather is a very jovial, very peaceful man. But whatever happened between them was bitter, and doesn't even pale in this sad event of his gradual passing.

"Has someone called Layo?" my mother asks her younger brothers, Uncles Juwon and Gbenga, as she walks past them on the corridor leading to Grandpa's room.

"She arrives Saturday," Uncle Juwon replies.

Aunty Layo is my grandfather's fifth child, the second one from Grandma Kike.

"Who is with him?" my mother asks as she pauses with her hand on the door handle.

"Sesan, and Ladepe," Uncle Gbenga replies. "He wanted everyone else out of the room."

"At least I can tell him I'm around." My mother hands her bag over to me.

"You know Baba doesn't like interference," Uncle Gbenga starts to say.

My mother marches into the room without a word. I follow with a hasty curtsey to my uncles. They don't look happy.

"Morning o jare Femi," Uncle Juwon replies.

Uncle Gbenga doesn't speak. He looks worried, like he thinks Grandpa is in there dividing all his property between his first and third wives' children.

I slip into the room after my mother. There is a stale smell of urine and faecal matter in the air, along with antibiotics, methylated spirit, and death. It hangs above the room like clouds in the sky and terrifies me. My grandfather is emaciated. He looks tired and wrinkled, nothing like the yuppie old man who danced to 'Lady in Red' with Aunty Ladepe just a week ago.

There is medical equipment in the room—BP and sugar monitors, I.V. infusion packs and drip tubes, cotton wool, needles, and drugs of all kinds, ably monitored by a hefty guy who looks more like a gym instructor than a nurse.

My mother rushes to Grandpa's side and sits on the bed beside him. I don't think he sees anyone. He can probably hear the angels singing again. Uncle Sesan is on a chair with Aunty Ladepe beside him. Her eyes are red and swollen, and even with tears in them and at sixty, she looks so pretty.

My mother cradles his hand to her cheek. He looks peaceful. He is not going to watch me get married, I think. I want to get married. I want him there when I do, but I don't think those two things will happen. I feel the tear before it rolls down my cheek, and blink it back because I can't stay in the room with them all. I can't watch him die.

I hurry out and hear my uncles welcoming Uncle Deola and Aunty Norma in the living room. I don't wait to greet them. I step out and stand on the porch for a while and look around.

Grandpa's compound is huge—two plots of land with a duplex mansion sitting right in the middle of it. Ibadan land plots are slightly bigger than Lagos plots, so there's space. I see the grassy lawn on the right side of it and the car park on its left-hand side, the gravel-covered roundabout driveway, and the road that leads from the gate house to the outside world. It's hilly, un-tarred, and winding, like my Grandpa's life has been, a series of ups and downs that led him to the place of rest and recovery from the bruising that life gave him daily. He had lived in Ibadan, but had brought Lagos life with him.

I walk down the porch steps and turn right towards the back of the compound. Different flowers line the walls, and trees of all kinds dot the compound. I weave between parked cars to the place where the big, fat almond tree from my childhood shades a bleached red, yellow, and green plastic play house. It's old and small, but big enough to fit eight tiny children. Big enough that I think I can still get into it at my age.

The house brings back memories. Grandpa bought it on one of his trips to the United States, and it kept his grandkids eager to visit. Placed on the plot of grass growing beneath the tree, it has a swing set beside it and a see-saw behind it. It's the first place we all reported to during family events growing up, and a miracle to still be standing.

An urge comes over me to sit inside. I get down on my knees on the wet grass, pull open the faded green door, and crawl in. The opening is wide enough that I can pass through easily with space on either side of me.

My head is not more than half way inside when I realize I am not alone. The big fixture blocking light from the right-hand side window of the house is human.

"Cousin Toba!" I burst out laughing before crawling all the way inside.

"Hi." He is laughing, too, but I can't see his face in the semi-darkness. Our bodies are blocking the side windows, and the only light coming in is the one through the door. "I guess I'm not the only one with strange ideas."

"Nothing like crawling into your childhood play-pen to put you in a good mood," I reply, squeezing myself into the left-hand side of the play house. The roof is lower than I thought it was, but I raise my head once I'm inside. There's still plenty of space between my head and the roof.

I'm wearing jeans so I fold my legs to the side and lean back against the wall. He is seated cross-legged, scant space between us, and the remnants of his aftershave tease my senses with a delightful smell.

"What are you doing in here?"

"Hiding," he shifts himself and opens the window beside him to let in some air and sunlight, "and reminiscing. I saw the place and couldn't resist coming in."

"How did you manage to squeeze yourself inside?"

"I'm wondering same," he replies with a deep chuckle. "But I guess we never really grow old inside, do we? This playhouse, it brings back memories."

I open the window on my own side. "It does."

His smile wanes. "Have you seen him?"

I think of Grandpa lying sick in that bed and take my time to answer. He is a shadow of himself, more tired and old than the last time we had both seen him.

"Yeah," I breathe out loud and look up at Toba. I feel sorry for him—he is losing his father. I can't even bring myself to talk about his visit to Akpan.

"I just wanted to ..." he trails off and links his fingers between his legs with a sigh. "This was my happy place so I wanted—"

"*Our* happy place," I correct. He raises his head to look at me. "Brings back happy memories. You need them, now more than ever."

Toba and I have been in here more times than I can count, alone, with each other, with my sisters, with other relatives, and with friends. We cooked and played house. We hid, we sang, we told stories. It was where we went when we were scolded, where we went to read in peace and quiet, away from the noisier younger children. It was our happy place, one we now sit in to stop our hearts from breaking at Grandpa's passing.

"When did you get here?"

He exhales out loud. "Got the call yesterday and came in from Lagos last night. I spent the better part of the night with him."

"I'm sorry."

He holds my gaze. "Thank you."

"I'm going to miss him."

"Me too." Toba stares down at his hands. "How is your doctor friend?"

I conjure Esosa's face and smile in spite of myself. "He's good. How is Yinka 'with a C'?"

He shrugs. "She's fine."

"I heard you visited an old guy-friend of mine."

All of a sudden, there are worry lines on Toba's forehead. "He slapped you around a couple times, I hear."

I look down at my knees. The anger I had felt when I'd heard he'd visited Akpan dulled to shame at his words. How could I, Femi, the boldest girl in the family, have allowed that to happen?

"I handled it when we broke up."

"I know, but he'll be writing you an apology letter soon. He made me a promise."

"That's hardly necessary."

"He should, or we're slapping him with litigation. You visited an eye specialist! How dare he?"

I look up. Toba seems pretty serious, more than I'd ever seen him. Akpan had never apologized once. Not when I told him I had needed to see a doctor, not even when I told him it was over.

"I was angry when I heard you'd talked to him, but an apology would be nice. Thank you."

"You're welcome."

We fall quiet and study the plastic floor of the playhouse.

"Why aren't you in there?" I nod towards the house.

"Because I want to remember him different," he drawls. "Healthy, strong, not like this."

My cousin Toba fills up the space on his side and his head barely misses the roof. His huge shoulders are slumped, and his face is impassive. He's hurting. I'm hurting, too, not just because my grandfather won't be here any longer, but because Toba is hurting. The other children have siblings; he doesn't. He has always been alone, except for me and my three sisters.

"What did he say to you?" I ask, recalling the conversation I had seen him having with Grandpa, "that night of Aunty Ladepe's birthday."

Toba lifts his shoulders in a slow shrug.

"Stuff," he murmurs and falls into silence.

Stuff! Stuff he doesn't want to talk about. It's obvious I'm intruding. I think perhaps he wants to be alone to process Grandpa's death.

"I should go back in. My mum might need me."

"Don't." He reaches out a hand to me. "Stay with me."

I hesitate for a second, and then place my palm over his. We sit in silence, and wait for Grandpa to die.

There are so many things that I would like to tell my grandfather, like how I wish he could stay another ten years and how much I will miss him when he is gone. I'm losing my confidant, the only person I can talk to about how scared I am of getting married, and how scared I am of not. I feel my family is losing something special and they don't even know it. I am afraid that his influence over our lives is far greater than we realize, and that when he is gone, we will scatter and find it tough to come together again.

My eyes drop to our hands, and I sigh. My palm skims over his, exploring its tough-skinned breadth as my fingers run in-between his. I'm aware I'm playing with his hand, but I can't help myself. I don't know how to comfort him when I'm swallowed up in sadness and holding back my own tears. And he doesn't stop me. He keeps his gaze on our intertwined fingers and swipes his thumb over the back of my hand and knuckles. It's a thrilling sensation that shocks me and makes me look up at him.

In that moment, I want to fling myself at him and find comfort. Maybe give him comfort. The play house is cramped, and my feelings even more so.

"Everything is going to be okay," he says.

I nod to take my mind off the distracting feel of his wandering thumb. The words are as much for him as they are for me.

Just then, we hear a scream. I snatch my hand off Toba's and freeze. It's Aunty Ladepe's voice. We both know in that moment that Grandpa is gone.

***

Grandpa's burial takes us three days to celebrate. We plan it in a semi-sombre, semi-celebratory fashion. Lots of activities are ear-marked to celebrate the life he lived. The Wake Keep is organized by his church— the Anglican denomination—the Service of Songs organized by us, his family and the many friends he had, and the burial proper is held on the third day.

It begins with a church service, then an Interment at the graveside, and a grand reception party that resounds in Ibadan. Before it, however, there is the party planning and the antecedents that go with it. Arrangements for the washing and dressing of the corpse, picking of the burial vault and headstone, the choosing of pall bearers, publishing of a church program that includes family pictures and his life work, many details that get sorted.

In the days leading up to it, there is a crowd in and around the compound. Sober-looking elderly and middle-aged men, crying widows, young adults, children, the rich, the poor, politicians and top government officials, and people from all walks of life. The people my grandfather had touched with his philanthropic gestures. They throng the gate of the house, and the privileged few we allow in come and go.

There two policemen provided to us by the State Commissioner of Police, a valued friend of my late grandpa. They are stationed at the gate to keep the peace. Aunty Ladepe arranges food to feed everyone despite Uncle Gbenga and Uncle Sesan's strong objection. I know that wherever he is, Grandpa is pleased with this. My uncles aren't, however. It's our inheritance being fritted away again.

The family all deal with Grandpa's death in different ways. I don't cry when we view him at the mortuary, nor at the wake keep and service of songs. I don't cry at the church when I give the tribute on behalf of all the grandchildren, nor at the grave, where the songs are so sad and promising of meeting again, the tunes themselves invoke emotions. I don't even cry when they lower him into the grave, or when I watch Aunty Ladepe burst into tears and bury her face in Toba's arms.

It's at the party, when the guests have been served and the music is loud and the live band is calling us to come and dance on the centre stage, that's when it happens. I look at Aunty Ladepe sitting all alone, and I feel sorry for her. Over a month ago, we were all dancing at her party, full of joy and having our patriarch with us.

That is when I cry. That is when reality hits me and the dam breaks. My grandfather won't be at my wedding, or sit with me at family get-togethers, or tell me stories of the past, or mend my bike or twirl me around on his shoulder 'til we are both dizzy. I travel back in time down the years, and there is heaviness in my heart. All I have left is his voice, and his words of wisdom, his love, and his images.

He is gone, and I am going to miss him.
***

Going back to life after his burial hits me hard, I often burst into tears at the most inappropriate of times. Esosa is pretty understanding, but Grandpa's death derailed the relationship we'd built in over three months together. I am so sad, it drags on our dates, and I can tell he is reluctant for us to go out much. He holds me when I cry and tells me it's a phase I'll grow out of. He kisses me at other times, and I freeze. He thinks it is because of the sadness, but I know it's not.

I have this idea in my head that I want to save physical intimacy for the moment when I marry the man of my choosing. It's partly out of my religious upbringing, partly out of my strong moral code. Partly because I don't think I will hold any man's fancy that much anymore if I give it up to him too soon.

There are arguments for and against sex before marriage, but I'll just stick to being against it. Akpan and I had lots of arguments about it. I didn't give in because I don't have to do what everybody else does. Besides, Akpan was just not the one. Maybe it's why he felt okay hitting me.

Esosa thinks it's because I'm still sad about Grandpa's death. He's bidding his time but I know he will ask soon, and I will have to tell him that I am not going to sleep with him unless we walk down the aisle.

My mother cries in the bathroom. I heard her once when my dad was not home. Enitan cried every single day of the burial. The twins had their tears at the graveside. So did Uncle Juwon, and Uncle Deola.

The only people I fear did not shed a tear were Uncle Sesan, Uncle Gbenga, and Cousin Toba. The adults, I can understand, but Toba, doesn't even look like he's lost his dad. I think he mourned more before the old man passed. And when he was gone, he put his tears away. There was nothing on his face to suggest he even felt it. He went about the burial like an automated machine, did the vault and mortuary running around and arranged the pall bearers and graveside diggers with the ease of someone who did it often.

This annoyed me, but I didn't say anything. I know that somewhere inside him, Cousin Toba loved his father, and it's not for me to judge him.

Chapter Six

I love stories!

When I was younger, the highlight of my life was visiting my Grandpa's farm in Iseyin. A hundred kilometres north of Ibadan, and accessible by road networks from Oyo, Abeokuta, and Ogbomoso, we made sure to go there every time we visited him.

It is an hour and a half's drive from Bodija, and the journey is very boring. So my mother regaled us with tales of the Old Oyo Empire and its kings and princesses. Of course, we heard about the village of Iseyin, and how it came to be. I suppose that was how my love for the writing and editing of stories began, listening to tales spun in a chauffeured Peugeot 504 saloon car, on our way to Grandpa's farm.

History has it, that a certain hunter of no name or chieftaincy title, Aaba Odo Iseyin of the order of the Oro creed, ventured into a wild, fecund forest with a group of other hunter-farmers from Ile-Ife. They encountered some indigenes living under a High Chief of the Sango order known as Ebedi, and paid homage to him. In return, they were given chieftaincy titles, and the right to apportion land to any new settlers they deemed worthy.

In time, Ebedi became King of the whole land. In a bid to seek fortification for his ever growing empire, he travelled to Dahomey and did not return for a very long in time. Aaba and others voted to make his brother Ogbolu, king, suppossing he was dead. But Ebedi was already on his way home with a large number of slaves and warriors. As he neared the outskirts of his village, he heard the sounds of jubilation and found out that his brother had been installed as King in his place. Sad, but unwilling to make war with him, he sent the servants and warriors he had recruited as a gift to the newly elected King.

Now this is where the story got freaky, even for my ten year old mind. When Ebedi died, he and his six chief-servants transformed into the seven hills that border the forested village of Iseyin. Legend has it, that any King installed there must travel to the foothills of Ebedi to make an annual sacrifice.

Iseyin is known for cotton spinning, cloth weaving and dyeing. When Aaba settled there in those days, he brought with him the knowledge of the spinning of cotton to threads, and used hand looms to make them into Aso Oke fabrics. There was Sanyan, mostly brown and white, Alaari which is reddish in colour and Etu, dark blue with stripes.

The ancient inhabitants had cultivated tobacco, cotton, and vegetable dyes, mostly indigo in colour. My grandpa bought ten hectares of land and started his farm growing cash crops like maize, yams, cassava, and cocoa.

As the years hurtled by, the farm land became arid and needed an irrigation system to keep the crops viable. He paid huge sums to have water delivered to the farm daily, and then added poultry and goat rearing. His overheads increased because even animals need water. Being some distance from the Ikere Gorge dam built in the early eighties, the government promised aid to most of the farmers with lands around the area. As most things go in Nigeria, the promise has not seen the light of day, but Grandpa managed to keep his farm afloat and make it profitable. That profit, he put in various financial investments and land, so he died a very rich man.

I talk about this farm because it is important, and because we now sit around the dining table in Uncle Sesan's home discussing the issue of who gets it.

Grandpa's lawyer is here to disseminate the contents of his last will and testament. Everyone is here except Uncle Deola who is out of the country on work issues, and Aunty Layo who had to go back abroad immediately after the burial. She joined us via Skype, but network being what it is, had to abandon the idea after thirty minutes. Cousin Toba isn't around, either. He's on his way from Lagos, has been for about an hour. For some reason, the lawyer requested that I be present, too, and so after waiting for some time for Toba to show, the meeting began.

And it was hot, and expository!

You see, Grandpa divided his houses, shares, and 'stocks held in bonds' in various banks amongst his seven children and three wives. And that was fine. Everyone got a good semblance of something, including my maternal grandmother, his first wife, who had passed on years ago. Her share of the fortune was to be shared amongst her four children, and that was only proper.

Then Grandpa blindsided everyone and gave the profitable farm in Iseyin to his last-born son Toba, the only child of his favourite wife. I say favourite because it was obvious he loved her.

"This is ridiculous! This is nonsensical! This is cheating!" Uncle Gbenga paces the tiny dining room fuming with every fibre of his being. "I am not going to accept this! I will not allow this duplicitous piece of paper be entered to all of us as his last will and testament!"

Aunty Norma grabs my hand under the table and sniggers. Uncle Gbenga's penchant for using English words goes up a notch whenever he is angry. It's a favourite point of discussion when we get together at family functions to roast our parents. With him, the Ibadan accent is a little strong in his enunciation of certain English words, so 'cheating' sounds like 'shitting.'

"That farm should be divided amongst the seven of us. How can Baba give it to Toba? Is he the first-born? Is he the most qualified? That old man was senile, I'm telling you!"

Really Uncle Gbenga, calling Grandpa a senile old man in his absence is really hitting below the belt.

"Mr. Gbenga Awotunde," the lawyer says. "Please sit down."

"I am not sitting down! I'm not sitting down!" He turns to Aunty Ladepe and points at her. "Whatever vegetable you cook for my father to eat before he die is a potion that is not going to work!"

Aunty Norma jerks my arm under the table. 'Vegetable' sounds like 'Feshitable,' 'Father' sounds like 'Fadder,' and 'Eat' sounds like 'Heat.' The sing-song Ibadan accent isn't helping matters, either. It's obvious she wants to burst out laughing, so I pinch her to caution her.

"Gbenga, mind the way you talk to me," Aunty Ladepe warns. "Mind the way you talk to me."

I widen my eyes. I've never seen her this angry before.

"Keep quiet!" Uncle Gbenga says. "You see a married man with two wife, and you jump at him. Was there no single man in town? Where is your shame?"

I take in a deep breath. 'Married' sounds like 'Murried.' 'Man' sounds like 'Mon,' and somehow, there are no plurals in my uncles vocabulary.

"Gbenga, mind the way you talk to me!" Aunty Ladepe's voice goes an octave higher.

"*Huh, shioor!*" Uncle Gbenga continues. "*O mo boju e!*"

When he says this last part in Yoruba, Aunty Norma, who is beyond stopping at this point, actually titters with laughter and adjusts herself.

"Gbenga, will you sit down and stop making a fool of yourself!" Uncle Sesan shouts. "Mama Gbenga, *E ba omo yin soro!*"

"Please, let us have order!" the lawyer insists. I'm sure he would have banged on a judge's gavel if he'd had one.

"The boy is not even around," Uncle Gbenga continues. "And I'm sure Father gave him the farm at her insistence. He doesn't even take this reading of the Will as a serious something."

"Gbenga!" Uncle Sesan passes him a cautionary look.

"Please allow the lawyer to finish reading this Will *naau*," my mother adds.

Uncle Gbenga manages to find his seat, and the lawyer continues. He begins to name each grandchild one after the other and the amount of money accrued to them. I hear my name first, and something along the lines of a double portion inheritance. I look up. He has given me money, and a small piece of land in Bodija. It is land recently bought, and registered in my name.

"Land," Uncle Gbenga interjects. "He is giving her land? Which land is that?"

"Gbenga!" Uncle Sesan cautions again.

"So my own children will not get any land!"

'*Shuldren*' we hear, and Aunty Norma is swollen with laughter.

The lawyer goes on. Every other grandchild gets money not up to mine in amount, and none gets a piece of land. I'm perplexed and pained. I know more than anyone else seated in that room why Grandpa has given me that land. It's because I had told him once that if I clocked forty without a man, I would buy myself a house and start living in it. I don't think he ever thought I'd find someone.

Uncle Gbenga shakes his head and swings his knees back and forth. Uncle Juwon, seated on the other side of me, nudges me and whispers 'land owner' in my ear. I cringe. I don't know what the other grandchildren are going to think about this apparent show of favouritism.

The lawyer clears his throat and motions for everyone to be silent. "There is a video that I have to play at this point, and I will like to enjoin everyone present here to be quiet until it ends, regardless of what you hear." He makes a point of looking at Uncle Gbenga.

Video? I'm curious because the lawyer's voice sounds cryptic.

Grandpa's face appears on the laptop screen placed at a strategic point so everyone can see. It is a video made a year ago. In it, he says hello to everyone and mentions us all by name, including those not around. Next, he tells us to accept the details of his will as so. He had written it in his own hand, with his lawyer present. He gives us each a specific farewell message, starting with Uncle Sesan. To me, he adds that there is another video message to be played on the day of my wedding, so he can address my groom. There are tears in my eyes, but I am determined not to let them fall.

He talks to Toba last. It's unfortunate that Toba is not here to hear him. He tells him to keep the farm as they have discussed. He tells him to be strong and courageous and take risks with care. He tells him to keep feeding the farmhands and attending to his monthly poor clinic. My grandpa gives to the poor every last Thursday of every month. They come to the house, and he loans money, gives cash and food, employs some, or connects them to where they can find employment. Ibadan is a really poor town compared to Lagos, and my grandfather tried to do his bit to alleviate suffering. Toba is to continue this on his behalf. There is money set aside for it.

He then he says something that makes everyone frown.

"I have to let the cat out of the bag, so that you can be free, Toba."

Free? I'm wondering what it is Toba needs to be free from.

He calls Aunty Ladepe's name and tells her how much he loves her, how happy she made him, and how much he regrets that they couldn't have had more children.

Uncle Gbenga hisses, and Uncle Sesan frowns at him.

Grandpa goes on to tell Aunty Ladepe that the truth has to come out, for Toba's sake. He asks her to forgive him for letting it out like a coward.

I glance at her. She looks scared. Whatever it is he is about to say, Aunty Ladepe is well aware of, and it doesn't sound pleasant.

Grandpa drops the bombshell. "Toba is not my son."

Oh, snap!

"Not genetically, but he is as much my biological child as any of you. I would like you all to treat him as such. So accept him for who he is to me, and for the fact that he is innocent in all of this. You will share my fortune with him and not complain, because I love him as much as I love you all. I hope to meet you all someday in the future. This is my hearty farewell."

The recording ends, and there is silence in the room. I don't think anybody heard anything beyond the words *'Toba is not my son.'*

"Wait a minute." Uncle Juwon speaks first. "What did he just say?"

The lawyer switches off the video and looks at us. "Exactly what you heard, Toba was not fathered by Chief Awotunde, but he has chosen to treat him as his biological child."

"*What!*" Uncle Gbenga roars, and then looks at Aunty Ladepe. "You used juju on my father?"

Aunty Norma grabs my arm, and we both look at one another with raised eyebrows. Uncle Juwon is grinning from ear to ear, like he just won a lottery. I can bet he is busy splitting all the property six ways instead of seven. It's appalling, considering he is the one who has what looks like a half-decent relationship with Toba.

The door opens just then, and the subject of our conversation slips into the room without a sound. All eyes swing to him. This was a meeting slated for nine, and he just strolls in more than an hour and a half late, looking a tad disinterested and quite unrepentant about it. He closes the door behind himself and stares at everyone.

Through the corner of my eye, I see Uncle Gbenga give him a lethal look. If looks could kill, Toba would be joining Grandpa right now. Uncle Gbenga has never been his fan. Now with Grandpa's confession, he is very unhappy with him.

"Welcome, Toba." The lawyer peers at him from above the rim of thick lenses. "We were all wondering when you were going to join us."

"Good morning everyone," Toba bows his head to all the elders in the room. "my sincere apologies for being late. Egbon." He prostrates to Uncle Sesan and stands up. His movements are slow and half-hearted, like he doesn't even want to be in the room.

"So this is your nine o'clock?" Uncle Gbenga seethes.

"There was mad traffic on the way coming," Toba replies with an air of nonchalance. "I'm sorry I'm late."

He pulls out the only available chair and sinks heavily into it, dropping his car key on the table. It's the chair between Uncle Gbenga and Grandma Kike. It is not a comfortable place to be, between two people who don't like you and have now heard that you are not even meant to have a seat at the table.

It's opposite me, however, so I wipe the surprise off my face and give him a small smile of understanding, which he acknowledges. There's just something about Toba being around that puts me at ease.

"What have I missed?" He looks round at everyone. The closed office makes his voice sound deeper and richer than it actually is, and the tone resonates round the room.

"A lot," Uncle Juwon stares across the table at him.

Toba returns the stare unbothered.

"You should have been here yesterday night like the rest of us. You know this is an important meeting," Uncle Sesan adds.

"My apologies," he hangs his head and sits blank-faced, unaware that the bubble surrounding his parentage has been popped.

"Hmnn uhun hun." Grandma Kike squeezes her mouth and nose together feigning irritation. I've seen that look before. She is livid. But Toba is slumped in his chair next to her, somewhat oblivious to the fact that something is wrong and people are upset.

I have often wondered what goes on in that head of his when he sits through family meeting confrontations refusing to get involved. I wonder now what his reaction will be to Grandpa and Aunty Ladepe's best-kept secret. I look around me and realize that everyone is just as curious. We all stare at him, because we cannot believe what we have all just heard.

"We had to proceed with the reading of your father's will. Everyone else has places to go and things to do."

Toba nods. "I understand."

"You came in at just the right time because some interesting facts came to light in the course of the reading of the will." The lawyer peers over his glasses at him, "facts that concern you."

Toba tilts his head to his right-hand side and looks at the lawyer.

Get to it, I'm thinking as my eyes skim the faces of the people present in the dining room. I can't wait to see his reaction. Neither can anyone else.

"Toba, the person you have called your father for all of your life growing up is not actually your biological father."

Toba stares back at the lawyer for a moment. His eyes swing away from him as if in deep contemplation. "Hmnnn," he murmurs, and his head tilts backwards a little bit.

It sounds like a nonchalant grunt from the middle of his stomach in response to a question that requires a little bit of thinking.

The whole room is silent, albeit shocked for the second time that morning by Toba's reaction. *'Hmnnn?'*

Now, I like Cousin Toba, but he is of a stolid, calm, and even-tempered disposition which is as phlegmatic as phlegmatic temperaments usually come. He is composed to the point of annoyance most of the time and generally comes across as lazy, uninteresting, and uninterested in anything, in that particular order. Right now, he seems kind of uninterested in the news that his father is not his real father.

Most people are a blend of two major temperaments, say Sanguine and Melancholic, like me, or Choleric and Melancholic, like my twin sisters. With Toba, I am not sure that there is any other temperament lurking behind that closely-guarded, smiley face. A phleg through and through, he is so into himself that we sometimes forget he is there.

Like when he was away for three years getting his masters' in the UK. We forgot that he was on the face of this Earth 'til he showed up at Aramide's wedding with the cutest and homeliest girlfriend anyone of us had ever seen. He had every male person in the auditorium gawking. It was a jaw-dropping moment that most of us have never quite gotten over. That is until Yinka 'with a C' came along. Toba is like that. Mostly invisible when he is present, easily forgettable when he's not—because he kind of like doesn't say anything—and shocking when he stirs the waters, like he has just done.

"Toba." The lawyer's voice jerks me out of my imagination. "You do understand what I'm trying to tell you?"

He nods very slowly.

"*Yawah don gas*," Aunty Norma murmurs beside me through the side of her mouth.

My mum looks as flabbergasted as she did the first time she heard the news, and Uncle Gbenga looks like bread dipped in water.

"My darling," Aunty Ladepe wrings her hands as her voice shakes, "I was going to tell you."

Toba looks at his mum with disbelief. It's weird. For thirty-eight years, she doesn't say anything to him, and now, she tells him she always wanted to? Even I don't believe her.

"It was a difficult decision," she continues, "a joint one by your father and me to keep this news to protect you."

"He was not his father!" Uncle Gbenga roars.

"He was very much his father," Aunty Ladepe replies.

"He was not his father!"

"Toba is Awo's son!" Aunty Ladepe almost stands up from her seat.

"You are a conniving liar and a husband snatcher!"

"And you are just rude."

"That's enough!" Toba says in a voice loud and deep enough to command respect.

Everybody shuts up. I want to think it's because he wants to spare his mother any further embarrassment. Because all I can think about, all anyone can think about, is who his father really is.

"It's enough?" Uncle Juwon sounds agitated. "Toba, you find out that your father is not really your father, and you're not up in your mother's face, asking her who your real father is."

Toba shrugs. "I don't need to."

Why not?

"Why not?" Uncle Juwon asks out loud.

"Because it's not news to me," Toba replies him, straight-faced. "I've always known he wasn't my father."

There is a sudden uproar, and everyone starts talking at once. Aunty Norma holds down my forearm and squeezes it to make sure she doesn't jump up and scream. I am confused. Toba has known in all this while that he wasn't Grandpa's son, and he didn't say anything. To anyone!

The lawyer starts rapping on the table to keep things quiet. My mum takes in a deep breath. She can't quite comprehend how to react to the whole matter.

"How did you know?" Aunty Ladepe asks.

"He told me."

"For how long have you known?"

"Since I was twenty-three," Toba's gaze doesn't leave his mother's face.

Everyone is doing the maths. If Toba is thirty-eight now, then he has known for fifteen whole years that Grandpa wasn't his father. Shut up! And he didn't say anything. To anyone!

"As far as I'm concerned, he is my father. It's no big deal."

"It *is* a big deal!" Uncle Gbenga jumps out of his chair. Toba sort of glances at him for a second and doesn't flinch. "It's a big deal because despite knowing that you not his biological son, he left you the farm and his account to run! How fair is that?"

"Let us all calm down," my mother says. "There is nothing to be gained from tempers rising."

"I'm not calming down. I shall not accept this."

"Gbenga," Uncle Sesan finally speaks. "Sit down."

"I'm not sitting down. I'm not sitting down. We are going to scatter this place!" Uncle Gbenga points a finger in Aunty Ladepe's face. "And you, you are going to tell us who you cheated on my father with."

'*Shitted!*' I'm thinking. Aunty Norma can't hold back any more. She lowers her head onto her chin and starts chuckling, her huge shoulders shaking with laughter.

"Gbenga, I said sit down!" Uncle Sesan repeats as the lawyer raps on the table.

There is noise, and carnage. I watch Toba sit back in his chair, calm and clearly unconcerned. He toys with his car key and moves it about an invisible circle on the table with his right index finger.

It occurs to me in that moment that it was possible that he knew all along what would happen at this meeting. My grandfather already told him, that night of Aunty Ladepe's birthday. He probably already knew, long before any of us, that he was getting the farm. That's why he had looked so reluctant to be at the meeting. The keys to the farm were already in his pocket, and he was keeping them. There was no amount of commotion that Uncle Gbenga could raise that would reverse the decision, and he was secure in that knowledge.

He looks up just then, and our eyes meet. There is noise, shouting, and a lot of hubbub, but we both don't hear it. We are looking at each other. He, with tranquillity; me with the realization that he's not actually related to any of us, and that technically, he is not my uncle.

There is a flash of something in his face which intrigues me. Its stubbornness, determination, and strength, and I see it for the first time.

Chapter Seven

My twin sisters and I were at first confused about the fact that Toba was our mother's brother. He just seemed too little, and she just seemed too big. It was something that took us a while to accept, something we often giggled to one another about.

He was frequently put in charge of us but always failed at the task. He couldn't keep us obedient and quiet enough for the adults because the twins and I would pull incessant pranks that left him mildly disoriented. If he asked us to take a right on the way home from a walk, Aramide and Olamide would go left, while I would just climb a tree and taunt him to follow. Toba would call for us just once or twice and then give up.

Enitan was the only one Toba seemed to have a handle on. He'd walk her home, thumb stuck in her mouth and her tiny hand gripping his pudgy one. We would watch from a distance. In some way, he was like the brother we never had. Needless to say, my mother would chastise him on end for letting us get away from him, and he'd just go about his gentle ways, not having heard a word she said.

The meeting is over, and Uncle Gbenga is still complaining to everyone about Grandpa's unfairness. The lawyer tries extraditing himself from the conversation, but my uncle doesn't let him leave. I slip into the sitting room and watch through a translucent glass door as Toba and his mother speak on the balcony.

Toba is looking down at her, and for the first time, it strikes me that he is way taller than the average Awotunde male and looks nothing like them. I always just thought he picked more traits from his mother's side of the family.

Aunty Ladepe seems upset, and when he envelopes her in his arms, I feel a wave of sadness and wonder what the real story is behind it all.

"Favourite grandchild." Aunty Norma nudges me from behind. *"Na which kain fejitable you carry give grandpa chop."*

I eye her, and she starts laughing. She is not upset about the will, and neither is her husband. He is the most amiable of all my mother's brothers, and he married a lovely wife from another tribe whom we have all grown to love.

"When are you going to go and look at your land?" she asks.

I shrug. "I don't know, whenever I get the courage."

"Wetin you dey fear, you no know say land dey important?"

"I know. It just means Grandpa thought I'm not going to get married. He gave me land so I can build my own house."

"Haba, no!" Aunty Norma squeezes her forehead. "Why would you think that? The old man loved you and everyone knows it. He even made a video to your future husband."

"On the off chance that I get married—"

"You are going to get married and have beautiful children with beautiful brown skin and a heart-shaped face like yours, *haba. Abi you no know say you fine, that handsome docki nko? Abi you no wan marry am?"*

I had forgotten about Esosa. I'm dating, and worried about not getting married. I look at Aunty Norma; her words fill me with hope.

"Thank you," I say and put my arms around her.

The door to the balcony opens, and Toba strides out looking a little stern. It's not surprising, considering all that has gone down.

"Femi," he says. It's impersonal, devoid of the usual warmth. "Do you mind dropping my mother off at home?"

He has always called me Nifemi, and I had never noticed the difference 'til now. Femi puts this space between us that makes the whole situation real. There are things I can't do with him again. Like hug him when we meet, or hold his hand in a plastic playhouse.

Everything is awkward now, but it doesn't have to be, I tell myself.

"I don't mind," I say, releasing Aunty Norma.

People troop out of the dining and avoid Aunty Ladepe. I can't help but feel a little angry about that as I recall the last dance she had with Grandpa, and how much in love they were. He's gone now, and he left her this big mess.

I go round to say my goodbyes. My mum is still in discussions with her brothers over Grandpa's house. It's to remain a family house for everyone to land in whenever they come down to Ibadan, so it doesn't belong to any one person. I can see it causing problems in future, especially because Grandpa mandated that Aunty Ladepe live in it.

When I get outside, Toba is speaking to his mm in soft tones while she dabs her eyes with her handkerchief. He looks up and hands me his car transponder.

"I'll meet you guys at home. And," he pauses to eye me, "don't crash my car!"

"Yes, sir," I salute him. I crashed his car once, at Uncle Sesan's birthday while trying to move it out of the way for someone.

He doesn't smile. I get the feeling he is staying back to get some backlash from his older siblings, and my heart goes out to him. Nothing that is happening is his fault. And there is more to the story than we are all privy to.

"Are you ready ma?" I throw Aunty Ladepe's bags into the back seat of Toba's Ford Edge and smile at her.

"Obanifemi, thank you very much, my child, *ose gan ni.*"

"*Ko t'ope ma,*" I reply. "I'm happy to help."

We get into the car and drive away. Aunty Norma follows us to the bus-stop and drops, leaving Aunty Ladepe and me alone in a thick kind of silence that is filled with unasked questions.

"I didn't even thank you properly for my birthday," she begins.

"Ah, Aunty, you can't be thanking me." I concentrate on the cars coming up from behind me. "Thank Olamide. She planned the whole thing."

"But it was you I saw running around."

"Yes, her leg was in a cast." I shrugged. "Someone had to manage her event planning boys."

"Oh. All the same, thank you. The cake was lovely."

"You have Ara to thank for that. She donated it."

"I'm thanking all of you," she replies with a sigh. "You make me not miss having a daughter. The food was good, my friends were happy, your grandpa was happy—"

I realize she is making small talk so that we don't have to talk about the elephant in the car with us: the subject of Toba's father.

"I didn't know that you and Grandpa still had it going," I say with a huge grin. "That dance was really something else, Aunty."

She laughs, and then bursts out crying.

"Oh, Aunty Ladepe." I keep both hands on the steering wheel as two cars breeze past on both sides of me. I'm a tad confused about how to calm her and steer the car at the same time. "Are you alright ma?"

"I just miss Awo," she says, sniffing.

"I know, I know. We all miss him, too."

She digs for her handkerchief in her handbag and wipes her face and dabs her nose. "It's just that, when he was around, I felt safe, and now, Toba is angry with me."

"I seriously doubt that, Aunty." I look ahead out of the windscreen as we slow down into a hold up. "He hasn't been upset in fifteen years."

"He doesn't understand the circumstances."

"You are his mother, and Toba doesn't keep scores. Grandpa loved you both, and he wanted us all to accept him. That settles it for me."

We drive on in silence, and I don't ask her who Toba's father is. I don't because I know she loved my grandfather and still grieves him. Even if she had an affair, it doesn't matter. Grandpa loved her with his dying breath, and he had obviously forgiven her. So who were we to judge?

There are still a few little questions, like if Toba should still bear my grandfather's name, or if his biological father is still alive and if Toba would even like to meet him. But we don't talk about those things. I respect Aunty Ladepe in spite of what happened, and I know she's dealing with feelings we all can't possibly comprehend.

***

"Whooaaaat!"

I roll my eyes at Pariola's exaggerated response to the news about Toba when we tell her.

She grabs a chair and pulls it up to the dining table where Olamide, Aramide, and I sit planning Olamide's upcoming wedding.

"Tell me more," she says, placing her bag on the table and sinking into the chair. "So Toba is not an Awotunde! What! Somebody pinch me."

I've a good mind to if she doesn't stop yelling.

"Yeah, this is how I was a-looking when Femi told me." Aramide stays still and crosses her eyes. "The information was just scrambling my brains."

"Haaaaa," Pariola sinks her chin into cupped hands with her elbows on the table. "Aunty Ladepe had an affair?"

"Yeah, just like you to jump into the easiest conclusion," I say, turning the page of the wedding cake booklet I'm looking at.

"So what happened?"

"We don't know," Aramide says. "Just that Grandpa is not his father, and Uncle Gbenga is raising dust and trouble."

"And shitting bad grammar all over the place," I add.

"And there is a big fight over the farm. Grandpa left it to him," Olamide adds.

"Yes, the farm and—" Pariola turns to me. "—I heard he left you a piece of land and forgot the rest of us. You have some explaining to do, young lady, but we'll get to that in a minute! So, Toba's father is who exactly?"

"Nobody knows," Aramide says. "Except Aunty Ladepe, of course, she would know who knocked her up."

"So she's not saying?"

"I think both Toba and his mum want to keep that piece of information private," Olamide says, "because Toba always knew Grandpa wasn't his dad."

Pariola looks perplexed. "But why, so they could wrangle Grandpa into giving them money and land?"

"Which he did give them," Aramide points out.

"And I always thought Toba was the epitome of uprightness. Why would he do this?"

"Maybe Grandpa just loved her." Olamide looks at Pariola. "We all saw that at the birthday."

I start laughing, and the others peer at me with concern.

"According to Uncle Gbenga, Aunty Ladepe gave him fejitable to heat—" I can't stop laughing. "You should have seen Aunty Norma's face. I had to pinch her so she wouldn't start laughing out loud."

Olamide chuckles. "But seriously, the question needs asking. What in the world did Aunty Ladepe do to make Grandpa love her so much?"

"She gave him good sex," Aramide mutters and pushes her mouth to the right-hand side like she didn't just say anything. Olamide starts laughing.

I look up and stare at her. "Ara, really ..."

"She has a point," Pariola says with vigorous nodding. "No offence to your grandmother, but Aunty Ladepe was thirty years younger and quite the looker."

I try to imagine Grandpa and Aunty Ladepe together, and the images just don't form. I soon shake my head. "It's got to be something more."

"Maybe—" Pariola holds up a hand, "—she had an affair with Grandpa's best friend, and passed Toba off as his own. Then he found out. Maybe that's why Toba came to live with you guys when he was ten."

Aramide and I look at one another. We can both remember that Toba lived with us until he went to university. We had never really known why.

"I always assumed it was Grandma Kike who didn't want him living with them," I say to everyone.

"I thought it was because Aunty Ladepe was worried they'd poison Toba." Aramide stares at me, and I can't erase that possibility from my head.

"I thought they just wanted someone close in age to be Toba's companion." Olamide shrugs. "Uncle Sesan's kids were schooling abroad, but we were available."

"Hmmm." Pariola's chin is in her right fist now. "So, does Toba know who his dad is?"

"You're as curious as the rest of us," I reply, "but coming to the party late. Me thinks he just doesn't care. You should have seen the way he told us he knew, like yeah he's not my dad, and Uncle Juwon was like, you are not up in your mother's face asking who the heck your dad is, and Toba's like, yeah whatever."

"Have you guys thought of all the possible ramifications of this?" Pariola says, looking from me to Aramide. "As in, there is literarily no blood between him and any of us. And you know what I mean."

"So?" Aramide looks at Pariola and raises a shoulder.

"I have always wanted to lock that skinny girlfriend of his into a toilet and throw away the key." She raises her eyes to the ceiling. "But Toba is so boring. Y'all know we can't call him Cousin Toba anymore, right?"

"Pari, you won't find a husband by jumping from guy to guy." Aramide flips through the iPad on the table searching for possible wedding colours.

"Toba is still family. We can't throw him away now just 'cause his dad is not who we think it is. What if it had happened to anyone of us?" Olamide adds.

"Are you kidding me?" Pariola drops her mouth open. "We should abandon Toba to that fake skinny girl with an abominable letter that does not exist in the Yoruba alphabet scheme in her name."

"She's got her hooks sunk into him," Olamide lifts her hands and curls her fingers. "And I think Cousin Toba likes it that way."

"So we should remove the hooks and kick her out!" Pariola replies.

I snigger. "And who is going to do that? You?"

"And why not?" She turns to look at me. "I'm from your dad's side of the family and not your mum's side, and it isn't these two 'cause they are married. You can't, either. You're busy entertaining the affections of a certain young doctor."

I think of Esosa and blush.

"By the way, when is your cast coming off?" Pariola turns to Olamide.

Olamide raises her casted leg and places it on the dining table with a loud thud. "Next week. I'm taking an X-ray."

"You better not let Mummy see you putting that leg on the dining table!" I warn.

"I'm going to ask Mummy," Aramide announces. "About Toba."

I stare at her. "I doubt Mummy knows. She was just as surprised as the rest of us."

"Yeah, but if anyone can get the truth out of her, it will be Mummy."

So we pile into my mother's room before Aramide leaves with her twins. We want to know the deal about Toba.

She is propped up in bed reading a novel. It's one of those days that my father has decided to watch ball late into the night. Diran, Aramide's husband who has come to pick them, is watching with him.

"We have all heard what happened at the reading of the will and everyone is curious," Aramide begins. "Why did Toba come to live with us when we were younger?"

My mother removes her glasses, and puts her book down. "You ask after almost thirty years."

I'm leaning against the wall opposite her. "Mummy, just tell us, okay? We finally asked."

"It's nothing," she said. "Your grandpa wanted him to school in Lagos. I think he listened to you all speak well and concluded he wanted Lagos education for Toba, not that Ibadan doesn't have great schools. He just believed in that Lagos the centre of excellence thing."

Olamide looks disappointed. "Nothing to do with a scandal?"

"No. Your grandpa felt that Toba was a little too—" My mother struggles for a word.

"Slow?" I offer.

"Needed a little less codling. He felt his mum was smothering him and he wanted Toba to grow up." My mother's eyes find mine. "He was intelligent, but my father wanted him to lose the, I don't know—" She struggles again with her explanations. "He wanted the Lagos smarts to rub off on Toba so he could grow up. And he did, to be a charming young man. Who'd have thought?"

"Guess the frog turned into a prince," I say.

"So who is his father?" Aramide asks.

My mother shakes her head. "I never knew he wasn't Grandpa's son."

"But you talk to Aunty Ladepe." Aramide is reluctant to give up. "You guys are close. She will tell you if you ask her."

"Whoever Toba's father is, if she wants us to know, she'll tell us. My father regarded Toba as his son and raised him."

"You helped," I say from beside the wall and take my weight off it. It's apparent we are not getting any answers from talking to her.

"I did." My mother looks at me.

"And you don't mind him having the farm?" Aramide folds her arms.

"One needs time and dedication to run that farm, none of which my brothers and I have. It's good that the farm is with Toba, he has grown up to be everything that we wanted him to be and more."

"I saw Aunty Ladepe crying the night she left Toba with us," I say.

"Yes, it's not easy to abandon your own child for someone else to raise. When you have your own baby, you'll understand what that means." She is looking at me, and I get the message. I must have a child, she's expecting it.

"Good night, Mum," I say. Yeah, she just had to find a way to rub that in.

If I have babies, I'm definitely giving them to someone else.

Chapter Eight

Nigerian wedding parties are the highlight of catching fun. Typically a conundrum of too many things happening, they are filled with music, drama, and tempers rising around Jollof rice coolers.

Particularly notorious for being an extravagant show of wealth, people save towards weddings, borrow to fund weddings, and guilt family members into paying for their weddings. The average Nigerian wedding is just an excuse to throw down and have some good old-fashioned fun, because a typical day in Naija, is full of a whole lot of stress.

Planning starts with a vision of the bride's dream wedding. Then a date is picked and venues are booked. You'd be amazed at how far into the year these bookings go. Two hundred million people nationwide, makes the probability of ten people picking the same date, venue and time very high.

Several things qualify the expenses a high society (Yoruba) wedding brings to the table, that is, if the wedding doesn't even take place overseas. The pre wedding photo shoot; the list of traditional wedding requirements; the couple's engagement attire; the family's *Aso Ebi*; the well-known comedian aka Master of Ceremony hired to make us all laugh and forget the sorry state of our economy; the contemporary musician and entertainment of the day; and the bride's beautiful, imported (worn only once in a lifetime) wedding gown.

The average Nigerian wedding is a fashion show that has the couple's family members sporting an *Aso*

Ebi fabric that's different from that of the couple's friends. The invited guests purchase it, and an *Aso Oke gele* that earns them a party favour and admittance into the reception venue. A guest list is prepared in advance. No matter how high your 'gele' is, if your name isn't stated, you are not getting in. Everyone's tailor is put to the test and the accompanying make up has got to transform. The best ones have people walk right past you and you don't even recognize them.

So a multimillion naira industry has sprung up as a result of these wedding day dress ups. Jewellery; Hair and Makeup; Fashion Photography, Soft sell magazines; Blogging, the literal works! Weddings provide an opportunity to get snapped and end up as a style icon in a magazine that millions of Nigerian women browse for the latest fusion of styles. So, it's mind-boggling, what Nigerian weddings have done for the West African fashion scene creatively, and economically.

Back in the day, the couple's family appeared in two different colours that informed the whole bridal theme. Today, weddings are viewed as a union of families, it makes sense that everyone appear in unison, saves the bouncers less of a headache trying to pick out wedding crashers. Then the colours were simple, red, blue, orange and green. Now we have magenta, teal, and burgundy, colours most people have to look up in the dictionary to get their bearing right.

So the colours make the day, and that hasn't changed. They inform the venue décor, party favours and wedding cake, which is rarely ever shared at receptions anymore. More a part of the décor than dessert, they make the hall look grand because reception menus now feature three course meals with desert afterwards.

The cutting of the cake preludes the couple's first official dance, and dancing, is something Nigerians enjoy. No wedding is complete without it. Competitions arise between the bride and groom; the bride's maids and groom's men; and between the bride's family and groom's family. It's the main attraction to weddings asides food.

While dancing, the couple is showered with different currency denominations by family and invited guests. Care is taken, so the people helping to pick up the money don't pocket some of it themselves. Everyone is sprayed, so it's often tough to tell which belongs to the couple and which doesn't. The music band leader isn't left out. He calls the rich and influential to dance with the couple and praises them enough that they are swayed into giving him part of this money. Most people comply. There is this force that takes you over when you hear your name being called in a song. It drags you over to the music section and draws wads of naira notes out of your pocket and unto the band leader's forehead. I've seen it happen countless times.

Nigerian weddings also show social influence. Everyone with a smart phone and pixel capabilities compete to capture the first looks of the new couple. When these pictures make their way to magazines and social media platforms, the wedding becomes an overnight sensation. It's a status thing to have your wedding covered by a popular blogger or an e-magazine. No one wants to feel like they don't matter on the Nigerian social scene.

So in conclusion, there are things that now exist at weddings that didn't a mere fifteen years ago, and planning for Olamide's wedding makes me realize why I want a small one with just family, close friends, and simplicity in every way possible.

***

We execute Olamide's wedding in a big Lagos way at Ibadan. My dad consented to it long before Grandpa died, because our family church is there and Korede's family lives in Ibadan.

The wedding colours of lilac and marigold carry into everything. Olamide's off-white dress is beautiful, her train decorated with dustings of lilac and marigold, and her bouquet a delicate arrangement of marigold flowers interspaced with tiny lilac drops. Her bridal train, a length of eight girls, dress in matching lilac dresses. Aramide's twins join them as ring bearer and little bride, and the whole affair projects as an Ibadan royalty wedding.

The reception is filled to capacity. I find myself wondering if the ushers and bouncers used the guest list. Aramide and I coordinate the food vendors and take turns to ensure Olamide sits in place and doesn't barge out to correct some wrong she has noticed with her ever-roving event planning eyes.

She is on pain meds for the day, pre-taken on the advice of Dr. Esosa because the engagement ceremony the day before knocks some pain back into her ankle. We want her to smile for the camera at every juncture, but I follow Esosa's advice and take away the rest of the meds so Olamide doesn't get into a habit she will find very difficult to break.

Weaving through the seated guests, I greet people I haven't seen in ages and thank them for coming as I hurry over to my table of friends. Lilian has been keeping them fed and entertained. I'm more than grateful to her. As I sit to take a break, I spy Aunty

Norma heading in my direction. I do not know why she thinks that the more she gives Jolomi to me the more we will like each other. I've been sorting guests and coordinating ushers all day, the last thing I want to do is hold a baby.

Up on the gallery where my parents are seated, I see Mama Bimpe talking at the top of her voice and my mum beside her. They are heading down to the stage to dance with the latest couple in town. My mum beckons to me. I groan. I would rather hold the baby than discuss my unmarried state with Mama Bimpe.

No, she hasn't met Esosa, and no, I have no plans introducing them.

"You no go dance now, abi Femi," Aunty Norma pushes Jolomi in my direction.

"This baby has an older sister," I reply. "And my mum is calling me."

"Bring, bring, bring," Lilian holds up her hands with a huge smile. She loves babies. So do the litany of my other friends seated at the table, so Jolomi will have a wide cross-section of eager babysitters.

"Thank you jare, don't mind this alako," Aunty Norma eye-balls me a couple of times before handing the baby over.

"You can trust Lilian," I say, ignoring her look. "You should not trust me with your baby."

"You no know wetin dey for your front. Call me to come babysit now, see whether I go answer you!"

"Who told you I plan to have a baby?" I throw back while heading towards the gallery.

I don't know if its fear or something more, but the idea of getting married and having babies with Esosa distresses me. We will be too busy. I worry that I won't have the heart or the patience for child care, and I'll become an Aunty Norma, always sourcing people to hold my child.

"Your father needs food for three of his guests who just arrived." My mother points at the table where he is, laughing at the top of his voice in the midst of friends. "Please sort them out. It's my turn to dance with the bride."

"Sure," I say with a lot of reservation.

I have been told over and over at this wedding— by almost everyone—that they thought it was me getting married. I know that. I don't need anyone to remind me. I do a good enough job reminding myself. My father's friends, however, they like to joke a lot about unmarried older girls who still live in their parents' houses.

I plaster a smile on my face, grab an usher, and head towards their table. Once I get the orders down, I leave the usher to return with the server and the food. As much as I love my sister, I can't wait for her party to be over.

Pausing at the railings, I stare at the festivity below. My mum and her friends are dancing to Ebenezer Obe's *'What God has joined together.'* Mama Bimpe is waving her bust at the couple with her index fingers high in the air. She's having the time of her life like she always does at parties. Everyone has those family members that contribute nothing to the party organization but leave having eaten the most, drunk the most, danced the most, and gotten every single souvenir available. That's Mama Bimpe. She'll eat at least twice and ensure you do her a takeaway pack.

My eyes slide over to my own table where Jolomi is with Esosa. He is cradling her in his arms with so much care, I'm impressed. I watch with a smile on my face. Esosa looks like a proud new father rocking his kid like a pro. Jolomi is gazing up at him, quiet and enjoying whatever song he's singing.

"Paediatrician?"

Cousin Toba's voice startles me. I find him standing next to me looking down the railings at Esosa.

"Esosa? Oh, no, he's a surgeon. Orthopaedics," I add with a grin and turn to stare at Esosa with affection. "He fixed Olamide's leg. That's how we met."

"He seems very handy with the baby." Toba turns full body and leans an elbow on the top of the railings so he can look at me, "sort of complimentary to you."

"A side of him I've never seen before, I must confess," I reply watching everyone surround Esosa as he rocks the baby. "Yeap, he's good with the baby."

Toba clears his throat. "So, how are things going with you both?"

I eye him and understand what he means. "Good. He doesn't, I mean he isn't violent, yet. Nor do I think he will be." I shrug. "We're great."

He wrinkles his forehead at me. I sense he wants to say something but doesn't quite know how to put it.

"Esosa's a great guy," I say before he speaks. "So don't worry."

"I—"

"Toba darling!"

The British voice is unmistakeable and cuts into our conversation. Toba and I turn to see Yinka slide up to us wearing the fabulous dress I'd been admiring all day. With little left to imagination, Yinka shines. Huge white, feathery ruffles cover most of her upper chest, and the sides are cut so low, we can see some semblance of her bust flattening out into a tummy to die for and a trim, narrow waist.

"There you are." She pauses beside him and places a manicured hand on his elbow. "I'm seeing a friend out for a bit. I'll be back for that dance you owe me." She winks at him.

"Okay." Toba nods.

"By the way," she continues, turning to me. "It's a keeper you've got down there. You shouldn't let him get away."

I start out in a shrug and glance back down the railing. "I won't. Thank you."

Yinka doesn't wait. She sweeps around after a soft squeeze of my cousin's forearm and strides away, hips swinging. Toba and I both watch her leave, he with a smile, and me with a pensive look.

The back of her dress drops to her waist, exposing fair, flawless skin. A feat possibly achieved by expensive creams and designer skin products. I'm wondering how the dress holds without straps. Only Pariola could carry off that look as confidently as Yinka does, and only Yinka could wear it and look elegant.

"She always looks good," I say to Cousin Toba when she's out of earshot.

"Yes, she does," he replies with a sigh and turns his smile over to me. "Be honest with me. You guys haven't been roasting her up, have you?"

I try to keep a straight face. "I can neither confirm nor deny that rumour."

My face dissolves into laughter, and Toba narrows his eyes at me.

"Okay, yes, we have, but only because she always gives us something to talk about. That dress, practically every dress she wears, attracts attention.

Her makeup is always on point, and I'm sure it takes her three or four hours to put her whole look together."

"Yinka is an interesting girl, and she's nice when you get to know her."

"And you are the king of finding interesting girls."

His smile returns. "Is that so?"

"Yes. You always change your side squeezes every now and then."

"Side squeezes?" He chuckles. "That implies I have a main squeeze somewhere, I don't know about."

"Okay, she's your one and only squeeze, pardon my language."

Toba shakes his head like he's sorry for me. I see Mama Bimpe and my mum leaving the dance arena and hear announcements for the couple's dance with the father of the bride. I can't stay on that gallery any longer.

"I have to run. Have fun with your girlfriend," I say to him. "And, good talk."

"Sure!" He turns his attention back to viewing the crowd in the party below and folds both arms over the railings.

Toba, I recall, has never really been a fan of small talk and crowded parties.

***

When the party ends, Olamide gives Aramide, Enitan, and me a long hug. There are tears in her eyes, and happiness that I can only imagine. She goes to my parents for farewell prayers—weird, since we are all coming to church for thanksgiving tomorrow morning—and to her in-laws for welcome prayers.

A few of the guests following us to church bunk for the night at Uncle Deola and Uncle Sesan's houses. Esosa and Yinka join us at Grandpa's house, and I find Lilian a ride to Lagos. The church service the next morning is by ten, so everyone gets right to bed as we hit home. Toba offers Yinka his room and sleeps at a neighbour's place. Esosa bunks with Deji. I stay with Aramide and her kids in my mum's old room while Diran, Aramide's husband, follows Uncle Juwon home along with other guests.

It's a happy affair after the three-hour church service that ends at eleven. We say our farewells to the new couple who are headed out of Lagos to catch a flight to the Caribbean Island of Barbados for their honeymoon. While the older adults stay back in church to appreciate those members who were present at the wedding, the rest of us head home to eat and catch up on some much-needed sleep. I don't even have time to feel blue about being the only unmarried sister left. Food is a high priority on everyone's mind. Esosa's packing up to leave, but I don't want him to go on an empty stomach.

Unfortunately, the rest of the Jollof rice and meat from the wedding reception were stored in Aunty Ladepe's room the night before. That's food everyone agreed would be best for brunch, but Aunty Ladepe is way back in church, and her room is locked.

"I have a spare key," Toba booms. "I'll get it."

"Nifemi, follow him and get the key, please. We are starving." Aramide says this with a groan as she plops onto the sitting room sofa.

I eye her. Who's she sending on errands? This apparent disrespect will be corrected, I promise myself while hurrying up the stairs after Cousin Toba. I know I'm being antsy and that Aramide's kids are really just hungry, but she has got to watch the way she orders me around. Just because I haven't changed my name doesn't take away the fact that I'm older.

"We should be gearing up for your wedding next, abi?" Cousin Toba says from three steps ahead of me.

I eye his huge shoulders and catch his teasing look as he waits for me to catch up to him.

"Yours too, right? Or is Yinka still a side and not a main?"

He chuckles out loud. Oh, God, I love his laugh! It makes me smile, even when I don't want to.

"You already have a main. You'll get there before I do."

"I have a main, but I'm keeping my fingers crossed."

"The doctor seems like marriage material."

I'm quiet, can't say the same about Yinca.

Talking about marriage with Toba does not annoy me. Maybe because I know he's not malicious, or maybe because we're both rocking that unmarried boat.

We get to the door, and he gives one knock. Waits a moment, then opens the door. I follow. He stops halfway and takes in a deep breath as if surprised. I run into him, and after glaring at his broad back, wriggle round and walk into a scene I had only read of in books and seen in movies.

There is a moment when I understand why Toba made me run into him, and another where my mind rejects the image in front of me. Then there is the now, the moment I watch my relationship go up in flames. I want to scream and shout and pull Yinka 'with a C's hair extensions out from within her scalp. I am not angry with Esosa—I am upset with her, and by extension Toba, the person who brought her into our lives.

"Toba!" Her husky British accent is flushed with embarrassment. "It's not what you think."

Wait, why are those words always the first line of support people hang on to when they're caught doing stuff they are not supposed to be doing? Like we are crazy and didn't see what we saw. It's gas lighting, in a subtle way.

"Femi—"

"Don't call my name, you two-timing cheat!" I snap.

"It didn't start out that way."

"It didn't start out what way? You just decided to hump my cousin's girlfriend on the side out of boredom? At an event I invited you to?"

Really, was he really trying to explain away their half-nakedness and his arms around Yinka 'with a C's ultrathin body by saying it didn't start out that way?

"Femi, listen to me—"

"Get up, and get out!" I snap through my teeth.

Yinka slips out of the bed, dragging the covers with her. Esosa is stripped to his boxer shorts. And they had had the un-decency—or stupidity, I don't even know which—to leave the door unlocked for whatever they were about to do.

"Toba, honestly, I can explain," she says, pulling the covers up to her neck, her eyes dove-like. "It's — it's—"

She is short of words. I am devoid of words, and repulsed. My repulsion gives way to surprise when I turn my head and see Toba smile and hand a shirt hanging on the wardrobe door over to her. Esosa is trying to get as much of his clothes back on his person as quick as he can, but Toba is smiling at Yinka in this fond way that I cannot understand.

I can't tell if he is angry or not. He has this amused look that bothers on irritating, because I feel that this is his fault. If he had not brought her for any of our family functions, she would not have met Esosa. And I would still be in a relationship right now.

"Toba—" Yinka begins again.

"Just get dressed," he says as he turns and walks out of the room.

Chapter Nine

I am hiding, in the bedroom I share with my sisters whenever we stay at Grandpa's house. It's my mother's old bedroom. The only window in it overlooks the car park, and I'm standing by it watching for Esosa's exit. He hasn't left, and I won't let him into the room.

I can't bring myself to share with anyone what has just happened. Aramide, oblivious to what happened, sorts lunch for everyone and leaves me alone after trying twice to get me to come out of the room.

I see Toba come into view carrying Yinka's overnight bag. She is not clinging to his arm like she usually does, the shameless girl. They are walking side by side with space enough for a third person between them. A car drives into position, and Toba opens the boot and puts her luggage in. Yinka doesn't get in. She stands in front of him, begging or explaining herself, I don't know which and I don't care.

Toba watches without a word, like a father would an errant toddler. He shrugs and looks around, uncomfortable, I can tell. She reaches for his hand, and I lean closer to the window, heartbeat soaring. I wish for a moment that I can hear whatever it is she is saying to him. It can't be anything but lies, I'm convinced. I don't want him to believe her.

She leans on tiptoes and kisses him on the lips. He smiles and steps sideways so he can open the car door for her. She gets in, he shuts the door, and then throws his hands into his pockets, stepping away from the vehicle as the gateman opens the gate for them.

Then he stares after her when the gate closes and doesn't look in the least bit angry. And that's what infuriates me!

The first time I fell in love, I think I was fourteen. I'd grown up watching movies and reading novels and nursing these outrageous ideas about how boys ought to be, and how girls should behave, and how things must evolve when love happens.

I assumed that love is a thing that smacks you in the face when you are going out and about with life and not expecting it. I had even read that it makes you ill, or makes you lift one leg in the air when the object of your affection kisses you.

And so when Soji Olapade helped me out with opening a rusty window in the Biology lab one hot Wednesday afternoon, then followed it up with a sparkle in his smile, I thought I had evolved and gone to love universe. I walked on air for most of that day, with him voted the most handsome boy in class. That is, of course, before I heard he was planning to give Lolade Green a gift come Valentine's Day. Safe to say my heart was bruised and it took a while to get over my first crush.

My idea of love, like me, has matured. Every romantic encounter I have had has shown me the full picture of the rounded shape that love can take when the heart ripens and the mind grows and doesn't jump with every single feeling that enters into it.

Love is tough to define. It's a solid emotion with many sides. It has been thrown about by people who have no clue what it really means, confused with infatuation, jumbled up with sex, and substituted with desire. Manhandled, mislabelled, and misunderstood, it has become a farce, a funny mirage.

But love is not blind. It sees all of who a person is and makes a decision—consciously or unconsciously—to stay with them. Love is not deaf. It hears the unsaid things and feels the unspoken words and brings them to life in actions we can all see. Love is also not chaotic. It doesn't take over your mind and shut down your brain and flow however it wills without allowing you any say in the matter.

It is not something you cannot control. It is not the erratic beating of the heart or the loss of speech, nor the clumsiness of mind and limb when the object of one's affection passes by. It is not found in a kiss or in clammy hands, or in nervous behaviour or happy laughter. And sadly, it's not based on if the other person even loves you back or treats you right.

Love has character. It is intentional, unconditional, compassionate, empathic, and translational. It enacts an emotion that begins from a place of feeling and ends in a place of doing. It's an action word, full of passion and commitment and dedication. It reasons and thinks and decides. It's selfless, thinks of others first, and seeks to bring out the best in them. It wants what they want and not what it wants, and it honours them. You can control it, and master it, and empower it. You can own it. And you can own your brain, as well.

Love should be handled with respect. If it stays in that place of feeling and doesn't progress into actions that back it up, then it's immature and incomplete and should not be trusted. Because the heart is fragile, and sometimes when it shatters, it's really tough to put back together again.

I sit in the room, with tears sliding down my face. I don't even want to see Esosa or hear his explanations. He did not handle our love with respect, and I am not averse to letting him go.

I finally walk him out of my grandfather's house. I know I will forgive him, but it doesn't mean that my heart is not broken or that I didn't even like him in the first place. It just means I need space. Love encompasses forgiveness, but also includes wisdom. I can't let Esosa have my heart again. He knew fully well what he was doing when he jumped into bed with Yinka 'with a C,' clearly, I wasn't enough to make him restrain himself.

When I come back into the house, Aramide tells me we've run out of Jollof rice but Toba is cooking if I want some. I wander into the kitchen and find him cooking some form of noodles with beef, shrimp, bell peppers, onions, and egg. I watch him stir the wok and sprinkle sea salt into the mix. He is calm and cooking like he didn't just find his girlfriend in bed with my boyfriend. I am perplexed, because I've lost my appetite. I cannot imagine how he can even think about eating.

"So, how far with the letter from Akpan, did you read it yet?" he asks without looking at me. "I heard he sent it."

I'm stunned.

"You are going to ask me that now? Now, with what just happened? Now, like you and I didn't just find our relationship halves in bed together. You're seriously going to ask me that now?"

He looks at me and lifts up one shoulder. "They were both just in the mood."

"Your girlfriend cheated on you, and you give her an excuse. You walk her to the gate and get her a cab, like she's some prima donna ballerina." I am aware that my voice has gone up, but I can't help myself. "Seriously, like who does that?"

"They're gone. Life moves on. We should, too." He licks sauce off his finger with a glance in my direction.

I am so angry at Toba, I don't even know when the words burst out of me.

"You apathetic, emotionless slob!" From that point onwards, I can't help myself, nor hear myself. "You're not even angry. You don't even care. I doubt you care about anything in that bland, clueless life of yours. You didn't care when Grandpa died, nor did you care when you found out that he wasn't your father. Nothing moves you. You are like a thick piece of wooden block with no nerve endings. You are so numb about life, so accepting of everything that ever happens to you, so passive, so lazy, and so lackadaisical. You're so damn relaxed about everything that it's downright irritating."

I am shouting now, shouting at the back of his head, and he doesn't even flinch. I am further infuriated.

"Someone steals your girlfriend, and you want to just move on? Didn't you love her? Didn't you care about her? I can't believe that you didn't order her out of this house like the pathetic little tramp that she is. I can't believe you didn't hit Esosa. I can't believe that you would smile at her like she just gave you the best birthday gift and walk her to the door like some majestic queen from some royal family. Instead, you are here, asking me stupid questions and cooking like nothing even happened."

I storm towards the kitchen back door as Aramide walks in.

"What's going on?" I hear her ask. "Why is Femi shouting?"

"You might wanna go check on her," I hear Toba reply. "Esosa just broke her heart."

I hiss, slam the door, and stomp away. I can't believe Toba is not yelling back at me. I want him to yell! I want him to care! I want a reaction from him!

Aramide finds me sitting on the swing beside the old playhouse.

"Toba told me what happened," she says. "I'm so sorry. He is not worth your thinking about him."

"Who, Toba?" My eyes are blazing when I look up at Aramide. "He gets her a cab, can you imagine? Walks her out the door, takes her hand, and helps her into it like she's one dainty Disney princess, that phony *naija* girl."

Aramide smiles and sits down on the other swing beside me. "I was talking about Dr. Esosa."

"I literarily just watched my life go up in flames, and Toba treats it like it's an everyday occurrence. Why should he care? In another week, he will have another *lepa shandy* girl clinging to his forearm." I wipe the tear sliding down the right side of my cheek as my sister puts an arm around me. "And that lying, two-timing excuse of a man!"

"He is not worth your thinking about him."

"I'm not thinking about him. I'm thinking about me! I had shut that door. I'd given up on ever getting married, and he opened it with his charm and his fine boy baby face and perfect medical doctor qualifications. And I was taken for a ride."

"We all were," Aramide replies.

"No." I wiped my tears. "I had thought that window of opportunity had passed me by, and I was comfortable with myself and in being single. I wasn't even really looking. He gave me hope, got me to start dreaming again, then he yanks it all away. Now I have a hole in my heart."

I sniff, and Aramide rubs my back.

"A hole I now have to fill and sew, and cover up. And I can't. I don't have the strength to do it all over again." I shake my head as tears fall. "Teach myself to forget what it's like to be in a relationship, or how to get back to that place of serenity where I had accepted the things that were not going to change. I don't know if I can be comfortable and confident enough again in being alone and being fine with it. And Toba is just there, cooking like he—"

Aramide places her other arm around me and puts my head on her shoulder. I'm too upset to even realize that she is not snapping at me or saying it's because I'm too opinionated and serious and that is why Esosa slept with Yinka.

"You will be strong again, and I believe you will find someone again," she says.

"Don't give me hope," I whisper. "I'm not planning to find anybody."

"Hey." I hear Toba's voice behind me. "How is she?"

She sighs. I can't see her face, but I can tell she has a helpless look on it. Through the corner of my eye, I see his legs as he walks round the swing.

"Here," he says, his voice so deep, and yet soft at the same time. "Have something to eat. Take your mind off it. They don't call it comfort food for nothing."

I look up and see him with a steaming plate. I don't even want to know how hot it is. I stand up, grab the plate, and pour the contents all over the front of his shirt. Toba sort of sucks in a deep breath and steps back in a bid to get away from his shirt. He looks at me, and I want to hit him.

"I don't want your stupid food," I say and throw the plate on the grass.

Aramide jumps out of the swing in alarm.

"Femi!" she screeches behind me. "Oh, Cousin Toba, I'm so sorry. She's just—Femi, why did you do that?"

I march off into the house not caring or listening to either of them.

***

Okay, so my anger can chime with the size of a nuclear bomb blast. It leads me to call people names and throw things, but it also fizzles out pretty quickly, because just like that, I'm feeling guilty about pouring that plate of noodles all over Cousin Toba. For one, it was disrespectful. Secondly, it only just occurs to me that it was piping hot and I might have burned him.

It takes me some time, after Aramide had come into the room and given me a piece of her mind about the *'shit stunt'* I had pulled, to pick myself up and go and find him. At this point, I'm just empty of all the anger. My conscience nags me towards an apology because Toba is not to blame for any of what had happened. If I hadn't been too wrapped up in finding myself six years ago, I would have said yes to Adenrele Thomas and probably would be married right now.

I come out of the room subdued and hear Aramide and Aunty Norma in the living room arguing with Diran and Uncle Juwon about license plates and state laws. I don't need the reprimand, so I run into the kitchen and into Deji who's munching on Rich Tea biscuits.

"Where is Cousin Toba?"

"Car park." Deji raises his arm and the hand holding the plate of biscuits towards the kitchen back door. "I think he's going out."

"Thanks."

I tear through the kitchen and step outside. Toba isn't there. Following the space behind the kitchen towards the swing set and play pen, I enter the wide-open car park and see him at the gates. His blue Honda pickup truck has the engine running, and the gateman is nowhere to be seen. He's changed his shirt and looks, well, not angry.

"Cousin Toba!" I hurry towards him, hoping that the softness in my voice will give him the respect that I owe him. "Can you please hold on for a second?"

He looks at up as he secures the second gate and stares at me like he is not sure if I am coming back to finish my verbal assault on his character. I am too ashamed to look him in the eye as he walks towards me.

"I want to apologize for calling you a slob. It wasn't your fault Esosa did what he did, and I had no right to be rude." I look up at his face and take in a deep breath. "I'm sorry."

Toba has stopped in front of me and is looking down at me with an expression that has softened considerably and is bordering on hiding a smile.

"I'm going to the farm." He nods at the truck. "Come with me."

Without waiting for my reply, he walks over to his truck and climbs into the driver's seat. I'm left staring at the truck, wondering why he's not mad at me.

I get in with him, and he backs it out of the compound with scant effort as the gateman runs up, holding his cap on his head.

"I'm going to the farm." Toba leans out of the open window on the driver's side and glances with a worried brow at the sky. "Barring any rain, I should be back in four or five hours. Biko, try and stay at the gate, okay."

"Yes, sir," the errant gateman replies, amidst frequent bowing.

He throws the truck's gear into drive and speeds off down the bumpy, un-tarred road leading out of my grandfather's house. I buckle myself into the passenger seat and lean into the back rest. The truck's motion throws me out of balance with each bump on the road.

"Are you okay now?"

"I am. Thanks for asking. I hope I didn't scald you too much with that plate of food?" I add a second later.

"Yeah, you did." He glances at me for a second before swinging his eyes back onto the road.

"You are not angry?"

His chuckle barely escapes his lips. "Just a little."

"I'm sorry."

"It's okay."

I am supposed to be uncomfortable at the idea of riding with him after my horrible outburst, but I'm not. He makes it so I'm not, and that is just it with Toba. He is like a comfy, old armchair. The kind you want to sink into after a taxing day at work. He is so welcoming, that it's easy to step all over him and still feel at ease, because he won't bug you. I hate passive guys, but I'm happy that it is Toba that I had lashed out at. Had it been anybody else, a family meeting would have been called, and I would have been facing a panel of angry elders for daring to throw shrimp at my uncle's shirt.

The Yoruba tradition of respect for an older person is strongly adhered to in my family. No one must hear what had transpired between Toba and me. It would call into question my character as a woman, and point to the reason why at thirty-five going on thirty-six, I'm still unmarried.

My mother would ask me what I had achieved that gave me the effrontery to speak to Toba like I had. And Uncle Sesan would reiterate the fact that respect goes out of the window with the learning of English language.

"So," Toba says, "seems like you use a lot of big words in your writing."

I stare at him. "Why do you ask?"

"I had to look up the word lackadaisical in the dictionary."

I turn away, glum. He is smiling, however.

"Don't worry I know I'm painfully laid back." He glances at me. "My mum never lets me hear the last of it."

"I'm sorry I called you an emotionless slob."

He laughs out loud, and we don't say anything anymore 'til we get to the farm. I am lost in my thoughts, and he just lets me be.

It's almost four p.m. when we arrive. Toba manoeuvres the truck into a large clearing and two men come running up to us.

"Give me a minute," he says and jumps down from the cab.

My eyes follow his hulking frame around the the vehicle as he speaks with them. I don't for the life of me understand why I have followed him to the farm. Perhaps as part of my apology, I had not wanted to refuse him. Deep within, I know it's something more. I feel I've lost face. I like Toba. I don't want him to stop liking me.

He walks over to the passenger side of the truck and opens the door.

"Come on, hop out," he says, holding out both hands.

For any other person, I might have snapped out, *'Keep your hands to yourself, what makes you think I can't jump out of a truck?'* or muttered something about not being a damsel in distress. I don't call myself feminist, but I have major reservations about having a guy open the car door for me, or assist me with scaling a gutter, or paying for my meal, or driving my car to the mechanic. I have friends who love it, but I hate feeling weak and incapable of doing things on my own.

For Toba, however, I bite my tongue. I reach for his shoulders, and he lifts me by the waist from the vehicle.

The so-called attraction women have for strong-looking men must be swaying me a little bit because I leave my hands on his shoulders for longer than I should. They feel strong and sturdy underneath my fingers, nothing like Esosa's slight build I can see why Yinka kept clinging to him.

"Why are we here?" I ask, letting his shoulders go and looking around. I'm ashamed to be feeling up my uncle.

"I just took possession of a large herd of goats, and poultry. I want to inspect them." He grabs a pair of black wellington boots from one farmhand and points them at me. "It looks like it might rain, so I say boots over shoes. Come on."

A few minutes later, we are trudging through a wide hectare of farmland in knee-high wellington boots.

Toba is an astute businessman. The farm is a little bigger than I remember, and he is showing me everything there is to be seen. There is fire in his eyes and energy in his voice that hints at the crazy love he has for the soil beneath our feet. He will do anything for the farm, and I can see that as I listen with rapt attention.

He talks about the oil palms with pride, and describes the oil processing plant beside them. He's turned the chaos I had always known growing up into this organized, financially viable business, and I see passion, pride, and meticulous work. I can't deny that so much has happened in the six months that Toba has taken over Grandpa's farm, and I can see why he willed it to him.

We stop to look at the goats and talk to the workers. They all greet him with cheerful respect. I can measure the regard they have for him, and I'm impressed.

"So you gave up your fancy desk job at the oil company to come and march around a bush in big boots," I tease as we walk up the dirt pathway to the farm's lodge.

"There is a lot of money to be made here if I can do the work."

"And I can see that you enjoy it."

"I do." He exhales and gives me a rueful look. "Farming is in my DNA. Our ancestors were farmers. The farm has always been—"

"Your playground," I cut him short. "I remember when we used to run around this jungle climbing trees and raiding mangoes and guavas off their branches."

"And almond fruits."

I laugh out loud. "And almond fruits, because you recall being stuck with the arduous task of breaking them open to find us the seeds inside. After, the twins and I would eat piles and piles of them."

He grins. "That was the life back then, me waiting on y'all hand and foot."

"You were always sitting up in a tree reading a book, or trying to help Mr. Lasisi weed the plantation. We literarily had to drag you away from the farm animals to come and play with us."

"Well, I've been reading up on farming, and visiting other farms. It's a tasking job, but it's honest, and challenging, and healthy, exactly what the country needs right now. More people leaving the cities to find work in the hinterland." He looks up at the sky as the rain that had been threatening to fall starts to trickle down. "I love the farm. Beats sitting at a desk doing boring paper work."

"I love boring paper work. I love reading manuscripts and correcting grammatical errors."

The walk through the farm leaves me panting. It makes up for the lack of exercise that had been seeing my tummy take a more rounded shape in the days I'd been in Ibadan. I glance at Toba and see the V-shaped outline of his chest underneath the inner white shirt he has on. He's lost weight. The dark blue, long-sleeved shirt on him is matted to his toned upper arms and turned up at the wrists, revealing thick, somewhat hairy forearms. If Toba was walking the length of the farm at least once a day, it made sense that he would.

With a dark stub of facial hair that never gets cleanly shaven, he looks good. He was never the tall, dark and handsome guy that most girls like to fantasize about. He was chubby and clumsy growing up, with thick arms and legs, soft pudgy hands, and a big belly. Now, his solid build invites second looks because he found a way to turn most of that fat into well-defined muscles. And because his warm eyes and mouth remain in a constant state of likeable hilarity.

It starts to drizzle a little harder, so we walk faster towards the farm lodge. Lasisi comes running down the path with a wide umbrella. Toba steps forward to take it and shield it over both our heads. He puts a hand behind my back and guides me towards the lodge. It's an innocent gesture, but it invokes a warm feeling that leaves me with tingles down my back. An invisible energy surrounds us and fills me with nervousness, but I chuck it up to being cautious of walking a line I can't allow myself to cross. The other side of it harbours feelings I can't allow myself to feel. He is still family—I shouldn't be trembling at his touch.

It has to be the idea of seeing him take charge, I rationalize, the idea that he is not as lackadaisical as I thought. He is just one of those guys with gallantry in his DNA like he claimed farming was, or Aunty Ladepe—and my mum if I think about it—just raised him well.

The rain starts to pour all around us, and I am happy for the umbrella and the boots. The dry earth turns muddy in seconds, and we find ourselves running along the path and up the creaky, wooden stairs into the shaded veranda of the wooden lodge house.

I laugh and remove myself from any more contact with Toba's hand as he folds up the umbrella. I'm confused about how jittery it makes me feel.

"We have to wait for the rain to go down before we head back," he says as he shakes rain water off of the umbrella. "Let's go inside. It will get colder on this porch."

I nod, and he lets me follow the farmhand inside, taking up the rear as the rain descends on the lodge house with ferocious intensity.

Chapter Ten

The lodge, a single storage room built when I was younger, seems to have taken on a new lease of life. There is a wide sitting area with cane chairs, a long sofa, a woven centre rug, and a curtain that hangs along a wall with a door beside it.

"Wow!"

He grins at me. "I expanded it to include extra rooms. It's where I bring farm's guests, stakeholders, and friends. I also sleep here when I stay late at the farm, and there's a kitchen. Do you want something to drink?"

"I'm fine," I say, astounded at the simple beauty of the front room.

"We're going to be here a while. Why not sit down and try our bottled orange juice?"

"We have an orange farm?" I turn around and look at him.

My use of the word 'we' comes back to haunt me. The farm doesn't belong to Grandpa anymore, so it's not ours. It's his, Toba's.

"We do." He walks towards the open doorway and sticks his head in. "Lasisi."

I help myself out of the wet boots and place them by the main door. Then I pad, barefoot, over a neat, wooden floor to the makeshift sitting area. It's clean. I love well-swept floors. Not a grain of sand in sight.

I sink into the cane sofa and stare through the open window at the falling rain. The cold air breezes in with raindrops that wet the floor behind it. I watch and remember when the lodge was just a shabby, over-stuffed storage room for farm implements. Grandpa always warned us not to play in it, but someone always made sure to pick it as a spot for hide and seek.

Toba plops onto the same sofa a moment later and exhales.

He looks tired, like the walk around the farm has drained him of energy. He also looks like he needs someone to take care of him. Someone like a wife.

"Uncle Gbenga isn't fighting you anymore for control of the farm, is he?"

He shrugs. "He's not ready to put in the amount of work this place requires for it to thrive. So I'm not worried about him. I'll ensure they get their five per cent of profits every year end. All of them, including your mum."

"Mummy doesn't have a problem with you running this place. She has zero interest in it. She wouldn't mind the profit share, though."

Lasisi comes in just then with a tray and two bottles of orange juice.

"Fresh from the farm," he says as he hands me one of the short, fat bottles.

Toba watches me stare at them. "We transport it to Lagos weekly. I'm hoping it will do well in the market."

I pick one up and look at the label. "What's it called?"

"Osan," he says in a thick Yoruba accent, and I see his cheek bulge as he looks at me with wide innocent eyes, waiting for my approval.

I burst into crazy laughter, "oh my goodness, who came up with that name?"

He shrugs. "I wanted something catchy."

"And you think Osan is catchy?" I continue laughing as Lasisi hands him his own bottle.

"Well, it attracts second looks." He twists open the cover and takes a sip.

My eyes follow Lasisi and swing back to Toba.

"You said you entertain guests here," I begin, opening mine. "Did you bring her here?"

"Who?" He stops drinking.

"Yinka," I reply, "with a C."

Toba puts his arm around the back of the sofa and shifts so he can look at me. He looks amused. "Why do you ask?"

I shrug. "I'm just, I don't know, trying to figure out how serious you guys were."

"Nope, I have never brought her here. She's just a friend."

"A friend, tsk—" I roll my eyes. "Aunty Norma started planning your wedding the moment we saw the way she was guarding you at your mum's party, like if she left you alone for a second, you would get stolen."

"Really," he drawls with a smile that puts dimples the shape of moon crescents in his cheeks as he raises the bottle to his lips. "She was not my girlfriend."

"Oh, please!" *Why have I never noticed his dimples? They're so cute!*

He takes a sip and swallows fast. "Honestly."

"Cousin Toba, everyone saw the way you were carrying her about like one expensive artefact. You even let her sit on your thigh. You only do that with the girls you like."

"There were no more free seats that day. I had to offer her something."

"Come on, Toba, that beautiful girl with perfect features, I find that very hard to believe."

He shrugs. "She was just someone I brought for show and tell, so my mum can stop fretting and trying to match me up with one of her numerous god-daughters."

I giggle but understand. When you are of marriageable age and unmarried in our family, its hide, find, or be matched.

"I even told her it was all the way in Ibadan but she showed up, *said* she took your invitation to heart." He points a finger at me.

"My invitation?"

"The one you gave at the recital. I didn't mind, though. It was better than being unattached at that party and having everyone badger me."

"You can't be having it as bad as I am."

"Don't kid yourself, girl. We guys are under pressure, too. We just don't let it get to us."

I roll my eyes. "Please, you don't get as many jabs on it like we do."

His trademark amused smile wrinkles his eyes. "You think?"

"I do. Everyone is telling me I'm going to end up with a man twice my age the way I'm going. My father doesn't ever forget to remind me that my sisters are all married and I'm just chasing education all over the place. I just wonder why he didn't just go the Biblical Laban style and tell Aramide's husband that we don't marry the younger child before the older."

Toba chucks out his signature belly laugh, and it's so loveable. It's a bottomless throttle that lifts my spirits and makes me give him a second look. I like him in that instant for no reason I can think of. I just do.

"My mother has picked out her attire for my wedding day. She's just waiting for me to set a date, says she'll show up with a bride as long as I promise her to be there on time."

It's my turn to laugh. Aunty Ladepe is usually so calm about things. To hear that means the matter has reached a neck-breaking point.

"My mum figured out how to use a dating site app just so she could find me a suitable husband. All her friends' male children are either married or younger than I am. It doesn't stop her setting me up on blind dates, though."

"And you go for these dates?"

"Have you seen those guys? At least you've had some good-looking girlfriends. I have had a series of douchebags."

He doesn't say anything, so I start rattling off a list of his exes. "Ann, Shade, Temidire with the funny laughter, and then there was this girl you were with for almost five years."

"Bimpe," he offers.

"Bimpe. Yes." The chubby, cute-faced girl was always all over the place giving Toba all the accolades a traditional Yoruba husband would love, including cooking, washing, and making everyone feel at home. "She had that homely-wife thing down to a tee. You showed up with her at Aramide's wedding, and everybody fell in love."

Toba grins. He remembers.

"She was a whiz at tying *gele*, and her Jollof rice, oh la la, was Heaven on Earth." I close my eyes and shake my head. "Why the heck did you ever let that girl go? Aunty Norma said she lost all hope for you the moment you broke up with her."

He utters a deep sigh. It is obvious to me, and him, too, that Bimpe was the one that got away.

"My mum didn't speak to me for almost three months," he says with regret. "She's married now, to an investment banker. They have two kids."

"Awww, I bet she is making him a great wife."

"An excellent one, we catch up on FB from time to time."

I think of the pretty girl and smile; I had liked her, too.

"Why did you break up with her?"

"I didn't break up with her. She broke up with me."

"She did?" I'm shocked. "Why?"

A despondent look crosses his face. "She had the same ideas you have about me. Said I was too content with life and headed nowhere. Plus, I wouldn't set a wedding date."

I feel guilty. I had not really meant those words. Now seeing all I had seen at the farm today, I realize that I had been unfair to him. He was certainly laidback, but there were some choleric tendencies to him.

"She didn't call me an emotionless slob, though," he says with a smile in my direction. "But she wanted me to get off my sorry ass and do something meaningful with my life."

I toss him a smile halfway to being encouraging. "I'm sorry it didn't work out between you."

"Yeah," Toba drawls.

"What about Theresa, that slim Warri babe?"

"Theresa," he says with an element of fondness. "Mother detested her."

"After Bimpe, I can't imagine why not. I heard she couldn't cook to save her life."

His brow falls into a frown, but a smile hovers around his lips. "We mostly ate out, so that didn't bother me much. She had other skills, and they were pretty amazing."

"Skills, as in?"

He tilted his head. "She was creative, flexible, unpredictable, and rife with ideas for interesting positions." He runs a hand down his chest with a deep sigh. "Gave me a run for my stamina."

"Oh my goodness, Cousin Toba, do you want me to cover my ears?"

His face takes up the endearing look of a cuddly teddy bear. "You're all grown up. We should be able to talk about sex without you cringing."

"Should you be telling me all about your sexcapades?"

He looks a little bewildered. "It's a little hard to believe that the all-bold, all-action Nifemi is squeamish about discussing sex. You mean you've never ..."

I hold up a hand. "Stop it right there, cowboy. That's none of your business."

"Ahhh, never been kissed."

"Uncle Tobaaaa, you should be telling me not to get into it before marriage."

"Okay," he says in a flat voice. "Don't get into it before marriage."

I groan and cover my face while he laughs.

"You are not convincing. Is that how you would say it to Jumoke?"

"No, I'd just tan her behind and rough-house her boyfriend. One chokehold and he will think twice whenever he looks at her."

I shake my head. I can't imagine the cool, calm, and collected Cousin Toba rough-housing anyone. "I'll believe that when I see it."

"Oh, Akpan didn't write about it in his little note to you?"

"No, he didn't."

"Well, he can tell you."

"You choked him?" I'm alarmed. "Toba!"

"I just threatened him a little. Safe to say he'll be more careful with his next girlfriend. She might just have a big, scary cousin."

I drop my mouth open and stare at him. "Thank you for embarrassing me."

"You're welcome. Sex—" Toba says holding out his hands, "—is a beautiful thing to be enjoyed but handled with care and maturity."

"Cousin Toba." My voice has this frank tone to it. "Can we drop this?"

"Uncle or cousin, you really need to make up your mind about me." He glances at me with amusement. "But Toba's fine since we are discussing sex."

His voice has this soft teasing quality that makes me blush.

"Sex is for adults, Femi. You're an adult."

"Who can make her own decisions about whether or not to have it. Right now, I feel it should be with someone I can trust."

He is quiet for a second. "I agree."

"So she had great bedroom skills."

"Outstanding bedroom skills," he replies before I'm through with my comment.

"Can we change the topic, please?" I say, chuckling.

"Yes, ma'am," he says as thunder rumbles in the distance.

In all our talk, I had forgotten it was raining.

"I'm not too sure I'm going to get married. Aramide says that my eggs are getting frozen, and my joints are getting stiff, and my window of easily bearing children is narrowing." I roll my eyes, "whatever that means. I don't even know if I want children, or if I'll ever find someone who won't mind not having them."

Toba straightens in his corner of the cane sofa. "And you believe that?"

"No. I think my life should matter for much more than having someone's children." I look at him. "By two p.m., Aramide's scrambling from wherever she is to go pick up the twins from school. She's got mum brain, doesn't even remember simple stuff sometimes. Holidays are a headache, school runs and home works are a solitary job for her."

"Femi, you can plan for whatever you want in life."

"Yes. But I don't want to resent a person I'm supposed to love because taking care of them doesn't allow me to focus on what I really want in life. I hear my sisters moan, I hear my friends complain. I know it sounds selfish not to want kids, but it also sounds selfish to want them just because I think they'll sort me out when I'm old."

"How about wanting them for the joys they can bring? But then, it's you prerogative. You don't have to do what everybody does."

"So why are you running away from getting married?"

"I'm taking my time. My mum has warned me that raising a child in your old age isn't the best thing. But sex and children are not my priority in marriage."

I take a sip of my drink. "What's your priority?"

"Companionship; I've been in enough relationships to know that it's what I want in my future. So I won't make that move because everyone says I should, but because I've found a friend willing to share life and its ups and downs with."

My smile fades. I understand what he means. The idea of being alone, and making decisions alone, and doing projects alone for the rest of my future, was beginning to give me a gloomy outlook. Life is tough and complicated and doesn't belong to any one person. Finding someone to share that complication with is important. Perhaps children are not a bad idea, aside finding someone to love.

"I promised myself that if I clocked forty without a man, I would get myself a house, and plan for retirement."

There's a frown on his face when he looks at me. "What makes you think you are going to be forty and unmarried?"

"I don't know. I just lost hope."

He tosses his head back on the sofa's back rest and exhales. "For what it's worth, you shouldn't listen to anyone. You are a beautiful girl. The right person will show up when you least expect it. The age you are when you marry is not as important as it being to the right person. It will happen, when it will happen. And if it doesn't happen for either of us—" he turns his head to me, "—we could always just get married and save everyone the hullabaloo."

His words are so quiet and serious that I almost think he means it. My heart races at the ridiculous thought. Toba and I, married?

Pariola's statement on all the possible ramifications of Toba not being blood-related hits me, and I start laughing, because it means Toba has thought about it, too.

"You are funny."

He's family. Whether my grandfather had him or not doesn't matter. I see him as my uncle, my older brother, and my grandfather's son. The family would just keel over to hear that we want to get married to each other.

"I am." He looks away.

I see the crescent-shaped dimples and realize that he is just joking. But for a moment, the idea had held fascination.

***

As Toba and I drive back to civilization he seems lost in thoughts. I wonder if he is still thinking about us getting married. It would be an unusual solution to our mutual problem, but I'm not even sure Toba wants marriage. Nor sure my mother won't kill him for even suggesting it.

I'm quiet in the passenger seat. I've just had a conversation about nothing and everything happening in my life right now so I'm light, and empty, and optimistic. Esosa and I might be over, but life goes on. And life, though complicated, is beautiful.

The drive back takes an hour, fifteen minutes, and it's dark when we get home. Just as we hit the stretch of un-tarred road leading to Grandpa's house, he decides to speak.

"Great!"

I watch him struggle to manoeuvre his truck through the rough terrain of the muddy road.

"We should think about tarring Grandpa's road," I say.

"Tell that to my brothers, and the six other families that live on the street," he mutters back.

"Ibadan is a town filled with lacklustre people with a penchant for financial issues. They're going to tell me there's no money, or they have plans for the little they have."

I smile at him. "Big words, I seem to be rubbing off on you."

He returns the smile, and it cheers up the quiet atmosphere in the truck as we bounce around. Toba drives right past the gate and heads for the gorge at the hilly end of the road. It's filled with a thick wild forest of trees. As kids, our mothers always yelled for us to avoid the place.

"Where are you going?" I quip, fear from the past finding its way back to me in the form of my mother's voice.

"I want to back the truck into the compound," he says but scrunches up against the steering wheel and peers out through the windscreen.

I'm startled. "What is it?"

"The grey Hyundai Getz that keeps parking at the side of the compound every now and then has people in it today."

I don't know what he's talking about, so I try to peep through window of his door as he slows the truck to a stop.

Now Toba is built like a bear. His broad back and thick shoulders block my view of the unknown driver's car. He opens his door and jumps down. I hurry too, eager to see who it is he is going up to challenge. I'm thinking this will be interesting.

I'm just in time to see him yank open the left back seat door and drag a shirtless young man out by the scruff of his neck.

"What the—" The boy pales on seeing Toba. He is an average-height, skinny, scrawny-looking thing compared to Toba's hefty six-foot-four.

"You were saying?"

Toba rarely gets angry, but looking at his face under the security lights, I'd say he was pretty close to it.

"Uncle Toba." I hear a familiar voice, and my eyes widen as Jumoke scrambles out from the other side of the back seat, fully dressed but very embarrassed. "We were just talking."

Toba looks at her.

"Just talking? Get in the truck," he says and points a thumb backwards in my general direction.

"We weren't doing anything—"

"Get in the truck," Toba repeats, the thumb still pointing backwards, fist holding onto the back of the shirtless young man's neck.

"I can—"

"*Get in the truck!*" he roars, picking the words one by one.

Jumoke slams the door of the vehicle and walks towards me. Her face is all made up, and she's wearing a jean jacket over a boob tube and shorts that show off her lean, long legs. She looks like a seventeen-year-old university student, and I won't be surprised if that's what she told the guy.

She avoids my eyes, but I can't resist turning to watch her hurry round the front of the truck to get in via the door on the other side. She is no longer a young girl, and the thought frightens me.

"I can explain," the young man says.

Toba takes his hand off the boy's neck and pushes him against the Getz. "How old do you think she is?"

"I'm sorry, sir."

"How old?" His voice goes an octave louder.

"Sixteen, I don't know."

"Thirteen," Toba replies, "that's statutory rape."

I am impressed. Toba keeps showing me a new side to him by the hour.

"I'm guessing you're a student of—" Toba waits for him to fill in the blanks.

"Ibadan Poly, sir."

"Ibadan Poly." He puts two fingers on the poor boy's chest and shoves him against the car. "See, I'm going to cut you some slack today. Next time I find you or your car here or anywhere near our house, I'm going to impound it and throw you in jail. Do we have an understanding?"

"Yes, sir. Yes, sir."

"Good. Now beat it, before I change my mind."

The boy scrambles into his car as soon as Toba lets him go. He drives at top speed down the length of the compound's wall and rounds it in less than ten seconds.

"Cousin Toba," I begin as we find our way back to the truck. "Don't you think that yelling at the two of them might have been counterproductive?"

Toba glances at me. "He was French-kissing her in that back seat. What did you want me to do? Wait 'til she's pregnant?"

"She was a willing party. What's to say she won't sneak her way out of the house to go be with him?"

Toba stops in front of the Truck. "That's why you are going to have a talk with her. Sex is a beautiful thing, but wait 'til you're married."

I raise my eyebrows. "Me?"

"Yeah, you, because Norma will just tear through the girl, and Imisi will not even know what to say."

"I'm hardly qualified."

"I did just give you a talk about sex within marriage, didn't I?"

I laugh and get into the truck. "Yes, about how to grow my bedroom skills enough to keep my husband happy."

"True, but mostly about maturity and the role it plays."

We throw a backward glance at Jumoke. She has her hands folded under her armpits and is scowling through the window. Toba turns an amused smile from her to me as he starts the truck. "She's mad at me. Better you than me."

When we drive into the compound, Jumoke jumps down and runs off before Toba and I can get down.

"Toba!"

We look up and see Yinka 'with a C' standing on the front porch. I instinctively glance at Toba. He's just as surprised as I am. He switches off the truck's engine and gets down without a word and without taking his eyes off her.

I follow, slam my side of the truck's door, and glare at her. What in the world is she doing back?

Chapter Eleven

Forgiveness is a conscious, deliberate decision to extend grace to someone who doesn't deserve it. It requires letting go of what someone has done to hurt you, and forgoing the desire to seek revenge, no matter how painful it is to see the other person go scot-free.

Forgiveness is the essence that builds relationships, the variable that adds depths and layers to friendships. Few people understand it, because it's easier keeping scores and holding onto offences. Fewer still practice it, because it's a very, very difficult thing to do.

Bitterness locks you in a prison that slowly poisons you. Forgiveness opens the door, and gently heals you. It's an act that tells you more about yourself than the person who hurt you. It's a sign of maturity, a character strength that makes you stronger on the inside and weaker on the outside. Many people will tell you they exacted revenge from the people who hurt them and didn't feel any better afterwards. Rarely will a man say he forgave someone and didn't immediately—or sometime afterwards—experience peace.

Forgiveness doesn't come easy. It's not a once and for all time package that makes you all smiles with the person who hurt you immediately. It is a hard agreement you enter into with yourself every day before your mind is free of anger. Every time the matter resurfaces, you must forgive, because the heart might soften but the mind doesn't forget. Forgiveness is tough but liberating, painful but therapeutic, and easier to say but harder to follow through on. It is something we must all do ever-so-often on Earth as long as we live on it because offences will always come, people are not perfect, and life is not a fairy tale.

So I'm thinking about this as I look at Yinka 'with a C.' I can't help envisioning her and Esosa entwined in each other's arms. I know I ought to forgive them, but I'm finding it really difficult.

"I wonder how Olamide is doing," Aramide says as she packs up her bags.

We are all going back to Lagos in bits. Aramide's husband and children had left after lunch, but she and I had stayed back to help clean-up.

"The first night of marriage with an eager new husband can be a lot to take," she continues. "I did try to prepare her, but you know Olamide—she believes Korede is a gentle guy and everything is going to be splendid."

I stand beside the window and fume. I don't know what Yinka is doing back, or what Toba is doing entertaining her.

"What's going on?" Aramide asks, perplexed. She has stopped folding her dresses and is looking at me with a frown.

"It's that skinny two-by-four," I reply, leaning into a tiptoe and peering through the glass of the window. "She's back."

"Are you serious?" She drops the dress in her hand and hurries over to stand beside me and peer outside.

"I don't even know why she would show her phony face here again. Worse, I don't know what Cousin Toba is doing listening to her."

Toba and Yinka are standing by the pickup truck. It's dark, but we can see Yinka in front of him, gesticulating. Toba is flat against its passenger side door with his arms across his wide chest. There is this soft look and calm feel about his demeanour that tells me a lot.

He is buying whatever crappy story she is selling!

"Ha," Aramide exhales. "What kind of explanation does she want to give now?"

"He is being a total and complete idiot if he lets that girl back into his life," I say bitterly.

Just then, Toba leans away from the truck and reaches out to grab Yinka's hands. For some unknown reason, my heart sinks into my stomach.

I turn away from the window and lean against the wall. "He's forgiven her."

"You don't know what's happening out there. Maybe she is threatening to kill herself and he is just calming her down. You don't know these types of girls and what they are capable of."

"Either way, they get to rebuild their relationship, but mine is gone. She just came here and ruined everything, and she gets to go scot-free and win her man back."

Aramide turns to me. "Did you pick any of Esosa's calls?"

I lower my eyes and shake my head. "How do I know he hasn't slept with some other girl besides Yinka?"

"How do you know he has not?"

I stare at Aramide. "He wanted to be with me, but I shut him down, and he went to the next best thing—no, the next available thing. I don't want a guy who wants me for my body."

Aramide doesn't say anything.

"Maybe that's why he went to her, because I wouldn't give it to him." I am still frowning at this point.

Aramide pulls me into a hug. "Perhaps you should just pick his call and talk to him."

I shook my head. "It will be a little hard to trust him. I'm not sure I'm ready for that."

She leans back. "And that's okay. You guys should meet and just talk things through before you end it completely. I'm sure that somewhere inside, he is sorry."

I know Aramide is right, so we pack in silence, but I can't help listening for the slam of the kitchen back door signalling that Cousin Toba has returned indoors. When it doesn't happen after about an hour, I sneak outside to take a look for myself. Whatever apology Yinka had come back with, an hour was stretching the limits of it.

I find my way past the playhouse to the front of the house and look around in confusion. I can't believe I'm acting so petty. I want to know what is happening with Yinka and my uncle, and I cannot deny that I'm a tiny bit upset that they've been talking this long.

I walk towards the garden and see them both lying in the grass next to one another. Toba's form is long and huge. Hers is dainty, curled into a ball beside him. They are holding linked hands in the air with their elbows on the grass. I can't hear what they are saying, but there is laughter, and I'm angry that he can forgive her and be a total idiot.

***

Esosa shows up at my place of work by the end of the week. I am forced to go outside and talk to him. He looks a bit sheepish, and my heart softens. I take him outside to the side entrance where it's private, and we talk.

"Femi, I'm beyond ashamed of myself. I know you have every right to be angry with me, but please, let's work this out."

I take in a deep breath and fold my arms.

"She was just a—"

"Side squeeze?"

He shakes his head. "I don't know what came over me."

"Do I mean anything to you?"

"Yes," he says, stepping closer to me. "Of course."

I stare into his eyes, but I don't believe him. I'm not hanging onto any notion that things will work out between us. On the outside, however, I smile and let him take my hand.

"Let me make this up to you. How about a boat ride to Tarkwa Bay? A couple of friends and I are planning a day out soon. I can't think of anyone else I'd rather go with."

"Okay. But I want us to ease back into this. I can't just—" I look up at him. "It will take a while for me."

He nods. "I know."

I smile, genuinely this time. I wouldn't mind going on a boat.

So we don't get the boat trip opportunity 'til the first week in December. Tarkwa Bay is a delight. An island, off the coast of the Lagos Harbour, it's a twenty-minute ride from the marina, and fifteen from the jetty stand near Bonny Camp.

Years ago, the bay had had the unfortunate luck of being notorious for criminal activities. A former haven for drug pushers, hoodlums, and people seeking cheap sex, it sold excitement of a different kind for folks of a different breed. People flocked there more for the thrill of engaging in illicit acts than for the simple joy of exploring one of Lagos' little islands. I'm told a police crackdown one day lasted almost forty-eight hours and rid the bay of its disreputable occupants. Now the island is a charming getaway spot for anyone looking to escape the stress of Lagos life.

The speed boat journey knocks the wind out of me, but I put up a brave front. The girls on the boat, three of them, are squirmy and giggly and excited by the ambience of wind in their hair. The guys, five of them including Esosa, are all in shirts and shorts, ready to party.

While I'm modestly dressed in a sleeveless tie-up top over jean shorts, the others have swim wear under wrap skirts. They don't hesitate to take them off when we settle into the bay to play beach volley ball. I notice pleased looks on the guys' faces, but I don't care—I don't plan to show off any more skin than I'm already showing. Esosa's wink calms me.

It's nice to run around in the sun, toss a ball around in beach shorts, and laugh. The girls are sweet at first. They want to know what I do for a living, where I work, and how Esosa and I met. They are tickled by the story of Olamide's bouquet-catching trip and how it landed us in Esosa's office. In time, a jetty drops off a few more people on the island, and we see a fair-skinned girl running towards us with a hand holding onto her wide-brimmed sun-hat.

"Hey guys, I made it!" she yells.

"*Adora!*"

I'm about throwing the ball across the net, but no one is paying attention. The girls are all running to give her a hug and scream with delight. The guys all seem happy that she is around, but Esosa looks subdued. I am confused. Who is this new girl?

"Sosa," she says, after exchanging pleasantries with just about everyone except me. "Won't you give me a hug?"

I watch as my boyfriend hugs the pretty young girl and try not to get jealous.

"Okay, so the girls are now complete," someone yells. "Let's play ball."

"Yes, lets." Adora places her things with the rest of ours and take off her one-piece jumper suit. What's left is a baby-blue two-piece bathing suit, long yellow legs, and Esosa's distraction.

When some of the guys go swimming along the beach front, one of the girls, Elizabeth, asks if I can setup the food with her. I go, ignoring the fact that Esosa and Adora are standing a little way off talking.

"So what's the deal with you and Esosa?" she asks as we sort paper plates. "Just friends, or something more?"

"Friends." I'm curious about her response.

"Oh, good," Elizabeth's laugh has relief in it. "Esosa brings a different girl every time we go thrill-seeking. I'm just trying to figure out what his deal is."

A different girl. I'm surprised.

"Really, how often do you go for these thrill-seeking adventures?"

"You know us doctors, hectic work schedules and over-bearing bosses. We try to find time every three months so we don't collapse from stress." Elizabeth starts dishing miniature spoons of Jollof rice and prompts me to put a piece of grilled chicken and beef kebab on each plate. "Last time, we went paint ball fighting at Omu Resort. And the time before that, Ikogosi Springs."

"That must have been fun!" I say mechanically. Mentally, I'm doing some calculations. Esosa and I have been dating for about eight months. "So what's the deal with Adora?"

"She's the daughter of Senator Rowland, her mum is the MD of the State Hospital in Abuja. Mad money, beauty, and brains combined."

I stare at her. Elizabeth is dishing salad and fried plantain now. "I mean with her and Esosa."

"They broke up officially in January, after a four-year roller coaster of emotions."

That's three months before we met.

"It's why I'm asking what the deal is with you. I think Adora wants him back."

It's not long before we break into groups of twos and threes, and Esosa and I are together. He kisses my hands and acts unfamiliarly loving. I can't help but think it's all in a bid to make his ex-girlfriend jealous.

"I hear you and Adora were once an item," I say, popping a piece of puff-puff into my mouth and watching the smile freeze on his face. "If you had told me you wanted us to just be friends, I would have agreed. I would have come here fully expecting to enjoy myself and not felt bad when I met your ex-girlfriend."

"*Adora?*" He glances at her and starts laughing. "Adora and I were over months ago."

"You were with her at Omu Resort two months ago."

It was a guess, and I was correct. His face betrayed him.

"Femi ... Honestly, I didn't know she was coming. You were busy, and I didn't know if you'd want to go to Omu—"

"You didn't ask," I say quietly. "I thought we were trying to get back together."

"I'm sorry I didn't ask. But we only just met, and I'm not ready for marriage."

"I'm not asking for marriage; I'm asking for exclusivity. You are dating other girls, and I don't know where I stand."

"You're foremost," he jokes.

"I'm serious. For me, there is just you. But for you, it was so easy to jump into bed with Yinka, and Adora is here on our supposed get back together. How do you think that makes me feel?"

"Okay, Femi." Esosa touches my arm and looks into my eye. "Stop getting paranoid about Adora. I want to build something with you, but I will always meet other girls—"

"And you might ask them out just for fun."

He starts to laugh. "That's not what I meant."

I don't believe him. For me, the issue is less about marriage and more about focus. I want to know if we are still in the stage of seeing other people. I haven't, but apparently Esosa has.

"We're taking this slow," he continues. "You're not ready for intimacy and I get that, but it tells me we're not strictly a couple—"

"So you can see other girls?"

I don't want to listen anymore. His betrayal with Yinka is fresh on my mind. It had more to do with disrespecting me in my grandfather's house with my uncle's girlfriend than with him seeing someone else. But he thinks it's okay if he dates other women as long as I don't find out about it. That, for me, is a deal-breaker.

"That day in the hospital, it was me because I was the only one who looked single."

He frowns at me. "What are you talking about?"

Stop talking, Femi, I say to myself, but I can't. I'm too hurt.

"Aramide was married; she had the rings to show. Olamide's fiancé was standing just outside the door." I say this with the realization that Esosa was just looking for a cheap thrill. "I was the only available option, perhaps the only option you'd seen all day."

"Come on, Femi. Why would you say something like that?"

"It wasn't because you saw me and you liked me." *Stop it!* I'm breaking up with Esosa, and I can't help myself. "It was because you needed a replacement for Adora."

"Femi, that's not true. I am very attracted to you."

"That's the thing. I don't want someone who is merely attracted to me. I don't want to hang with you for a year or two to see where this goes. I've done that a couple of times, and I don't have the luxury of time. I want to settle down and build something real with someone who loves me. I'm not going to settle for any guy who shows interest because I need to fill a void in my life—I want a real relationship. But if you're still seeing other girls because I'm not ready for intimacy, then I think we should just stop."

"Femi." Esosa grabs my hands, but he doesn't say the words I want to hear. "I like you a whole lot, but I'm not ready for a commitment I can't make unless I'm absolutely sure it's what I want. Doesn't mean I don't want to be with you."

"Because you're still in love with Adora," I say gently.

What happened to wanting to be a part of my family? I muse, thinking about our dance on the night of Aunty Ladepe's birthday.

"That's not true."

I smile at him but don't respond. He is going to go back to Adora. She is younger, slimmer, richer, and full of more than he realizes he needs in a woman. I'm not what he wants. I never was.

Chapter Twelve

We are constantly told that we are unique and special, and we believe it, 'til someone comes along and challenges those labels. We are told to have a list of what we want from life and relationships, and we forget that the probability of others messing up, or falling short, or just plain being more or less than what we'd hoped, exists.

So when it happens, our mind takes a beating. We kick ourselves in the gut for failing to be perceptive. We berate ourselves, and imagine that we need to become the person we want or expect to see in others for our own lives to change. We resent our stupidity, and overshoot or underachieve in order to avoid the pain that comes with disappointment. And we attribute negative life experiences to our personal failings.

We are not told to study life and learn from history. Nor told that sometimes needs are unmet and anticipations unfulfilled, and that it is not always our fault. So we lose hope, and the courage to hope, and then decide not to. We are disappointed.

Some say that disappointments are healthy. That anything that crushes your hopes, or cancels your plans, or ruins your dreams, makes you stronger. That it's in those experiences that we grow, and come up with new ways of doing things, and find something far better than what we lost in the first place.

I see disappointments as shame-based, not so much entrenched in the experiences that cause them, but in the rejection that follows them. We mourn the hurt of falling short of expectation, the pain of losing face, and the feeling of being inconsequential. And we feel disappointed, because we think the world views us differently.

That's how I feel now, because after five failed relationships, I should have known better.

"How was your trip?" Aramide asks when they pick me up on their way to Ibadan the following weekend.

"It was okay." I hand my bag to Diran and get into the backseat with their twins. He picks up on my dreary answer from behind the car boot's lid.

"Just okay? Don't tell me you didn't enjoy Tarkwa Bay. I've been begging your sister to let us go for months now, so we can spend time lounging on the beach before the New Year."

"What happened?" Aramide turns round in the front seat, "with Esosa."

"The guy is a douchebag, baring him being a doctor."

"Nifemi!"

"He brought his ex-girlfriend, who by the way he is still in love with, along for the trip."

"PG in the back, can we talk later?"

I nod. Aramide faces forward so she can secure her seat belt, and Diran slides into the driver's seat, still talking about the finer points of Tarkwa Bay.

I don't want to talk, but I'm stuck in the back seat with the twins. Darasimi, the girl—the chatterbox who finds it impossible to stop prattling— hugs me and lifts milk-white teeth in my direction. "What did you buy for me, Aunty Femi?"

I hang my head and groan. She's five, which is difficult to believe because she is several vocabulary levels ahead of her twin brother Iremide, the one who never grew out of the Terrible Twos. I know I'm not getting out of her chubby arms any moment soon.

"Biscuits."

"Yeaaa!" she announces with glee and hugs me tighter. "Where are they?"

"No biscuits until we get to the toll gate," her mother replies. "And everyone should let Aunty Femi rest."

"So," Diran says. "I hear there are chalets there we can rent for the night as a family."

Aramide looks at him. "When I say everyone, I mean everyone, Diran. Femi was hoping to catch some zzzs on this trip."

I'mgrateful for my sister's protection.

So Aunty Norma, Uncle Deola, and their brood are at Grandpa's house when we get there. My mum is around, as well. Grandpa has been gone almost five months, and life must be lonely for Aunty Ladepe. It's why we are here, spending time with her and Cousin Toba.

She is more than happy to see us. She grabs Aramide and Diran in a bear hug while I greet Aunty Norma and her family.

"Hey, Femo, I have not seen you in a while." Uncle Deola gives me a side hug. He is balding in a U-shape and is my second favourite uncle. "I hear you are dating a doctor now," he says, eyes twinkling behind his glasses as he gives Diran a firm hand shake.

"Oh, yeah," I quip. I want to keep the information about Esosa for as long as I possibly can.

"I'm hoping to meet him soon so I can give him a pep talk."

"Daddy already did some of that," I say, waving a hand.

"Well, it can never be too much."

Aramide catches my eye. All the pep talk in the world won't keep Esosa from chasing other women, and she knows it.

"Aunty, we are so sorry to burst in on you like this with the house so full," she says to steer the conversation in another direction.

I meet her eye and communicate my thanks.

"Nonsense, you are more than welcome here. This is your home. I've ordered for a cooler of Jollof and fried rice and it should arrive soon. Deji, too, has friends over, so the more the merrier."

"And meat, I hope Aunty," Diran says.

"Plenty of fried meat and chicken."

"Aunty, don't indulge him." Aramide swats her husband. "He will eat your meat and leave your rice."

Everyone laughs.

"Has anyone heard from Olamide? Is she coming?" my mother asks.

"Korede said they are visiting his parents. Perhaps they'll meet up with us in the new year," I reply.

"My dear," Aunty Ladepe hugs me and holds me at arm length, "how are you?"

"Very well, thank you, Aunty."

She cups my cheek and looks into my eyes, and for a moment, I'm scared that she sees the sadness in them. She would know about Esosa; Toba would have told her about Yinka. "I am glad you're here."

The noise level rises as everyone starts talking all at once trying to catch up. It's going to be a fun Christmas, as long as no one asks me about Esosa.

"There are drinks in the fridge, and lunch will soon be here!" Aunty Ladepe announces to everyone.

"So where is Toba?" Diran wants to know as we pile out of the kitchen into the living room.

"Out," Uncle Deola replies, "took the kid next door and his mother to the shopping mall."

"Kid next door," I say with a frown. I'm annoyed that Toba is with another woman. There are many kids living on my grandfather's street, and I don't know which one specifically they are referring to, or the reason why I'm annoyed to be perfectly honest.

"Ladun's son, you all remember Ladun, right, the youngest of Pa Adekunle's children," Aunty Ladepe explains. "She moved back home earlier in the year."

"Oh, I remember Ladun," *Tiny, scrawny-looking girl with three brothers.* "Didn't she get married like three years ago?"

I recall the long wedding ceremony and the constant heat in their church hall during the reception. Olamide and I had attended.

"I heard rumours of a break up." Aramide's joins the conversation as she gets a drink from the refrigerator. "She's been back home for a year."

"Yes," my mum says. "The man has not been kind to her at all. I hear he beats her."

Aunty Ladepe sighs. "Toba wanted to do something nice for the boy since its Christmas and the father is absent. He took them to see the farm, and they called to tell me they stopped at the mall."

"Really," Aramide pops open a can of malt. "That's mighty nice of him."

"Have you all been to the farm? We should go this weekend. I hear Toba is turning the place into some kind of haven." Diran steals a sip out of his wife's malt.

"*Han han* Diran, get your own," Aramide grumbles, and my mother gives her a disapproving frown.

I can almost hear her disappointed voice chirping out loud about disrespectful wives.

We are all in the big living room settling into plates of rice and chicken when we hear the kitchen door open. A young boy of about five runs in followed by the young woman I assume is his mother, Ladun.

"*E kaa san ma, e kaa san sir,*" she curtseys as she enters.

My mum and Aunty Ladepe smile as she comes into the room and goes on her two knees before them. I roll my eyes. Yoruba folk and their patronizing need for respect!

"Welcome." Aunty Ladepe gives her a hug.

"Help me thank Uncle Toba. We really enjoyed ourselves. Ibukun was so happy with all the gifts he bought for us. I don't even know how to thank him. Aunty Norma." She goes over to kneel and greet her, too.

"*Abeg no greet me. Abi na me take you out?*" Aunty Norma says, laughing.

"You know Aramide and Femi *abi.*" Aunty Ladepe points us out to her.

"I do ma." She beams at both of us, and I return the smile. She reminds me a little of Bimpe, Cousin Toba's former girlfriend—overtly happy, overtly respectful, and overtly wife material. "Please help me thank Uncle Toba. He really made me happy today."

Aramide nods. "We will."

"Where is Toba?" Aunty Ladepe asks.

She stands up. "He is talking with the estate chairman outside. He will come inside later."

"Okay," Aunty Ladepe says.

Ladun beams at everyone and calls her son. "We are going back home. I just wanted to come and greet you ma."

"Alright, please greet your mother for me."

"Yes ma." She curtseys—on her knees again—as she says her goodbyes, and leaves with her son.

"That boy looks older than the twins," I lean over to whisper to Aramide.

"They had the child pre-marriage. I'm so not a fan of marriage because you have a child together. People change, and sometimes, the change is not pleasant."

"True!"

I watch my mum and Aunty Ladepe talk about the girl. How respectful she is, how nice she is, and how much of a shame it is that her marriage didn't work out. I can't help but think to myself that it would be better to remain unmarried than to fall into the wrong hands, get divorced, and then have to endure the *'Oh, what a pity'* side talk. I feel better about my breakup with Esosa, and I throw the thoughts out of my head.

As I look around, I realise that my worry about us scattering after Grandpa's death was unnecessary. We're still together, we still enjoy each other's company, and there is still life as a family outside of Grandpa's influence.

***

I'm the only one in the bed I shared with Aramide and her daughter, Darasimi.

"These guys didn't wake me," I moan, yawning and stretching.

Everyone is downstairs. I can smell yam and eggs and hear their voices floating up from the living room. I hurry with my bath rituals and dress in slacks and a three-quarter length top.

"Morning everyone," I sing as I hurry down the staircase.

"Iremide is a douchebag," I hear Darasimi say to Cousin Toba. He's crouched low in front of her and holding her by the shoulders. "He took my toy and broke it on purpose."

I slow to a stop and widen my eyes. *OMG, that little imp! Did she just say that out loud?* She was apparently awake the whole time her mother and I were gossip-shaming Esosa.

"Hey. Don't call your brother the d-word. Where'd you hear that from?" Toba's deep voice floats up to me.

"Aunty Femi said it," Darasimi says matter-of-factly. "I heard her tell my mummy that Dr. Esosa is a douchebag!"

I cover my face with one hand.

"Did she now?" he says.

"She did!" The girl's vigorous nodding looks like her head is about to snap off.

"Why don't you call him a naughty boy instead?"

"So Dr. Esosa is a naughty boy?"

Toba recoils from the smart-ass statement and raises his eyes to mine as I take slow steps down the rest of the staircase. "I guess we will have to ask Aunty Femi."

"That—" I say, holding up my hands in defence, "—is not exactly how I put it."

"Yeah," he holds my gaze as he rises to his feet. He does not have a smile, but his tone tells me he's amused. He knows without doubt that Esosa and I are finally over. So I am ashamed, staring at his perfect solid frame and wondering at the futility of girls letting a guy like him slip through their fingers.

"What's a douchebag?" Darasimi continues unfazed.

We both turn and stare down at her.

"Darasimi!" Aramide shouts from the dining room table. She stands up with her plate in her hand and pulls her away from Cousin Toba. "How many times will I tell you to stop eavesdropping on people's conversations, eh? And don't ever let me ever catch you calling your bother names."

Eavesdropping? Yeah, when she puts it like that, the five-year old is supposed to know not to do it.

"I take it the good doctor has been acting out of character," Toba says, causing me to look up at him. I open my mouth and snap it shut as Jumoke heads over with a breakfast plate for me. There is laughter in his eyes, but I'm ignoring it.

"If Radio Lagos over there were a couple years older, she'd know not to broadcast everything she hears out of context." I accept the plate from Jumoke and sit on the last step of the staircase.

Jumoke steps out of Cousin Toba' way as she passes by him. His eyes follow her movement. She is worried we might tell her mum about her way older boyfriend and is probably glad the seats in the dining area are all occupied.

"What happened?" He walks over to slide onto the step beside me.

"Don't even ask." I roll my eyes and pop a piece of yam and egg into my mouth.

"Guess that means Esosa is out of the picture."

"And I want to keep that piece of news on the down low, please." I lean over and whisper to him. "There are people here that believe I don't know how to keep a man, even though the men out there are just, I don't know. My mum might decide to set me up with Ladun's older brother, but I'm kinda like taking a break from relationships."

"You mean from men?"

"Yeah."

Toba leans his elbows on the step behind us. "He's a douchebag," he says out of the blue. "Knew it the moment I laid eyes on him."

"How could you tell?" I ask, balancing my plate on my thighs. "How does one pick up on that on your first meeting with a guy?"

"You usually can't."

"But you did."

"I'm a guy."

I look at Toba, and he turns his head to look at me. His gaze is prolonged, mine seeking clarification.

"He was with you, and he was checking Yinca out. That's disrespect if anything, but then my standards might be high. In truth, we all do it, but he was making no effort to hide it. And you were right beside him."

"He's a doctor. I thought he was decent."

"He's a man."

"So you check out girls?" I tease.

He shrugs and gives me a sluggish smile. "Which red-blooded man doesn't?"

"Right, so how do I know a douchebag before I give him full access to my life?"

"You've got to be their friend first," he says. "That way, you'd know the real guy before he hides the parts of himself he doesn't want you to see."

"That's what I thought I'd been doing all along."

He sits up and puts his elbows on his thighs. "Sometimes, you can't let a guy know you like him, while you're vetting him."

"Explain."

"Yinca wanted us to take the relationship to the next level, but I just didn't see it happening. She didn't care about that, though. She wanted a friend with benefit kind of thing, but there was no point leading her on. You guys have emotional entanglements. Even when you claim it's just benefits, there are always ties. Been there, done that, made the mistakes."

I stare at him, and he stares back.

"Your point being?"

"It didn't hurt when she strayed. We were friends. I already knew she wasn't the one for me."

"I had a long-time friendship with Akpan, then a relationship, and he hurt me badly, physically, too."

"You didn't see the red flags. Subtle things that point to a guy you need to watch carefully."

"Like?"

"Well, how he drives, for example."

I'm curious.

"Does he give people chances to get ahead or does he block them? Does he cut into lines with no apologies? Does he flaunt rules? When someone hits his car or brushes past him, does he chase them down and exact vengeance, or does he let them go?"

I raise an eyebrow.

"How does he treat beggars, with impatience or with some form of dignity? If he holds a car door open for you, does he do it for others or is he just trying to impress you? Little things," Toba shrugs, "things that are already a part of character."

I try to look back at my past relationships and pick these things out.

"A guy who doesn't care so much about them could turn out to be aggressive. A guy who cares too much and brings you flowers all the time is probably trying to hide something and make up for it. These are all general assertions, though. There should be a right balance."

I look away and nod.

"But you got out of it just in time. A guy like that, he wouldn't have stopped. After marriage, it would have only gotten worse." Toba is looking at me with calm thoughtfulness. "If you're with a guy and he wants sex before a week is up, then you need to check if that relationship is real. Not saying some guys aren't good at heart or that there shouldn't be attraction, but the wait period refines a guy's intentions. If a guy's really into you, he can wait a year, two, doesn't really matter. He knows you are his in the end, and he likes you for other reasons. And those reasons, they cement relationships. He's not going to source out another girl to replace you."

I think about Adenrele and wonder where he is. He was my first real boyfriend. We dated for more than two years, but I broke it off because, according to me, he was too passive. But he was kind to people, he was a gentleman. He never pressured me into anything I didn't want to do.

He just wasn't exciting.

"Are you saying that a guy who wants intimacy right from the start shouldn't be trusted?"

"No. I'm saying friendship outweighs sex. Build that first, and keep your eyes on the lookout for how the guy treats other people whenever he thinks you're not looking. It's usually a strong indication of what kind of person he truly is."

I glance at Toba.

"Thanks," I say with a forced smile.

"You're welcome, little niece."

I chuckle. "I'm not your little niece."

He just sits still beside me and doesn't respond.

"Hey, are you ready?" Aramide comes back into the dining room with Aunty Norma.

"Yeah." I stand up from beside Cousin Toba and hurry to drop my plate on the kitchen side cabinet. Jumoke is also doing the washing up with her brothers. "Been waiting for ya'll to get ready."

"Where are you headed?" Toba asks, getting up from the step.

"To look at my land," I reply, turning round to face him. "I haven't seen it, and I want to determine if I'm going to keep it or sell."

"Don't sell!" Aramide replies. "Lagos is not the best place to settle down, trust me."

"So I'm going to uproot my whole life and move to dreary Ibadan because Grandpa gave me land?"

"What's wrong with Ibadan?" She grabs a malt from the fridge.

"Are you seriously asking me that question?"

"Yes. All you need is a good enough reason to stay."

I snigger. "Yeah, speaking financially and economically, I don't think there will ever be."

"You don't know how I envy the people who live here. Lagos is stressful. Look at Cousin Toba, for example." Aramide takes a swig from the can and points at him.

He straightens up, slides his hands into his pockets, and waits for her assessment of him.

"He looks fresh and healthy. You can't tell me Ibadan has not been good to him."

"I work on a farm, Ara. And bet you a whole lot of stress lies there," he replies with a candid look.

"Yeah, but looking at you, we don't see it. You can't tell me that the air on that farm has not been good for you."

He smiles, and our eyes meet. I catch my breath for a moment. Ara is right—he does look better than he has in years. Like aging did its work backwards and peeled off his imperfections.

Aunty Norma's arrival breaks up my random—inadmissible—thoughts. I can't be caught thinking about my uncle like that. Toba is my new crush, and I'm looking to clone him.

"My yard people shey una don ready? Toba come and carry us now. I wan enter that your fancy car again. Make you no use that truck o!"

He grins and looks from me to her. "Sure, let's go."

Chapter Thirteen

I've surfed the ocean of being 'single again' so many times, the waves are familiar. I've ridden the highs and lows of my emotions, snubbed the gnawing itch to troll an ex's social media pages for signs of progress, and spent countless sleepless nights pouring over how to handle running into an ex. It's the shame of uncomfortable discussions that get me, and the avoidance of mutual friends.

I've found that losing myself in activities that span huge portions of my day help. Going out becomes a lifeline, travelling, a way of masking pain in lieu of getting high on doughnuts and ice-cream. So I welcome them, any and every opportunity to do anything but sit around and mope.

The problem is, my mum is conversant with my methods of distraction. She knows, without my saying a word that Esosa and I are over, and she's unhappy that I've decided to go to Ibadan to represent my office at the ANA Oyo state chapter's get together.

"You need to stay at home and enjoy the New Year," she says, standing at the door to my room, watching me pack.

"It's just four days. I'll be back on Sunday."

"But we haven't even spent a week in the New Year!"

I know she wants me to talk about what happened. She wants us to examine my relationships together, and figure out what keeps going wrong.

"I'm going to Ibadan. Not Abuja, or Port Harcourt, or anywhere scary. Don't worry."

"That's hardly the point. It's the travelling, in strange cars."

I never change my mind. So she always comes up with creative ways to get her point across, or have her way stamped all over mine. Finding Cousin Toba seated at our dining table that morning is not a surprise. It's my mum, up to no good.

"Hi, Femi," he says, all innocent.

"Hey, pleasant surprise." My countenance is anything but happy to see him. "What brings you here?"

He grins at me from behind a plate piled with fried eggs, sardine sauce, and sausages. "I came over to drop some foodstuff, and your mum insisted I stay for breakfast."

Liar! I know why he's here. It has nothing to do with delivering anything because my mum and his mum send their things through me.

"Femi." My mum saunters out of the kitchen carrying a golden-coloured dish filled with more sardine sauce. "Look who dropped in on us this morning. I'm not letting him go anywhere without breakfast. I can't remember when last he visited, and it looks like he's losing weight."

She gives him a reprimanding stare before walking back into the kitchen.

"I'm not going to escape from this without eating, am I?" Cousin Toba says to me.

I shake my head and stuff my handbag with the book I plan to read on my way to Ibadan.

He glances at the travelling bag on the floor. "She mentioned you are going to Ibadan today."

"I am. Work stuff."

"Are you going to stay over at the house?"

I look up and hold his gaze. He returns the stare and doesn't blink, nor give any indication that he knows that I know my mum asked him to come over. "Nope, my company booked a hotel."

"We have plenty of room at the house."

"I know."

He searches my eyes and smiles like he has thought of some elaborate plan to make me stay over at Grandpa's house. Whatever he's planning, it's not going to work.

"She is going to Ibadan." My mum tosses a net curtain out of her way as she comes out with a tray of fresh sliced bread. "She has been travelling up and down like Nigerian roads are that safe, in cars with strange drivers I don't know."

I place my bag on the table and exhale. "Mummy—"

"Don't you think it's dangerous for a young girl to be travelling around on her own?"

"I'm not young."

"You are compared to my age."

"Mummy!"

"Toba!"

We both turn to him helpless, but he sits still doing what he knows how to do best, refusing to get involved.

"If she was married or in a relationship now, and it was her husband or fiancé driving her, I wouldn't worry."

"It's Ibadan, less than an hour's drive away. I went there a billion times last year, and on my own in a cab."

"You know why I don't want you to go alone? There are men kidnapping people, and that Lagos-Ibadan road is full of potholes."

"Taxify is relatively safe. And for goodness' sake, they've fixed major portions of that road."

"Kidnappers can use Taxify. Toba can take you. Toba, you can take her, right?"

He looks from me, to my mum, and back to me. "Sure."

My mum leaves the dining room looking victorious.

I narrow my eyes at him. "I'm sure you have work, something else that brought you to Lagos."

His eyes soften as he considers this. "I'm done with it. Let me give you a lift."

"No thanks. I already called my cab guy."

"Come on, Femi. It's a chance for us to hang out for a bit. We haven't done that in a while."

"We hung out plenty last Christmas."

"My heart will be at rest if Toba takes you." My mum comes back into the dining room and stares at Toba. "You're not eating?"

"I am." He reaches for a thick slice of bread.

"Please, convince your niece to go with you."

I eye my mum, and she smiles at me before going back into the kitchen.

"You really don't have to drop me," I say, turning to Toba.

"It will get your mum off your back." He dips a piece of bread into the sauce. "Besides, I wouldn't mind company on the drive back."

He shrugs and pops it into his mouth.

I glare at him. The honest truth is, I want to be alone.

"Femi, make your uncle some tea now, or would you prefer coffee, Toba?"

"Coffee would be nice, Aunty," he says and tosses me his famous amused look.

I slam my bag on the table and go and make the coffee. I don't even care that I'm being childish.

***

When we get out of the house, Toba helps me to the car with my travelling bag.

"Tell me the truth. My mum coerced you into coming," I say, hoping to force him into a confession.

"Does it matter?" He tosses the bag into the boot of the car and comes round to open the passenger side door for me.

"You let my mum bully you into things. You don't even object to any of her suggestions."

"She didn't have to do much to convince me. I had work in Lagos." He leans over the open door and peers at me. "And I like spending time with you. Aren't you glad I rescued you?"

I scowl at him and slide into the car. He grins, slams the door, and walks round the bonnet to the driver's side.

"What exactly did she say to you?" I ask when he's settled and prepared to drive.

"That you needed some cheering up." Toba throws his gear into drive, and we speed off. "By the way, I'm going to make some quick stop-overs along the way."

"I need to be in Ibadan by three."

"We'll get there." He chuckles as he catches sight of my face. "It'll be an adventure, don't worry."

Three hours later, we are at another stop-over. This time, I'm following Toba and his friend, Mr. Noah, down a path behind a brick office.

"You promised my mum you'd take me straight to Ibadan, but you've dragged me to a poultry farm, a juice bottling industry, and now, a Shagamu pig and fishery farm," I whisper at him. "I'm not going anywhere else with you if you keep this up."

"You are having an adventure, aren't you?"

"You've been talking farm stuff all day. Does that sound adventurous enough to you?"

"I promise to have you in Ibadan well in time for your cocktail party. Our meeting will be a quick twenty minutes at the farm proper, which is a long distance to walk in this heat."

"We're there," Mr. Noah announces as we step into the field behind the office.

I'm surprised at the expanse of unending land. It's green and brown, and set against a backdrop of blueness that takes my breath away. I suppose it's the price we pay for living in the city: the abject amnesia of how big and beautiful God's Earth is.

"This—" Toba says holding his arms out, "—is why I farm."

"Beautiful," I reply.

Mr. Noah waves us over to his truck.

"*Oya* come inside!" he says with pride.

I stare. The vehicle he has promised will take us to his fish-farm is a rusty, four-wheel-drive jeep with no roof or doors.

"That?" I mutter out loud. "That's what we're taking?"

"Yes," Toba says. "What were you expecting, a limo?"

I eye him. What actually hinders me is not the rickety look of the vehicle, but the two muddy-looking farmhands seated in it.

Mr. Noah slides himself into the driver's seat as Toba nudges my arm with his and nods at the truck. "Let's go."

Go? Go where? There are four seats, and three are already occupied. Toba and I will have to squeeze into the back with the farmhand, and I am wearing a dress I still want to wear to my cocktail party.

I look up at him. "I'll stay here and wait for you."

"I can't leave you here, come on." He strolls towards the jeep.

I watch him duck his head under the frame that once held the jeep's fabric roof and slide his huge build into the rest of the backseat. There is no space for me.

"You just go and do your business. I'll be fine. Twenty minutes, did you say?"

"Mr. Toba, Madam cannot stay here alone oh, it's dangerous," Mr. Noah says. "There is no one at the office. You have to come with us."

"I'm fine," I reply, raising a palm.

The farmhand in the front seat shakes his head. "*Anti, plenty kidnappers dey here oh, those people wey dey drive cow, E no safe.*"

"Femi," Toba's look is worried. "I kind of like agree with them. Come on, we'll be back in a jiffy."

I stare at him and chuckle, "to sit where, exactly?"

"Here." He pats his thighs with two hands and looks up at me, "a quick five-minute ride. Hop on."

"On your laps?" I dare to look in his face and find him grinning. "Do I look like Darasimi?"

"Nifemi, I can't leave you here all by yourself. Let's go."

"*Anti, we go quick go.*" The farmhand at the back lends his voice to the plea. "*Make you manage for oga's leg.*"

Manage for oga's leg, are you alright? My eyes are on Toba's.

"Five minutes," he repeats.

Mr. Noah starts the jeep. I'm wasting everyone's time.

I take ginger steps over and climb in. This will be between Toba and me; no one has to know. The farmhand is muddy and wafting a peculiar odour. As ridiculous as I feel sitting on Toba's laps, sitting next to him would have been horrendous. I'm wondering how Toba can do it and not puke.

Toba leans backwards and shifts his feet to make space for mine. He catches my eye as I lower my butt across his thighs and tries not to touch me any more than is necessary. But the space is small and awkward, and his gaze is on the right side of my face.

"Tell anyone about this, and I will murder you myself!" I say to him, blushing through brown cheeks.

He smiles, pulls an imaginary zipper over his lips, and keeps right on staring at me.

The jeep jerks to a start and winds off down a path between tall, green stalks of growing maize. The sounds of it rumbling along on the dirt path fills the air between us, but the unruly farm scenery with its wild grass and rows of plantation steal my attention. I don't want to look at Toba. It's embarrassing. It's hard to remember when last I took a ride via lapping, and on a guy's laps.

The truck runs over a bump and tosses me. I put a hand out to break my fall, but he leans forward and his right hand encircles my waist and draws me in just in time. I find my face inches from his chest, staring at his bearded chin.

"Thanks," I say, inhaling his manly scent.

"You are welcome," he replies, his voice low in my ears. "You do know you're my favourite niece, I can't let you to fall off."

I freeze and look up at his face. I'm at that line again. That confusing line that's too close for comfort, yet low enough to trip over. "You know you'll have to answer to your sister."

He chuckles. "I know."

I'm holding my breath.

Okay! You may let go now, I'm thinking, but he doesn't. His hand is warm against the left side of my waist, arm taut against my stomach.

"You're not as light weight as I imagined you'd be," he continues.

"Are you comparing me with Yinca?" I ask, confused. *Toba can't be flirting. Can he?*

"No," he grunts, the rich baritone of his voice lending weight to the word and pressure to my soaring pulse rate. "Just commenting."

"Don't. A woman's weight is a sensitive subject."

I can't even let him know what I'm thinking, or feeling. I trust Toba. He would never do anything untoward, but I want him to take his hand away. It's distracting, and I'm at a very vulnerable point in my life.

"You've trimmed down a lot, and it's a good look on you."

"Can we not make this anymore awkward than it already is?" I say eyes on his face. "And not talk about my weight, at all?"

He stares into my eyes and gives me a slow grin. "Okay."

"Thank you." I turn to watch the fast-moving greenery in front of me, and my heart starts thumping in my chest. The line reminds me that he is my uncle and warns me to stir clear, but my heart, I don't know where my heart's at.

"Relax," he utters low in my ear. "It's just a lift."

No, he's not flirting, he's teasing. There is a difference. He has, however, linked his left hand with his right, and I'm sweating slightly.

"You're not the grown-up woman sitting on her uncle's lap."

"Come on." He continues in that utterly provocative deep drawl. "I only let the girls I like sit on my lap."

Two warm spots deepen on my cheeks as Toba's voice in my ear takes an undecided tone. I can't tell anymore if he's teasing or flirting. "I'm not one of your girls."

That gets him laughing. "Your words, not mine, remember."

"Because it's your MO with girls at family events."

The grin doesn't leave his face. "But I had to offer you something. We were in a peculiar situation."

"I could have stayed back at the farm office. Don't justify this."

Take your hands away!

"I wouldn't want anyone to make off with you. Your mum would kill me."

"Stop talking."

He chuckles. "Yes ma'am."

I shake my head and exhale. What's confusing is my reaction. I'm nervous. I shouldn't be nervous around Toba. My heart shouldn't be fluttering, and I shouldn't be blushing. But I'm all those things that I shouldn't be. And Toba is—*flirting?*

"Mr. Toba I'm considering buying those tractors," Mr. Noah cuts in.

"You should, they're an investment." Toba's voice goes an octave higher as he turns his attention away from me and leans back into his seat. "They make harvesting a lot easier."

He relaxes his hold on me but doesn't take his hands away, and I release the breath I didn't know I was holding. What is wrong with me? Why will Toba and flirting be in the same sentence in my head? Losing Esosa must be messing me up.

We get to the farm, and Toba lets me down before stepping out of the jeep.

"Going back, you get your own seat," he informs me. "The men are staying."

"I'd better!" I say and walk away from him.

My runaway heart settles with this distance and I'm awed at the farm.

There are parallel rows of underground tanks with pipes of running water in between them. Most are covered with fish nets and have several catfish slithering around, free of worries and ignorant of the fate that awaits them.

I zone out, and for a moment imagine myself a fish swimming in the lake of life. Swimming into relationships, aware that something will happen but not knowing exactly what, when, how, or why.

I jerk out of the zone as Toba's hand grabs mine from behind. *'Oh god!'* I moan inside as my heart begins to throttle again.

"Come on," he says cheerfully as he links our fingers together, "lots to see."

***

An hour later, we are hurtling towards Ibadan, and I'm smiling at the setting sun. Following him around all day has been somewhat therapeutic. I don't know if it's the fresh air and natural environment or his generally pleasant disposition, but I'm grateful to my mum for calling him.

"Can I ask you a question?"

"Sure."

"Did you ever try to find your real dad?"

Toba is quiet for a while.

"I did," he finally says. "Wasn't what I expected."

"Who is he?"

"Can we not?" he asks, glancing at me. "Please?"

"Okay," I say. "So you want to bring a fish farm to *Iseyin*."

"I do."

"Grandpa made a wise choice," I murmur.

"About the farm ownership?"

"About a lot of things," I remember his frail shoulders and straight stance, and miss him for a minute. "But that especially."

"I'm just hoping it works with the water problem on ground, and the poaching locals, and my untrustworthy staff."

I turn. It's the first time I've seen him truly apprehensive about anything. "You're doing a great job."

He lets out a deep breath.

"I'm just running lucky." His eyes are fixed on the road in front of him, and there is no trace of his usual smile in sight. "I had to fire three people diverting produce last week. One of them has a wife and four kids. It's the last thing I wanted to do."

I understand. His heart is just like Grandpa's heart, golden. It hurt him to take away the man's livelihood. "But you have to look out for the farm. That sometimes involves making tough choices. You did the right thing."

"Did I?" he murmurs, brow knitted in a frown. "That man's going to be hustling to feed his kids now. How do I know he's not going to go elsewhere and do the same thing?"

"It won't be on you."

"No, but perhaps there was a better way I could have handled it and helped him. Yinka's got a tech guy coming over. Perhaps monitoring everything on the farm remotely might help keep the workers a little more honest."

"Yinka 'with a C'?"

"Yeah, her guy says we can do that with technology. We've been in talks, but tomorrow will be his first day on the farm. I'm nervous about the whole thing, but I think it just might work."

I'm not listening anymore; I'm thinking about Yinka 'with a C,' about the long night she spent lying in the grass curled up to him. "So, Yinka's into technology."

Toba glances at me. "Yeah, that's how we met. Her dad's part owner of a tech company in Lagos, and it was a hotly debated topic in one of my LBS classes, the aversion of native African farmers to the changing world of technology. I was on the side of inclusion, she was totting having things evolve more naturally. She grew up all her life over there, and this was her first visit to Nigeria."

I press my lips together and keep my eyes glued to the scenery outside the air-conditioned car. Why are we talking about Yinca?

"I know she took Esosa from you."

"No, she didn't. Esosa took himself out of the picture."

"Don't judge her too harshly."

"I'm not judging her."

"She comes from a different environment than we do, and some things are just ..."

"Wrong," I say turning to look at him. "Wrong, telling me to keep my boyfriend and then turning around to go do whatever with him."

Toba takes in a deep breath as we hit the stretch of road that takes us into Ring Road. "She feels bad about what happened. She wants you to know it."

"I hear you." I don't care about Yinka with a C's feelings. She had not bothered to care about mine.

"Listen, some doors close so others can open."

"Not everyone is going to be like you, Toba, all loving and forgiving."

"So you've not forgiven me?"

"For what? I'm not angry with you."

Toba glances at me and turns his eyes back to the road. "It didn't seem that way."

"Oh, come on, Cousin Toba." It is true that I was angry, but I wasn't any more. I needed him to know that. "Okay, yes, I was a little angry because she came in through you. But that's over and done with. I'm not angry."

"Anymore," he says.

"Anymore," I add with an exhausted sigh. "Sheeze, give me a break!"

He chuckles. "So am I invited to your cocktail mixer?"

I shrug. "If you're free, and you want to come."

"I'm free," he says. "I want to come."

***

I'm surprised at the turnout when we get there. We sip a mocktail of sorts and weave through a barrage of intellectuals arguing about Soyinka and Achebe and debating the reasons why they think feminism is un-African. While I scout around for new writers, Toba observes the crazy side that creative people sometimes have. Someone amps the music up, and people start jumping around in twos, dancing. A common effect when alcohol meets boredom.

"So, this was the event you wanted to rush off to," he comments as we stand by a wall watching the dancing.

"It's boring, *abi*? That's why my Chief sends me ahead. These mixers, she hates them. They're just to get people to loosen up and feel free with one another before the D-Day."

"Young people and boundless energy, they look well and truly loose," he says, downing the rest of his drink.

I grin. "I know this isn't your type of crowd, but can we stick around a little longer?"

"I'm not complaining." He wrinkles his forehead down at me. "After putting you through the horror of smelly farms and lapping in a wobbly jeep, this is more than enough payback."

I love the way he looks at me. I'm thinking.

"Dance with me," he says.

"What?"

My mind goes numb, and my grin disappears. I hate dancing. Worse, I think of the terse moment on his laps in the jeep and wonder if he is aware that we're crossing boundaries.

Toba drops his cup on the wall beside us and pulls me to the centre of the crowd.

"I'll step on your toes," I warn.

"Step on it. Nobody here can dance, not even me. The key is to move your body anyhow and enjoy yourself a little bit. Come on."

I groan, but we join everybody copying the latest Nigerian dance moves. He looks ludicrous doing them, but so does everyone else. I'm not averse to following.

In that moment, I don't miss Esosa. It's liberating to just let go and bury my worries in a fit of laughter and dance. I remember how much I enjoyed it as a child. Memories of dancing and generally being silly fill my mind. Somewhere in between then and now, I grew up and found shame. Someone told me to act like a reasonable adult, and I did. And I forgot how to have fun, and dancing became embarrassing.

Toba grabs my hand and turns me around under an extended arm. It triggers a memory, the night of Aunty Ladepe's birthday, and Esosa telling me he wants to be a part of my family. I'm sad again. Maybe the serious side of me scared him, and he realized he wanted different. Why else would Yinka appeal to him? Why would Adora?

Someone bumps me into Toba's thick build, and his hands instinctively encircle me. I stare at his chest, and he looks down at me with concern. "Are you okay?"

"I am." My voice is toneless. I've been nudged into the black hole of helplessness I'd been dodging for weeks, and it hits me that I'm single again.

I look up at him, and he can see that I'm about to cry.

"Come here." He pulls me into an embrace and cradles my head to his chest.

I cling to him and fight the desire to dissolve into tears. There are people around us, but we're standing still, matted in a hug. Ordinarily, I wouldn't have let the hug go on this long, but the memories hurt so much that I cave into him, and into my hidden feelings. I don't want to let him go. He doesn't seem to mind.

My mum was right. It would have been disastrous me coming to Ibadan by myself. I am glad that Toba is here with me as I come to terms with the idea that Esosa and every other guy I have been with probably left because of me. It makes me wonder if I'm broken, too broken to be loved by anyone.

"Do you want to leave now?" he murmurs above my head.

"No," I whisper. I don't want him to let me go.

"It's alright, whenever you're ready."

I nod against his shoulder and let the tears fall. I cry for the first time since losing Esosa, and Toba just holds me. I don't have to tell him anything. He understands. It's why he dragged me all over the place with him the whole day.

He knew, that I was still hurting.

Chapter Fourteen

Every day, I see new buildings come up in places that were previously residential and so archaic, they were falling apart. I get the sense that in its place will stand a new block of flats, a new shopping mall, a new restaurant, or a new hotel.

And I'm usually not disappointed.

I stare through the window of whatever vehicle I'm in and imagine myself relaxing, shopping, or even living inside them. If it's a restaurant, I'm hoping they will serve Mediterranean-themed food, for a change. If it's a hotel, I'm wondering if their hall will be affordable enough for any of our numerous programs. And if it's a group of serviced apartments, I'm convinced the average Nigerian cannot afford it.

Everything in hotels are designed to make one feel at home, from the clean, carpeted hallways to framed wall paintings and the fragrance of pot-pourri. The rooms are clean and spacious; beds large, comfortable and get made by themselves; and the bathrooms roomy. Some even come with tubs one can soak in.

My work assignments involve attending conferences or hosting book launchings at hotels. So I often catch myself wishing I was resident, surrounded by the ambience of wealth and charmed by the beauty of luxury. It's a surrealistic feeling, being waited on hand and foot—everything that requires attention and hard work is someone else's headache, for a change. The buildings are usually air-conditioned, and they insulate one from the Lagos heat and humdrum.

I like that when I'm hungry a phone call can bring meals that combine restaurant-styled cooking with fast delivery. I like that the bathrooms are cleaner and newer, and that they have well-lit mirrors and hot running shower.

It's the reason I insisted Toba bring me to the hotel. He thinks I should sleep in Bodija, but I want to enjoy that experience for a bit. I don't want to wake up in the morning and scramble to get myself to the venue in time to meet up with the conference. I want to wake up on freshly laundered sheets, shower with gel from a tiny tube under running water, and then go down to a breakfast buffet with so much variety, it kills me to make a choice.

Toba wants me to know that he can bring me in the morning from Bodija, but I decline. In truth, I'm embarrassed about bawling all over his shirt. I don't want to spend any more time with him. I can still remember introducing Esosa, the pride in my voice as I leaned in to clarify that he was medical, the scepticism I now realize was on Toba's face, and the shameless way Esosa had been staring at Yinka.

We get to the hotel car park at eleven p.m., and he leaves the engine running so the air conditioning can stay on.

"Are going to be alright?" he asks, placing a hand behind the passenger seat head-rest.

I get a whiff of his fragrance and nod. He still smells good this late at night, and it's a wonder.

I stare at my hands too ashamed to even look at him. I am afraid of everyone finding out that I'm out of another relationship; six to be precise, all down the drain of wasted years. But Toba breaks up with girls all the time, and no one gives him a hard time about it, so why the shame?

It's the subtle feeling of being mediocre that overwhelms me, the feeling of being less than I always thought I was. It engulfs me and answers my questions. Esosa thought Yinka was good enough to sleep with, and by inference, maybe better than me.

"Femi." Toba lifts my chin up with a crooked finger. "It's okay to feel a sense of loss when a person you've spent time building a connection with suddenly isn't there anymore."

"Don't mind me," I say and lower his finger with my hand. "I just didn't think that he was dating anyone else. I feel stupid for being so blind."

Toba watches me. "You can't beat yourself up for someone else's selfishness."

"It's my ineptitude. I've been down this road several times. How could I not have seen it?"

"There is a lot of pressure on you to get married. Sometimes—"

"It doesn't account for stupidity." I swallow my tears. "I was wanting him to be the one so badly, I—"

"Are you sure you should be alone tonight?"

"And miss the breakfast buffet, are you kidding me?" I say with a laugh and blink back tears. "I'm fine."

He doesn't seem amused. "I'd much rather have you with me at the house. The help can rustle up an array of food in the morning if that's what you want."

I shake my head. "This is what I need, time away to think and reflect. I'll be okay."

"When's your program ending?"

"Tomorrow evening, but the office booked two nights for me."

I'm lying. It's only one. I paid for the extra day.

"I can take you back to Lagos afterwards."

"Many people will be going back to Lagos."

"I just want to know that you're alright."

I stare at him. The concern in his eyes is adorable. It's obvious my mum has tasked him with the duty of looking out for me aside from driving. "Thank you."

"I can pick you up here on Saturday."

"I'll let you know," I say and step out of his car.

He stares at me with a worried frown. "I'll call you when I get home."

"Cousin Toba," I say with a fond smile as I shut his car door. "I'm not going to pop any pills before tomorrow morning. Don't worry."

He gives me a half-hearted smile.

"I'll call you," he repeats before he backs the car into the drive way and turns it towards the hotel gates.

My eyes trail his backlights. For some reason, I'm sad he is gone. He hasn't left the compound, and I'm missing him already. It will be lonely in the room by myself.

The next day passes in a whirlwind. Tunde, the event planning committee lead, and I clash often. I can't help but fault his level of preparedness for the event, and he can't understand why I'm snarky. But aside from the food service and technical hitches, the programme goes smoothly. At the end, Mrs. Olatoye, my Chief Editor, and I seek out a few key people and exchange business information before I see her off to her vehicle.

"Sure you don't want to come with me?" she asks. "There is still room in the car."

I shake my head. "Have a safe trip ma."

I have no short list of places I can bunk in for the night, top being my grandfather's house. I wave them off and head back up the stairs to the programme venue.

In that moment I hear my name being called. I know that voice; I would know it anywhere.

For a split second, I mentally gauge my level of attractiveness. I am in a knee-length Ankara dress with a V-shaped neckline and side peplums. My hair is a shoulder-length weave falling in layers over the sides of my face, and my face has a light touch of makeup. I'm wearing heels—a source of terrible pain—and yes, I stole the V-shaped neckline idea from seeing Yinca wear it at Aunty Ladepe's birthday party and look good.

So I'm confident when I face Adenrele and smile at him. I haven't seen him in six years. Since the day he proposed to me and I turned him down.

"Hi." He is on the other side of the entrance staircase. His smile is still amazing, full of sunshine and goofiness. If he aged at all, it doesn't show.

"Hi." I put up a smile that's forced. I don't know how I feel seeing him.

"You look great."

"You too," I say. He always looks good in native attire. "I'd ask what you're doing here, but this is Ibadan. You live here."

He is coming from a wedding, judging by the programme and goody bag in his hands.

"I live in Lagos now. How's everyone, mummy, the twins, Grandpa?"

"Great." I nod. "Grandpa died, though."

"For real? I'm so sorry." He takes a few steps closer as if to comfort me then probably remembers we are not together anymore. "When was this?"

"A few months back."

I don't want to talk about Grandpa with Ade. Grandpa had liked him for me, and I had let them both down.

"I was here for a literary event," I say, bridging the silence. "It's over, just seeing colleagues off."

"I was here for a wedding, friend of my brother's. He's got a job now, in Lagos. And I'm at a law firm, made partner."

"That's fantastic news!" I say, pushing all the enthusiasm I could muster into the words. "I'm very happy for you. Congratulations. Dating anyone?" I add with a teasing tone.

I'm panicking. There's a confidence in his demeanour that wasn't there before, self-assurance. He's grown. And he is not married. Yes! I shamelessly look at his ring finger and gloat. We're both still searching.

He laughs and looks a little forlorn. "I'm in a great friendship, trying to turn it into a relationship. You?"

"Yes, medical doctor, private hospital." I don't know how those words exit my mouth but they do.

I feel more panic setting in. I'll be thirty-six in a few months. I'm approaching the dreaded forty. So why am I not shouting it from the roof tops that I made a mistake walking away from the best guy that ever happened to me?

My pride won't let me admit the truth to Ade. I'm still single, confused about searching.

"That's good to hear." He nods at the group waiting for him at the bottom of the stairs. "I—"

"You have to go, I get it," I say. "It was great seeing you."

"You too, I'll call you."

"Sure." I turn around and leave without a backwards glance.

There is a painful squeeze in my heart that tells me he's not going to call. He hasn't in years. I know that chapter of my life is closed so I'm struggling to comprehend my nostalgia. He's moved on and is busy trying to make someone else his. I've moved on, and really, it's too late for us.

The hall is still full of people when I return. I run into Tunde.

"All's good and that ends well," he says, as he approaches. "Programme's over. You can stop fussing and let me take you over to the restaurant next door to get a proper meal."

I frown at him. "Do you have enough funds for me and each of the six other people on your team who also didn't get anything to eat today?"

He stops in his tracks and gives me an awkward grin. "We've been sparring all day, the meal's a truce. I'm not trying to score a cheap date."

No, you are not. I mutter. Coincidentally, I see Toba's head appear in the wide doorway of the hall. He looks worried, like he's missed me and I've already left. I watch him raise his phone to his ear and hear mine ringing in my purse.

"So, what do you say?" Tunde asks.

"I have a date already. There he is." I pick up my purse and programme folder, bid them all goodbye.

Toba saunters into the hall head and shoulders above everyone else, gathering scrutiny as he meanders his way through the outflow of people. The inspection doesn't faze him; he's had it all his life.

"Boy, am I glad to see you." I take his arm and turn him around.

"How did the programme go?"

"Great. My Lagos crew left a few minutes ago, and the head of the L.O.C is trying to pick me up. So no, I'm not going to ask what you're doing here."

"You sound moody," he says as I stir him in the direction of the exit.

"This guy is like five years my junior and so smug!" I say as we find our way to the nearest elevator. "I can't believe my options are now reduced to pretending like I'm in a relationship so I don't feel bad in front of my exes, and using you to get out of a date because the fishing pool is getting younger."

Toba chuckles.

"I'm done with guys, done wondering if they like me for real or just want to play around." I look at him and notice a small aluminium flask in his hand. "Please, tell me that is tea. I'm starving."

"It's—"

I don't wait for a response. I grab the flask and open it.

"Not tea," he says as I take a huge swig. "Are you hungry? We could order from your room or go out."

The drink is sweet, bitter, smoky, and chocolaty at the same time. And it tastes like Coke. It's too late to push it out, so I push it down, slowly. It scorches my throat and erupts down my oesophagus before exploding into a never-ending abyss of burning sulphur as it settles in my empty stomach.

I cough and splutter for the first few seconds afterwards and manage to look up at him.

"What was that?" My voice is hoarse and my stomach is boiling.

Toba's look is a cross between amused and guilty. "Bourbon, with coke and ice."

I stare at him. He drinks. Of course he drinks. My uncles all have their various vices, and I'm most often mad at Toba for not being a little more sanguine, but I hadn't even thought he would take anything other than malt or juice.

"Were you planning to come here and get me drunk?"

"My plan was to ensure your safety and head home to have my midnight snack all by myself, but you stole it. That's it there mixed to perfection. Is it burning your throat down yet?"

"It's scalding."

"Good. That's what happens to people with long throats."

I avoid alcohol. The benefits, as often gloriously touted, are far less than its harm. But this drink is a divine mix of caramel sweetness, chocolaty bitterness, and heady spiciness. It summarizes how I feel at the moment. Conflicted!

I raise the flask to my lips again and take another sip with my eyes fixed on his, daring him to stop me. It's fiery hot, and bittersweet. I cough. My face and throat heat up in seconds. My chest warms with a delightful zing, and my belly swirls. Most importantly, I'm no longer in a bad mood.

He raises his eyebrows. "You shouldn't have that on an empty stomach."

"It actually feels pretty good."

"It will feel like karma tomorrow."

"I can take it. I have had a few douchebags in my life. One more won't hurt."

He puts a hand behind my back and urges me on with a gentle push. "Let's go."

"Why are you drinking?" I ask as we make our way down the corridor.

"Sleepless nights."

"What's keeping you up?"

"The farm," he gives me a wary look. "And you. But you just called me a douchebag."

"Of course I didn't mean you," I moan as we step into the elevator. "I mean Tunde, Matthew, Adenrele, David, Gbenga, Akpan, and most recently, Esosa."

Toba frowns. "I don't recall a Tunde being part of that list."

"The guy who tried to pick me up tonight," I say, rummaging in my bag for my key card. "Okay, Adenrele was the only non-sleazy person on that list, but I lump him up with the others."

"Because?"

"Because I said no, and he just disappeared. Puff, like a chicken, didn't have the guts to fight me into saying yes." I take another large sip as we step into the corridor of the third floor. "He could have tried again. Maybe I'd have said yes. Instead, he ups and disappears, leaving me wide open for douchebags."

"What's your room number?"

"Three eleven." I take another sip, shut my eyes, and feel it burn going down.

Somewhere at the back of my mind, there's a buzz of warning, but I ignore it. I'm fed up of trying to be good all the time.

"Do I have a signpost on my head that says dump all your trash here and then move on when you're done?"

Toba looks worried. "Give me the key."

He finds the room and opens the door.

"The truth is," I say as I kick off my shoes and throw my bag and folder on the bed. "It's my fault, because I was either too scared, or too blind, or too worried, or just forcing what wasn't meant to be."

Toba walks over to the telephone, picks up the receiver, and presses three buttons. "Room service," he says quietly.

"I'm not hungry." I slide open the glass door and step into the warm evening night.

There's a generator on somewhere and cars honking in the distance. Light music fuses with the delicious smell of beef slices grilling over charcoal fire from the pool party below.

You need to stop, I say to myself as I drink some more out of Cousin Toba's flask and lean over the balcony. *Stop thinking about what could have been.*

Toba joins me. "I ordered chicken wings. Give it half an hour."

"I'm not hungry."

"We'll see when it gets here."

He leans back against the balcony railing and crosses one foot over the other. I stare. He is the perfect picture of careless, boyish charm, and next-door neighbour good looks. His sleeves are folded a quarter-way down and fit snugly around his huge brawny forearms. His collar stands straight around his neck, and his blue-black jeans and boot strap shoes tell me he'd been coming from the farm. The meeting with Yinca's tech guy.

"I said no," I say to him.

He raises an eyebrow. "To Tunde."

"To Adenrele. He asked me to marry him, and I freaked out. I thought I'd rather be his friend than his wife, so I said no, because I was afraid of settling. Scared that there was someone else more exciting out there for me."

I take another sip of the Bourbon, and Toba's eyebrow rises higher.

"How many swigs of that have you had?"

"Five, or six."

He stares at me for a while. "Tell me when the room starts spinning."

"Am I going to get drunk? There's Coke in it, isn't there?"

"Three parts to one." He leans away from the balcony to grab the flask and take a long swig himself. Then he stares at my face. "I'm here. I won't let you get drunk."

I am unravelling right in front of him, and I don't know what to do about it. I place my hands against warm cheeks and exhale. "I just want to be left alone."

He lowers the flask and eyes me. "By me?"

"By people, all of life's numerous judges."

He folds his arms and smiles at me.

"Why are you smiling?"

"There is a hole in your heart that needs filling. Not by a guy. By you, with the things you know you are. The things that won't matter or change with a relationship."

"I'm afraid of growing old alone." I raise the flask, but he stops me.

"I think you've had enough."

"No." I grab the flask with my other hand and pull it towards me, but he leaves the railing and comes with it. "I need comfort."

"You need to stop!"

"Toba, please—" He is not letting go, so I lean into him and place my forehead squat in the middle of his chest. "Is there something wrong with me?"

"Of course not," he murmurs as his right hand smoothens my hair out a few times. He tucks the stray strands behind my ear. "You're perfect. Beautiful, wonderfully made."

His voice soothes me. I hunch my shoulders against him as he lets go of the aluminium flask and envelopes me in his arms. I'm hugging the flask, and he is hugging me. I feel light-headed. His arms keep me warm, inside and out. They are a cross between vice grips and a soft, clingy material, and I'm too buzzed to question what I'm doing in between them. I snuggle further against the expanse of his chest and think that I want to stay in this magical place forever. A place where I'm protected, accepted and loved, regardless of marital status.

"I saw Adenrele."

"Where?"

"Here, at the hotel. He looks good."

"You took his number?"

"No, but I wanted to."

"Why didn't you?"

I sigh. "I slept with him."

I don't know why I'm telling him that.

I feel him stiffen. Then relax and hold me closer. "Today?"

The word reverberates in his chest, and I hear the shock in it.

"No, while we were dating."

Toba is quiet. "You'll be okay."

"Toba—" I stare through the transparent sliding door of the hotel bedroom and ask the question that has been bugging me from the moment I laid my head against his chest. "Are there two beds hanging upside down from the wall?"

He doesn't answer for a second. He pulls himself away from me and stares into my face with his hands tight against my upper arms.

I can't keep my glazed eyes steady as my head lulls backward. "I feel like I'm in a Dr. Strange movie. The walls are shifting. The floor is tilting, and everything is topsy-turvy."

"Alright," he says, "bed time."

He grabs the flask from my hands and half-carries me to the bed. As soon as my head hits the soft white pillow, I doze off.

I don't see him cover my numb body or admit the room service guy and pay him for the chicken wings. I don't even see him draw the curtains, put off the lights, and leave.

I'm not sure, but I think I felt his lips on my forehead, and his shadow by the bedside watching me fall asleep.

"You're going to be okay," is the last thing I hear. And I believe it.

Chapter Fifteen

There is a time for everything in life, and a first time for many things. We record our first breath, our first smile, and our first step on camera, then life continues, with other firsts.

Some firsts are monumental, like a first pay check, or the first time on an airplane. Others are cheesy, like buying your first bra, or getting hugged for the first time by your first best friend. Some firsts are scary and confusing, like getting your first period, or driving a car across the third mainland bridge. Others are sweet and delightful, like the taste of ice-cream, or taking a roller-coaster ride for the first time. Whichever way, firsts are bound to happen. And they will leave you either craving more of a thing, or deciding less of it is better.

It's the excitement that gets you about firsts, the simultaneous feeling of anticipation and apprehension. It follows the freedom of finally getting to do something you've always wanted to do, or something you've been afraid to do.

The great thing about firsts is that we never forget them. We remember our first drink and the feeling of getting tipsy; and our first crush, and the unmistakable tug of attraction that makes our heart pummel in our chest like a ticking time bomb. We remember our first kiss, the clumsy taste of dry lips, warm coke, and sweet popcorn. We recall our first embrace, the confusion of where to place the hands or if to close the eyes. The pain of heartbreak the first time it happens, and the wrenching sensation of the heart shattering inside like someone went at it with force and an invisible hammer.

We think about those initiating firsts and remember them often. The memories stay with us long after we've experienced them. We build our lives around them, cast our expectations inside of them, and unconsciously judge our subsequent experiences by them. We play the long-time game of this versus that with them. If they are good enough, nothing else will compare. If they are bad, then it will take a miracle to convince our scarred minds that the next time will be better.

That's how it felt like seeing Adenrele, remembering a first. He was first guy I ever kissed, the first I ever bared my heart to. After him, no other guy could compare. That was my role in my breakups, my expecting every guy to be like him.

I wake up on Saturday morning with a faint headache and an uncomfortable, uncontrollable urge to pee, my first hangover. I've heard that alcohol dehydrates you. Pools all the water from your system in your bladder, ready for voiding the moment you open your eyes. So I roll out of bed and rush to relieve myself. And as I wash my hands in the bathroom sink, I remember that Toba was with me the night before.

Oh my goodness, what did I blab out to him, and why was I clinging to him like a needy, obsessive girlfriend?

I don't understand why I have been behaving out of character and imagining in my head that Toba is flirting with me. I like him, but as family—I add in my head.

The good thing is that my head is clear, and I feel decidedly better about my relationship status. I'm going to be okay. It's a sentence that reverberates round my head as I munch on cold chicken wings and pray I hadn't said anything untoward to him.

Grandpa's driveway is overrun with cars when I arrive. People of all sizes and financial inclinations surround Mr. Abiodun, my grandfather's long-time secretary. Toba towers above them, stressed out and in command. He manages to smile when our eyes meet. They're handling my grandfather's clinic beside the house's veranda.

Ladun's boisterous and respectful voice in my head guides me as I curtsey and greet all the elderly people there including Mr. Abiodun. I am not really an Ibadan girl, so I might be showing too much Lagos.

Cousin Toba is scribbling into a chequebook and doesn't look up. "Can you give me like half an hour?"

His voice sounds impersonal but apologetic.

"I'll just sit with Aunty Ladepe while I wait," I reply and sweep my eyes across the crowd. Despite being overrun with requests, he orders a young boy to help with my travel bag.

My step-grand-mum is overjoyed to see me.

"The house has been empty since Christmas," she tells me. "I would be happy to have anyone visit. How is your mother?"

"Doing well, Aunty," I reply and find myself a seat next to her.

"Why did you not come and stay here? Toba said you have been in Ibadan since Thursday."

I grin. "My company booked me in a hotel. I have to chop their money sometimes, Aunty."

She's unsatisfied with my answer and goes ahead to chastise me further for not staying over.

Toba comes in looking a little less stressed but ready to head out. He's changed his shirt and sprayed up a scent that's musky with a faint citrus tinge to it. "Sorry I kept you waiting. Ready?"

"Sure." I turn to Aunty Ladepe. "I'm sorry to have to leave you, Aunty, but I need to get back to Lagos, and Cousin Toba has offered to take me. I'll come and visit when I'm less busy."

She stares at him for a second and then smiles at me. "I will expect."

"I'll be back tomorrow, but Ladun will come and keep you company. Plus, Mr. Abiodun will be staying the night. He just went out to run some errands."

Aunty Ladepe smiles. "*Ose omo mi*, safe journey."

He bends to kiss her cheek, and I kneel to say goodbye.

I think cheek-kissing is a rather un-African gesture, but Toba has been abroad for a significant portion of his adult life. The right thing is to lie prostrate and say goodbye, but then Aunty Ladepe was never a fussy person to begin with.

"How are you?" Toba asks as we leave the house.

"Good."

"No hangover?"

I eye him. "Were you hoping I'd be puking this morning?"

"It would have been a fun sight, the prim and proper lady with her head in a bucket."

"Wait 'til I tell mummy you got me breaking laws; maybe she won't mind the Taxify drivers the next time."

His teeth pop out between a lightly shaven beard and two dimples. A low growl of laughter follows. "Get in," he says and unlocks the car doors. "I'm taking you to watch a movie."

I'm thrilled, "yea! My trip to Ibadan is turning out way better than I expected."

"More for me than for you, I need a break!"

"I saw. Gramps really saddled you with responsibility."

He starts the car. "He did. I could always get Mr. Abiodun to handle it, but I know Daddy wanted a personal touch for these people. They like the fact that it's me. It makes them feel like they haven't lost him."

"He knew you'd do it exactly the way he wanted it done."

"He did."

We head out to Lagos around twelve-thirty, and it takes us two hours. We talk about Grandpa, and then music, books, work, friends, and circle back to family again. I mention that I like how he ensures there are people in the house with his mum every time he has to go away. He tells me it's the reason he wanted me to sleep over at the house that weekend.

"That is your excuse for ensuring I don't off myself before day-break."

He chuckles out loud, but I'm quiet.

"Thank you for being there. I was in a dark place."

"We all go there."

When we get to Lagos, he takes a detour to the Ikeja mall and we find a spot to park in the over-crowded parking lot.

"We are splitting the fees. I'm not going to sponge off my rich uncle, even if I'm a Lagos big babe."

He locks up the car and gives me a quizzical look. "You must be joking."

"I'm not. You've already driven me up and down from Lagos to Ibadan and back but—"

"Am I complaining?" he asks. "Take yourself out on your own terms some other time. Today, I'm taking myself out, and you're coming along for company."

I stand and stare at him. "I'm not Jumoke."

Toba tosses an amused glance in my direction. "Are you throwing a tantrum?"

"Sort of."

"I've taken Ara and Eni out before, didn't they tell you? They had a filled day on my behalf, and they weren't modest about it."

"Went for the most expensive thing on the menu, right?" I reply with a grin, imagining Aramide and Enitan gorging themselves out at Toba's expense.

"And had bags to go—"

I laugh. They had both told me about him driving over to Esosa's place of work and calling him out. That might have been when the said luncheon went down.

"Come on, Cousin Toba, let me pay."

"If I see your purse come out of your bag except to retouch your makeup—" he threatens, "—I will toss it in a bin. Now, which movie are we watching? Please don't mention a chick flick and bore me half to death."

I touch my hand to my face in horror. "Do you really think I need to re-powder my face?"

He glances at me and laughs. "You're fine the way you are."

We settle on a movie, get our popcorn and drink, and go find the movie hall. Toba takes water, I have a Pepsi, and we are lucky to enter the cinema as the opening credits roll. Fifteen minutes into it, I hear a tiny snore coming from beside me. I'm horrified to find Toba with his head thrown back on the seat, fast asleep, popcorn barely touched. I elbow him. He jumps to a start with eyes wide open and brings his head forward. Then he gives me a bleary, sheepish look.

"You paid money for this. Try to stay awake."

"Sorry," he whispers and sits up. "What did I miss?"

"Not sure when exactly you slept off," I reply as he sinks his chin into his right fist.

"Okay, so hero and heroine introduced?"

"Check!" I reply, amused.

"Back story done and dusted?"

"Check."

"Crises point set up to play out in the second act?"

I eye him. "Who told you about acts and story arcs?"

He eyes me back. "Theresa was a theatre-art major."

I smile at the reference to his ex with the outstanding bedroom antics. It's not hard to imagine why. I see his eyes narrow into slits and soon close again. A tiny snore follows.

"You are beyond redemption," I moan and roll my eyes. "We should have paid for four D X."

He doesn't respond. I get a glare from the lady on the other side of him, so I keep quiet and elbow him. He sits up, but struggles to stay awake throughout the movie. Feeling sorry for him, I let him sleep.

"You are not driving me anywhere in this state," I say when the movie ends. "Is this what happens on your dates?"

"I pretty much use their shoulders for a pillow." He dumps his popcorn in a bin as we amble down the corridor amidst a throng of satisfied movie watchers.

I shake my head at him. "You can take a nap at our place for a bit then head over to wherever you're going later."

"Meeting an investor at seven-thirty in Maryland, I don't think—" He glances at his wristwatch and looks up at me. "Yeah, I think I should crash at your place for an hour."

"My mum will be ecstatic," I reply as we get into the car with me in the driver's seat.

When we get home, Toba crashes in Olamide's old bedroom without taking his shoes off. He lies face-down, snoring just a tad loudly. For a moment, I'm scared for him. The work on the farm must be taking its toll far more than he realizes.

When I bend to take his shoes off, he opens his eyes.

"Thank you," he mumbles sleepily.

"Now I'm the one waiting on you hand and foot," I mutter and log the boots off his big feet one after the other. "What size are you wearing now, forty-eight?"

"Forty-six," he says as he turns over to his side, folds his arms across his chest, and watches me start on his socks. He is half-awake, but I'm not sure if its fondness or gratitude I'm seeing in his glassy-eyed look.

"Thank you for the movie," I say and start pulling off the second sock. "And the company and the cheering up, and the Bourbon, and for always looking out for me—"

When I don't hear a response, I glance up and watch him sleep. His face is relaxed, devoid of lines but no longer young or chubby. It's mature, full, defined by hard work but still pleasant to look at in sleep. I can't help thinking that there might be some element of truth to the ancient art of face reading. The Chinese believe that the shape and structure of a person's face gives a handy insight into their personality, and you can tell by looking at a face if a person will be difficult or unpleasant, greedy or generous, easy to like or tough to please.

Toba's face has a wide forehead, typical of a studious, quiet nature. His eyes are equally spaced and separated by a wide, generous nose, and full thick lips. His being bearded, even if lightly as is often the case, gives his face a soft look. I understand why the girls like him. Why it's easy for him to replace them every so often. His face tells anyone who looks at it that he is a kind and compassionate man. I bet he has taken care of each and every one of them in ways that any other guy they date after him will struggle to compete with. I wonder in that moment why I never met a man like him.

"Yinka," I whisper as I stare at him. "You made a big, huge, mistake."

***

I return to work more upbeat after my trip to Ibadan. Lilian can't help envying my relaxed attitude. I think it's because I finally had the good cry I'd been denying myself since the whole Esosa saga. Inside, I know it's because of Toba. It's relative, though, because by the end of the week, I'm moody again. I conclude that I'm going to ride this roller coaster of emotions for weeks on end.

When my phone rings, I'm not surprised it's him.

"Hi," I quip at him, a tad unfairly, too.

"Okay, day going goodly or day going badly?"

"Day just going," I groan as I scribble a side note on the manuscript with me. "What's up?"

"Fantastic, so I'm in Lagos again looking for company to a surprise birthday party."

"Yeah, and with the abundance of female numbers I know are on your phone, you pick a cousin to go to a party with."

He laughs out loud. "Fine, you got me. I'm just checking up on you because I made your mum a promise."

"You can do that via the phone. I'm okay. Go find a date elsewhere."

"I'm not in the mood for a babe who is looking to settle and trying all versions of ways to please me. Pack up and come downstairs. I'm in your office parking lot."

"I don't want to go to any party."

"Give it a half-hour. If you don't like it, I'll drop you back at work."

"So, I'm going to pay for breaking down in front of you with a visit every weekend?"

"Pack up and come downstairs!"

His voice tumbles into me, and I stand to my feet like a mechanical robot. It's nearing closing anyway, and a party might just cheer me up.

Lilian gives me a curious look. "Aren't you going home with me?"

"My uncle is around," I mumble. "He needs baby-sitting at a party."

"Toba?"

I eye Lilian. "Yes."

"Mention me!" Lilian whispers and I smile.

***

"Why are you dragging your feet about replacing Yinca?" I ask when we arrive at the venue and start up the stairs of the building where the party is being held.

"I told you before. She was not my girlfriend."

"Yeah, I believe you."

"It's the truth," he says as we run into two men at the top of the stair case.

"Awo!" one of them says. "You made it. This is the guy I was telling you about, walked away from a six-digit salary to go and own a farm."

Toba shakes their hands while I study the interior of the building we are in. It's brand new and packed with a cinema, gaming centre, a supermarket, and some other restaurant somewhere in it. "Congratulations," he says to the person I believe is the celebrant's husband. "I wish her a many happy returns."

"Thank you. The dip in my account balance is pinching my pocket, but my wife, she is worth it."

"Yep, this place will not bill in naira," Toba says, looking around.

"You got that right." His friend looks at me. "I don't believe we've met."

I shake my head and look at Toba.

"Gbenro, this is my ..." he trails off and stares at me.

I stare right back. This introduction thing has had Toba scratching his head for months. Years even, since he's known about the secret much longer than any of us. I don't know what I am to him anymore, but he's been really strong for me in the last couple of weeks. He's been a friend.

"This is Femi Ajayi," he finishes and turns to his friend, "my plus one. You said I could bring one."

Femi Ajayi, I think, confused. *Is that all I am?*

I don't have time to process this as his friend is holding out a hand.

"Femi Ajayi, it's nice to meet you." Gbenro clasps my hand with both of his for a brief moment. "I appreciate a lady with a masculine name, gives the idea of strength. It's a pleasure to meet you. Be the one to stay this time around."

I look from him to Toba. I've clearly missed a joke. "Why?"

"He's let one too many go. Been telling him he shouldn't have a son in the university in his sixties the way he's going."

"Idiot," Toba says and swipes Gbenro a fist he dodges.

"Oh. We are not dating," I reply, and Gbenro gives me a questioning look. "He's my uncle," I add and climb up the rest of the stairs, leaving Toba with the explanations.

"She's my step-sister's daughter," I hear him say behind me. "Too close in age to be my niece, so we just wing it."

I am no longer listening to them. I'm in the restaurant and liking the room. I don't want to go back to work.

Toba grabs my elbow when he catches up to me.

"Now I'm your uncle, right?" he whispers into my ear, "now when I'm not with your people."

I smile up at him. "I like your people. They look interesting."

"So you don't want to go back to work?"

I shake my head. "I think I'll enjoy Chinese food."

"You will. But first, let me show you something."

His hand is still on my elbow as we step out through a side entrance into a long, wide balcony. I feel a cold draft of air and hear water falling around us. On first instinct, I think its rain, but when I listen closely, I realize what it is. "Is that the Atlantic?"

"Right beneath us." He grins down at me.

"Are you serious?" I walk to the edge of the stone balcony and look over it.

"As sure as we are standing by it," he says, following me and folding his arms over it. "It's as close to the ocean as we can get. Fresh air comes from over the water, great for clarity of the mind. You can come here, appreciate God, and just sink all your troubles into the sea."

"And eat their pricey meals, I'm betting."

"And eat their pricey meals, yes."

We both burst out laughing.

I watch the greyish brown water crash onto huge boulders of rocks lining the edge of the ocean for miles. It's amazing, comforting and relaxing.

"Still moody?" Toba murmurs in my ear.

I shake my head.

"Not in this gorgeous place." I look at him, smile, and love his dimples. "Not with you."

He winds an arm around my waist and pulls me closer. "Hey, our society is conventionally geared towards marriage, but I need you to know that you are the most important factor in all of it. Being happy is what counts, the only thing that counts. So you should make it so you are, all the time."

I nod, and we watch the ocean together.

Chapter Sixteen

Newton's first law of motion states that a body at rest remains at rest until an outside force acts upon it. It also states that a body in motion at constant velocity will remain in motion, unless an outside force acts on it. The only thing that resists motion in either case is called inertia.

'Inertia,' derived from the same Latin root term as the word 'Inert,' means *'lacking the ability to make a move.'* It is the resistance of any object to a change in its position or state of motion.

I've become inert. My epiphany that not everyone finds love is my internal inertia. It's the force that put me in a sort of static motion and keeps me on autopilot. It keeps me doing everything to fill the void inside to stop myself from looking again. But I can't stay in this static state forever. It's exhausting. I have to move on, but I don't want to set myself up for failure again.

Esosa's betrayal made me wonder if there isn't some iota of truth to the idea that curses exist that halt people's lives and keeps them in a constant cycle of brokenness. Maybe it's the reason why my relationships have never worked. The reason why I don't like children, because somehow, my inner woman knows I'm not meant to get married.

When I catch myself feeling sorry for not having a partner to enjoy life with, I remember that I have my sisters and cousins and friends. I remind myself to soak in the present and relax. It's in the process of relaxing that we discover the why of our existence and stumble unto the path we're meant to be on.

It is now, that what I am really not looking for, comes looking for me.

I'm not planning to attend Toba's party, but my mum sends me to Aunty Ladepe with lace for a mutual friend's daughter's wedding. She gives me the lace with a prayer and tells me she hopes I'll be staying for Toba's party because his single friends will be there. She's hoping I will find someone new.

She doesn't know that I'm not keen on mingling at any family party. But I go, for her, and for Lilian and co. who have begged to be introduced to Toba, now that I can confirm that he is single and very much available.

We talk on the phone all the time now, Toba and me. He calls every week to check if I'm okay. I tell him I'm fine, but he insists on calling. We talk about everything and nothing. For me, it's an outlet, another form of diversion from my feelings. He claims it's an opportunity to vent about the farm. I don't blame him for calling, not after the way I just broke down at the ANA pre-event.

When I arrive, the party's in full swing. Toba is thirty-nine, and looking rather good for that age. He stands in a semi-circle with Uncle Juwon, Diran, and Korede, and they are all sipping from canned drinks and having a somewhat quiet conversation.

I stare at him and admit that the months on the farm have done his body a world of good. Still broad and thick-shouldered at the top, he tapers towards a narrower waist, with tough-looking looks dapper. My friends are awed, but I am indifferent. Sorry too, by the way. Toba doesn't seem like he ever will find that one girl.

"You made it!" Uncle Juwon is the first to grab my hand.

"Yeah, I thought to just breeze in."

Toba sips from his can and sweeps his eyes from me to my trio of girlfriends.

"In-law," I say to Korede and eye-ball him.

"Out-law," he replies, eye-balling me back.

"I hope you are giving my sister correct housekeeping allowance," I continue.

"I'm giving her everything she needs, and the outcome is visible."

We all laugh. Olamide is delightfully pregnant. It's the 'good news' everyone longs to hear months after a wedding, and I'm happy for her.

"I thought you weren't going to come," Uncle Juwon continues scrutinizing the parade behind me. "You know, you Lagos babes and your numerous engagements."

"How could I not?" I wink at Toba and reach out to give him a light side hug. "I brought him birthday presents too."

Toba lets me go and stares at my trio of friends. Men! I know I have to wrap up my greetings and make introductions.

"Lilian, Dayo, and Ebuwa came to gate-crash your party, the more the merrier, right?" I turn to my girlfriends. "This is my Uncle Juwon, who is married, by the way. My Uncle Toba whose birthday we came to. Lilian, you've met Toba before, right?" We exchange knowing looks. "And my in-laws, Korede and Diran."

Lilian reaches out a hand to shake Toba's. "Hi, sir," she says and laughs, embarrassed.

Toba hardly looks that much older than her so the 'sir' sounds—well, I know my friend is nervous.

"I remember." He returns the handshake with a nod.

"Toba is single, but there are other single people in the living room." I wave my hands towards it. "You guys should just go jingle, and mingle, and do whatever you singles do."

"You are welcome, let me take you inside." Uncle Juwon leads them, followed by Korede. I hear him take up an animated discussion with Dayo as Diran nudges me.

"*Why you come dey spoil show for awon boys now?*" he grumbles quietly as he follows them into the living room.

"Because Aramide is not here ehen," I throw at his retreating back. "Well done, you want to turn into an out-law too, right?"

Toba is smiling when I turn back to him.

"Turning in-laws into out-laws is very hazardous to the health," he teases and puts an arm around me.

"I'm protecting my sister's interests. I have to threaten them a little."

"You are not in the wrong. Someone needs to keep those three in line."

"My sisters don't deserve to share them with anyone, so I'll do the job, happily."

"You three were always as thick as thieves in any case, so I'm not surprised," he replies.

"Thicker now we are older. Aramide wouldn't have agreed with you fifteen years ago. She picked every single moment to fight me on every single thing, every single time."

Toba laughs out loud. "You weren't exactly a sweet piece of cake, either. And you three did always band together to give me trouble."

"We did, didn't we?"

"You most certainly did." His eyes crinkle at the sides.

His arm is strong and heavy around my shoulders, but I don't mind. I let mine slip around his waist, and we both take a slow walk towards the living room.

"I've kind of missed you," he says, glancing down at me.

It's been three weeks since I saw him last.

"But we talk on phone all the time."

"Not the same as seeing each other."

"True." I nod and recall the night of conversations by the ocean after his friend's birthday party crew had left.

We'd talked all night with the wind in our faces and the Atlantic billowing behind us, about stuff we'd like to put on our bucket lists and do before we grew too old to do them.

"We should find time and go out again."

"We should," he says quietly.

We pause at the door to the living room, and he lowers his voice as he takes his arm off my shoulders and grabs my hand instead. "How are you doing?"

"I'm fine," I reply, but he is still looking at me. I feel like a little child under his gaze, and keep my eyes straight at his chest. "I'm taking time to centre myself into the right frame of mind."

"And be happy."

"Yeah, be happy."

"It's showing. You're looking more like the Femi I used to know, less miserable."

I narrow my eyes and hit his shoulder. "I was not miserable!"

"I'm kidding. But you look good."

"Thank you. How is the farm?"

He shrugs and releases my hand as we enter the living room. "Doing great!"

"And Osan?"

"Selling." He gives me a rueful smile, "beyond my expectations despite the horrible name."

I laugh and shake my head. "Aw, come on, it's not horrible. I'm glad the farm is doing well. By the way, the girls are here for you to pick and choose from. I promised Aunty Ladepe I would bring friends."

"So you're now in sync with her? Both of you planning to get me married before I'm forty."

"What can I do, Toba? Between your mum and my mum, there is a noose around my neck about introducing you to my single friends. Please choose one. Just let me know which so I can put in a good word for you. Not that you ever needed help, anyway."

He raises an amused eyebrow.

"I'll see you around."

I turn to leave, but he grabs my hand and pulls me back.

"See me before you go," he says.

"Sure." I leave him smiling at me and dance towards Aunty Norma.

"Lagos big babe," Aunty Norma hails me from afar.

"Ibadan Edo girl," I reply and hurry over to her. "How far, them pikins nko?"

"*Pikins dem dey ooo. Dem dey chop my eba.*" She hugs me and scrutinizes my guests.

I eye her and roll my eyes. "*Abegi! No bi my uncle dey buy the eba? Why you dey complain?*"

"*True talk, but na me dey make am now.*" She glances at my guests again and looks at me. "*Wetin shele, I think say you go bring one broda come here now. Even if you don give up on yourself, we no dey give up on you.*"

"*Abeg leave that side,*" I say, hoping to change the topic. "Ebuwa and Dayo, come over here. This is the crazy Aunty Norma I've told you people about several times."

"Ehen, me, crazy." Aunty Norma pretends to be upset.

"Don't be angry, I'm only joking," I reply, laughing.

Olamide comes running from the side with her visibly round stomach. I cringe as she and Lilian both hug each other and jump around a bit. Olamide should be careful with the baby bump.

"You didn't bring Jolomi?" I say to Aunty Norma.

She eyes me. "*Make I dey fin person wey go hol am? Abeg leave me make I enjoy my life small. I leave am with the mama wey dey help me wash.*"

"And you think that's safe?"

"You think say this na Lagos?"

"Uncle Deola nko, where is he?"

"*Work no gree him. Even if he dey here, he go help me?*" Aunty Norma continues as she raises her hand to sweep my braids to the side and stare at my face. "*Haba, fine girl, you look take away, you sweet no bi small. I go help you find husband here today.*"

I'm alarmed at her intention. I'm just getting to a sane state of mind. A husband is the last thing on my mind.

"I'm coming," I say. "Let me greet everyone."

I run away from Norma and bustle about. The party is in full swing, and everybody is having a great time, but I don't want to stay. I want to return to Lagos. I say quick goodbyes to my friends who have opted to stay and head towards the living room hallway. Toba is there, chatting with a group of friends.

"Hey, Cousin Toba, I'm leaving."

He excuses himself and steps out of the group. I reach out to hug him goodbye, but he grabs my hand instead.

"Come here. I need your help with something."

He hurries me out of the hallway into the smaller sitting room where Grandpa used to entertain his close friends.

"I hope it's a quick something because I really have to go."

"I know, but you're the only one whose judgement I trust will be unbiased."

He shuts the door. My face is asking all the questions as he dips his hand into the front pocket of his jeans and brings out a black velvet box.

I know what it is before he opens it, and my heart jumps into my mouth for a second.

Now there is a fondness I have for Toba that I know dances around a line I shouldn't cross, things we do in private that will raise eyebrows if anyone ever heard them. I believe we have managed them with maturity, and I've accepted that holding his hand or hugging him is harmless, because it doesn't mean anything.

It doesn't mean he can give me a ring, or that I can accept it.

"I think I've found the person I want to share the rest of this wonderful life with." He points the box in my direction and opens it. "And I want to give her this ring. Look at it and tell me what you think."

I exhale with disappointed relief and stare at the ring. It's gorgeous.

"Oh my goodness," I say picking it up with my left thumb and index finger as my runaway heart beat slows down and the stupid thoughts fuelled by Pariola's crazy musings leave my mind. It can't be Yinca, can it?

It's a gold ring across another, one white, the other yellow. A tiny diamond stone embellishment links them together, and a worried look covers Toba's face.

"Is it too much? Am I going overboard?"

"It's beautiful. Is she here, the girl?"

He nods. "I don't know if I should give it to her, or just buy something else."

I frown.

"It looks expensive. Is she worth it? She has to be, this is a huge deal." I let the ring slip onto my index finger, and hold out my hand so I can look at it. "Wow!"

Toba watches me closely, a little too closely, if I may add, but I'm lost in the wonder of the valuable jewel on my finger. The stone glints for a second, and I'm mesmerized. I don't usually like jewellery, but this one is fine on another level.

"Ahhh," I sing as I admire it. "Cousin Toba …"

"I believe she's worth every carat," he says.

I glance at him. "She had better be! Have you been dating someone in secret while parading Yinka around? You guys are just devious. Who is she?"

Toba smiles. "You'll see."

My heart sinks. There is a girl out there I don't know about, that we've never talked about, that he loves.

"This ring is worth a lot of money. Where did you get it?"

He stares at it. "It's a family heirloom. That's why I'm asking your opinion before I give it."

I frown. "Then you really need to be sure that she won't break your heart or steal your fortune and run away with another guy, or with the ring."

"She doesn't seem like the type."

"You can never be too sure. Who did it belong to?" I take the ring off my finger and hand it back to him.

"My mum," he says. "Your grandfather gave it to her, before they got married."

I'm shocked. I have never seen that ring on Aunty Ladepe.

"He told me the story of how they met." Toba doesn't look up. "She was this scared, pregnant twenty-one-year-old, and he was her father's friend. She came looking for him, hysterical and seeking advice. She wanted him to talk to her father, or give her money for a termination." He shakes his head and laughs. "Her father wasn't the forgiving type, and her mother would literarily have slaughtered her on sight. Your grandfather knew that, so he took the blame for all of it. Marrying her was the only way out that her family agreed to, but his friend never spoke to him again."

I'm staring at him, understanding Aunty Ladepe's story. She hadn't cheated on my grandfather as everyone had thought. She had been saved by him. "Did my grandmother know?"

"She died believing I was Pa Awotunde's son."

"Did she love him, your mum?"

Toba looks up at me. "She was more worried about her reputation. There are lots of reasons why people marry, Femi."

"So it was an arrangement?"

"It was."

"I see."

"He bought her this ring as a wedding gift. He grew to love her, and she grew to love him. Even though it hadn't started out real, it became a real thing for both of them."

"That was so sweet."

He nods but doesn't say anything.

I smile at him.

"If you think she is worth it, you should give it to her. It has a great love story behind it, and I hope it finds you a great love story, too." I turn to look in the direction of the hallway and wonder for the millionth time who the girl is. "So no hope for any of my friends?"

I think of Lilian and how disappointed she will be.

He shrugs. "Will you wait and watch me give my birthday speech? I promise you, it won't take more than five minutes."

"Of course," I'm curious. I want to know who this girl is.

So we head back into the corridor and into the living room where the music is loud and people are yelling at one another in a bid to make themselves heard. Toba gets the DJ to lower the music and gathers everyone together.

He stays glued to one spot for a minute as everyone quietens and forms a rough circle around him. It's weird. He doesn't give speeches, doesn't have birthdays, and doesn't rally people round. But I know to an extent why he has called this, why we are all gathered in a circle around him. He wants to announce to the world his intention to marry someone, one of the girls at this party.

For the life of me, I can't figure out who it is. Yinca is not even around. He's been so quiet about who he's been dating in the last four months since he split with her—though he told me they were not dating and I don't believe him—that I'm speechless at the idea.

As Toba starts to speak, I look round at faces. There are a number of females, and I'm wondering if it's someone Aunty Norma arranged for him, or someone he's known for a while. I see Ladun, standing between Pariola and Diran, and frown. It can't be Ladun, can it?

He took her and her kid out during Christmas. Ladun has lived next door for as long as I have been aware of my grandfather's house. I know she had a brief stint of crush on him when we were teenagers. Then Toba went to school, and she grew out of it, I guess, and met her ex-husband. She's been back home for a year. Toba has been home for a year. Things could have happened.

I'm confused. Toba and I talk all the time—why is this news to me? Maybe they had both wanted to keep it all under wraps and his claim about Yinca was true, but why parade Yinca around in front of her? Or maybe this Ladun thing is a new thing. She is a respectful Yoruba girl. She would be good for him.

Whichever way, it's a somewhat mixed feeling for me. I'm going to be alone when Toba gets married. I'm happy he's found someone. At the same time, I'm sad that I'll be left alone in the singles' soap box at family events. I'm not going to be able to call him anytime like I used to, or see him when I'm down, or have him put his arm around me without his wife wondering what is up. This distresses me. I'm thinking it would be best for me to stop attending family functions altogether. I'm not sure I'll be able to stand seeing everyone in pairs while I log my lonely ears around.

Toba is looking in my direction at this moment, so I yank my thoughts back to the present. I haven't heard a word of what he's been saying. I'm surprised when he takes a step forward and gets down on one knee, right in front of me.

My eyes follow his movement in a daze as I navigate the corners of my mind, trying to understand why he is kneeling in front of me.

"Obanifemi Omolade Ajayi."

And calling my full name!

I turn my head to the side with my eyes fixed on his. He raises the box with the ring nestled safely in it towards me. I gasp. Everyone else in the living room gasps, too.

What are you doing? I mouth the words, but they don't come out.

"I'm asking you to marry me," he says.

I stare at the ring and then back at him. *Are you for real?*

"I have known you all my life," Toba begins. "I've watched you grow from childhood, to adulthood, and into the kind of woman I admire, a woman who is strong, and well-read, and beautiful, and funny, and very easy to talk to. I've loved you for a very, long time. Even when I knew it wasn't appropriate because I thought you were my sister's child, my niece, cousin for lack of a better word. I've struggled with the idea that loving you is a sin, and I've stayed away from you in order to fulfil what I think is right and proper."

Are you serious? This can't be right, or proper, or even happening, for that matter! Not in front of family!

"I don't think I can keep these feelings to myself any longer," Toba continues, "especially when you now know that my father, your grandfather, was never really my father, and I am not exactly your uncle."

I'm not breathing. I'm bordering on fainting, but Toba goes on, unfazed.

"Obanifemi, will you do me the honour of sharing life with me, of being my companion through thick and thin, of being my friend forever, and of being the woman on whose finger I put this ring?"

I open and close my mouth like fish in water because Toba has jumped that stupid line I've been so worried about. My heart pounds with furious fervour and my palms sweat. All I can think about is how serious he was that day at Grandpa's farm, and how serious he is now, kneeling in front of me—Scratch that, kneeling in front of our family and a lot of friends—asking me to marry him.

I want to say something, but I can't. I can't even breathe. I am speechless, and he is waiting for my answer.

I look up, and find everyone staring at me.

Aunty Norma with her eyes wide open; Olamide with both hands over her mouth; Uncle Juwon with confusion; and Korede laughing with his eyes shining bright behind oval-shaped frames. My friends Lilian, Dayo, and Ebuwa give me looks like I'm an evil person for dangling Toba in front of them and snatching him up for myself. Pariola looks shocked. The plastic cup in her hand clatters to the floor and splashes slush all over Deji's shoes, but her hand doesn't even realize it. It still forms the C shape a hand takes while holding a cup with no handles. Even Deji is looking at us, and I can tell that he is doing the sociological maths, trying to figure out if Toba is meant to be asking me to marry him.

The silence is palpable and painful, filled with all these accusing stares, like what have you both been doing behind our backs.

Nothing! I haven't been doing anything, I want to yell, but I don't. I can't. There is nothing I can say in that moment, that will make everyone believe that Toba and I haven't been sneaking around secretly dating.

I look at Toba, and in that miserable one second, I hate him. I want to hit him for humiliating us in front of our friends and family. He stares back at me, and his face is changing, from hope to worry. I don't look like I'm going to say yes, and he knows it.

I blink back tears and shake my head. "I need to get out of here."

I run. Everyone unfreezes and starts talking all at once.

"Nifemi!"

I hear Toba's strong voice behind me, and I suppose he stands up and follows me.

I dash into the corridor, out the front door, down the stony gravel pathway, and head straight for the gate.

"Nifemi! Wait!"

The gate is a blurry vision, and the man employed to guard it isn't anywhere around. I see that it's locked, and it's going to take me more than a minute to get to it and open it.

"Nifemi." Toba catches up to me. His large hands grab my slender shoulders and turn me around. "Come on, don't leave."

"Leave me alone!" I yell, pointing at the house. "What in the world was that?"

He takes in a deep breath and looks me in the eye. "A proposal."

"Are you crazy? You ambushed me, humiliated us both in front of our friends and family." I'm pacing up and down at this point. "How could you do that?"

"That wasn't my intention."

"Couldn't you have asked me in private?" I yell.

"I'm sorry. I didn't know how or when to do it, and I have been thinking about doing it for a long time. I wanted it memorable."

"Memorable? So you ask me, in front of everyone! What did you think? That I was going to just jump up and say yes, to you? That I am so desperate and hopeless and so can't get a husband that I would marry my own uncle. Are you alright?"

"Femi ..."

"I am your niece!" I explode. "Why would you ask me that?"

"There's no blood between us. We're just grew-up in the same house, that's all."

"No, you don't get to pull that excuse card!" I hiss upon noticing that a crowd has followed us out.

"It's not an excuse card. It's the truth."

"It's a half-truth. You are still my grandfather's son."

"Adopted son!"

"That doesn't give you the right to ask me to marry you," I shout at him, "right out of the blue! We are not even in a relationship."

I turn and try to get out of the compound. To think I'd been worried about crossing a line—Toba had leapt right over it, with no warning.

"Wait! Nifemi, please wait. Let's talk about this."

"Talk about what?" I screech and turn around. "We're not blood-related so we should get married and save the whole family the hullabaloo over our single status. Is that it? You said marriage wasn't important! Be happy, you said, my goodness, Toba!" My voice is hard.

"That's not the reason why I asked you."

"Then what is?"

The crowd stands around the front door, underneath the shade of the porches' rooftop. They are watching the ensuing drama, and it only serves to fuel my rage.

"Because you think I need rescuing? Because you and I can't find someone, so we are good together, is that it?"

He stares at me, and I see a little bit of regret in his eyes.

"How about because I love you?" he says in a quiet voice. "And because I don't want to torture myself, watching you get your heart broken again by another guy."

"I don't need rescuing!" I snap. "I don't need a husband to be functional. I don't need you to save me from every stupid guy that I date, and I certainly don't need you to marry me so I can save face and save my parents from shame. How dare you? I don't even—"

I stop in confusion and stare at his huge shoulders and calm, attractive face. I was going to blurt out that I don't love him. But I can't even say it. And it's absurd that I can't say it. It's ridiculous, because I know in that moment that it is not true. I like him, a lot. I like him more than I have ever liked anyone, and I like him too much to say that I don't.

It had felt right having him hold me in that hotel room and tell me I was perfect and beautiful. It had felt good snuggling up to him and having his hand stroke my hair. I had been angry when I heard he took Ladun out to the mall, and more than upset when Yinka 'with a C' had come over for Christmas to visit. They had spent all hours of the evening seated on the grassy lawn of my grandfather's compound, talking for what had seemed like an eternity. I had fumed to Aramide that he was being an idiot, but it hadn't been the only reason why.

I had been jealous, only I had not known it at the time.

We stare at each other, and I am shocked at my thoughts to the point of embarrassment. I like Cousin Toba a lot, and I have feelings for him.

When he had shown me that ring before the proposal, I had felt it, that stab of jealousy that surges through your mind when the guy you like loves someone else. That sad hole that swallows you and tells you you weren't good enough. I had thought it was just sadness at being left behind, but I realise now that it was much more. I had been jealous of the woman I had thought he was going to give that ring to, even though I didn't know who she was. I had for a split second wanted him to offer it to me, but I had not been prepared for what it would mean if he had.

"You know what, this is ridiculous." I turn away from him and figure out that I can still get out of the house through the foot gate. I don't want him to see the truth or learn the truth.

Toba doesn't try to stop me. I get in the cab, the driver takes off, and I realize that I'm shaking. I close my eyes and cover my face with my hands to try to calm myself down. All I can see is Toba getting down on one knee and offering me my grandfather's ring, the one with his mother's life story behind it.

A body at rest usually stays at rest, until an outside force acts on it. I had gotten back to my place of rest after Esosa, but Toba had come and stirred the waters.

Chapter Seventeen

When your life winds down a path you least expect, you begin to see things from a different perspective. You go through each minute leading up to it with a fine-tooth comb, and you catalogue where you went wrong and what you missed. Like the little flashes of warnings that you ignored, and little instances when the truth was staring you in the face and you didn't even recognize it.

You notice the things you were supposed to have taken note of, and you see your life with new eyes. You see things clearly. You see everything backwards.

"I only let the girls I like sit on my lap."

I don't know why those words come, but they sneak into my heart like quiet little mice scurrying through the dark corners of a house. I had spoken those words to Toba, and he had spoken them back to me on a rickety old jeep in his friend's farm in Shagamu. I haven't thought about those words since he'd uttered them, but they crowd my heart now as I sift through memories, and bring with them the same feelings I had the first time I heard them: endearment.

It was not just the words, but the way he had said them. Leaning close and whispering into my ear, smashing a hole in the niece and uncle relationship we had built over the years.

"Is there something wrong with me?" I had asked him.

"Of course not," he had replied. *"You're perfect."*

I feel his gentle hands pry the hair away from my face and slide down my hair, and I feel the care in them for the first time. I had been tipsy, but I remember.

As I sit in the back of the cab, a weird calmness settles inside me, an understanding. It's the kind of feeling you have the first time a guy hits on you and you realise you're no longer a little girl but a woman capable of rousing interest in a man. It's a feeling full of fear and exhilaration, of wanting something forbidden. It's a feeling of liking something you shouldn't like and doing something expressly wrong that feels somewhat right.

"Y'all know we can't call him Cousin Toba anymore, right?"

I close my eyes at Pariola's statement and scream inside, because Toba begins to appeal to me in a way that he never has before. I think about being in his arms and realize I hadn't just liked it—I had enjoyed it. I had thought it was the Bourbon stoking a fire in the middle of my chest, but it had been him. I had thought it was the warm night air and the feeling of being buzzed making his huge arms around me feel less like mechanical restraints and more like gentle caresses. I had smuggled into his chest and drowned my sorrows and thought it was just Toba taking care of me.

As we drive towards Lagos, I can't help but think about him and see everything in retrospect. Every conversation, every moment I'd ignored, the way he would sometimes look at me, and the way I would sometimes feel. Words I'd played down because I'd thought he was just joking, and acts that had pointed at something deeper between us.

"What makes you think you are going to be forty and unmarried?" Toba's voice teases into my memory. *"We could just get married, and save everyone the hullabaloo."*

The words register stronger than ever, and I laugh at the fact that I had not taken them seriously.

"You are a beautiful girl. The right person will show up when you least expect it."

You idiot! I lower my face into my hands again and struggle with the descending chaos of emotions—thirty-five and dumdum according to Aramide.

Toba had always been subtle with his attentions; I just hadn't picked up on them. The night that Grandpa had sat with him talking, he had looked at me and seemed to lose track of whatever Grandpa had been saying to him.

I see that moment now with different eyes. I see the restrained longing in his dark irises and sudden quietness. I remember his hand on my back at the music recital, and even under the umbrella at the farm, and I feel it again. It's warm and endearing, a hint at his desire for more intimacy than I was ready for. I even understand his refusal to be mad after I threw the plate of food at him and called him emotionless. He just couldn't be angry; I was the object of his affection. His silence in the truck on the way back from the farm had probably been a ploy to hide deeper feelings. I had laughed at his indirect attempt at a proposal, and it had hurt.

It's late when we get to Lagos. I veer straight to Aramide's place. I'm not sure I'm ready to face my parents and answer their confused questions. I'm not quite sure of anything, to be honest. I don't know what everyone in the family will think of Toba's proposal, worse now that I know how I actually feel about him.

There is some form of shame or fear that I can't understand when I knock on Aramide's door. She opens it and pulls me into her arms with a chuckle.

"You've heard?" I whisper.

"Pariola called me. Then Olamide called me. Then I saw the video."

"There is a video?" I ask, alarmed. "Oh my god!" Someone had had the bad sense to put their phone camera on record and capture my humiliation.

She pulls back and stares into my face. "Are you okay?"

I shake my head. "I'm not."

"Come on, come inside."

She settles me into the love seat in their anteroom and makes me a hot cup of tea. I really don't want to talk about Toba, but he's all I can think about and talk about when she comes to sit beside me.

"In front of everyone, Aramide, it was so humiliating. He didn't even give me a heads up." I stare at her. "Okay, I'm lying. He did act a little strange just before. He showed me the ring first. And there had been that moment when he looked like he wanted to propose in the privacy of Grandpa's smaller sitting room. Oh my Lawwd, why didn't he just do that?"

Aramide smiles like she knows some little secret that I don't.

"I don't even know what I'm going to do."

"About the proposal?" she asks with a naughty look.

"What! Of course I'm not going to say yes to him! I'm talking about what everyone probably thinks of us now. That we've been—" I grimace. "We've been, you know."

"Having sex?"

I look at my sister, and I can't even say it. I can't even imagine Toba and me in bed together.

"We have been spending time together, yes, but not like everyone thinks we have now."

"What we need to be doing right now is damage control, talking about how to handle Mummy and every other elder in the family. 'Cause by now, they've probably heard."

I groan and put my face in my hands.

"Why did he put me in this kind of situation?" I look up at my sister and hold out my hands. "But you know that I was not sneaking around with Toba, right? You know I would never do that."

"I know. He did it so you won't refuse him in private and let the matter die down."

"I don't understand."

"In the privacy of that parlour, you would have said no, repulsed by what you would think the family will say about it. Now that it's out in the open, you can think about it and decide what you want to do. I've long suspected that he liked you more than the rest of us."

"Oh pleaaase Aramide, that is so not true."

"It is. He is always cornering you in one place or the other at family events."

I exhale and look away from her. "I didn't come here so you could make things worse."

"I just want you to consider this proposal for a moment." She holds out her hands and stares up at the ceiling. "It seems genuine, and he's not blood-related."

"It was out of the blue!"

"Perhaps, but maybe it's been in his heart for a while."

"He is Mummy's brother Aramide, blood or no blood. I can't do it!" I snap at her.

Aramide lowers her head and turns her mouth to one side. "But you want to."

I look up in horror. "Want to? No, I don't want to!"

"Yes, you do."

I shake my head. "No. Don't put things in my head."

"I'm not putting anything in your head that has not always been there. You like Toba. There's nothing bad about that."

"I don't know what you're talking about!"

She laughs and settles herself into the couch. "Femi, you have always wanted more from him than you have from him."

I look at her with a little bit of confusion.

"That day that you caught your exes in bed together, you were not in the least bit upset with Esosa. You were raving mad at Toba."

"Yes, because he brought that skinny little destroyer into our lives."

"No," Aramide says. "Because he had so much potential, and he wasn't using it. You had a lot to say to him, and it was not about her, nor about finding your exes."

I raise my shoulders in the beginnings of a shrug, but nothing comes out of my mouth.

"Because you want him to be so much more than he is," Aramide continues. "Because you think he can do so much better than the kind of girls he dates."

"Oh my goodness, Ara, it's because he's our cousin," I say, pointing a finger at her. "Uncle—" I close my eyes and open them as I recall Toba's view about not really being my uncle. "Don't you care about him?"

Aramide straightens her back. "Well, not so much that I will yell at him out of nowhere, and then go with him somewhere for hours on end!"

My brows drop into a frown. I did lose it that day for no good reason. Then I'd just jumped into his truck and followed him to the farm. And I hadn't thought about Esosa for one single moment while I was with him.

His smile, the one he'd had when we found them both together, had infuriated the worst out of me. I think now that he'd been happy Esosa kicked himself out of my life. Esosa couldn't have done him a greater favour.

"When Diran hangs out with Toba and comes home late, I don't single Toba out and yell at him, my business is with my husband. I face my husband. But the emotion in your voice that day, Femi, your fury! It had nothing to do with Esosa cheating on you."

"So it has something to do with wanting Toba to ask me to marry him?"

"Maybe you are in love with him."

"I'm not in love with him!" I declare, and my face flames up at the idea of his arm around my waist and his voice in my ear.

My sister touches my shoulder. "Look, love is so much more than what a person looks like, or how he or she makes you feel. It's in the little things we do for one another without even realising it. Toba stood up against Akpan, when we all were too scared to do it. He hasn't done that for any other niece that he has."

"He's done that for Jumoke," I reply lamely.

"Jumoke is thirteen, you are thirty-five, and you have liver enough to tell a guy to back off if you don't want him around. You don't need a big brother to do it for you. And believe me, Toba knows, with first-hand experience, that you can do it yourself." She shrugs. "So why did he do it?"

I stare at Aramide and recall the quiet nod Toba had given Esosa when they had first met. It hadn't been anything inimical, but it had been full of cautionary contemplation. I hadn't given it a second thought. I had been too busy watching Esosa stare at Yinka to think that the tough grip Toba had given Esosa had meant anything.

"When Mummy and her brothers call you for the meeting that I know will happen, you should do more to remind them that Toba is not their brother, because he is not. Then when the dust settles, you two should go somewhere quiet and figure out this thing that has sprung up between you. I think it's lovely, I think it's sweet that it's Toba and I think it's romantic that he would propose in front of friends and family." Aramide's smile is reserved. "I think you should say yes."

My eyes pop open. "You think I should … are you insane?"

Aramide makes her mischievous face look and shrugs a shoulder.

"I thought you were on my side. Why would you be talking this way?"

"I'm on your side, and you should listen to me." She grabs my hands. "Toba is everything a girl could ever want in a man. He is tall, dark, handsome, brilliant, and has the character to match. We know him, we trust him, and we can vouch for whatever he says. He is one person I know would be perfect for you. I can't believe I didn't see it all this while."

I am looking at my sister with fear. "He doesn't stay long with any woman."

"Because you are the one he wants to be with!"

I look away from her and stare at the door for a long time. "Ara, what would Mummy say?"

"So that's what's been holding you back?"
***

I am quiet at the start of the meeting. My father's face is stern, and Uncle Sesan is doing his best to hold things together.

"You see what they are doing here, don't you?" Uncle Gbenga begins, angry. "He gets the farm, she gets land, and more money than any other grandchild. They get married—"

"And you have a whole duplex to yourself," Uncle Sesan snaps, "and stocks. Let it be enough."

Uncle Gbenga gets up, eyes me, and walks out of the room. I am relieved. I don't even want to meet anyone's eye. I don't know why Grandpa gave me a double portion inheritance. Nor why Toba chose to open his mouth and ask me to marry him.

"Now, Toba, I want to understand why you would ask Nifemi to marry you without permission. You should have talked to us first."

Toba is seated in his favourite position, slumped in his chair and indifferent to the whole inquisition.

"I wasn't aware that I needed permission to ask a girl to marry me," he says in his usual lazy drawl.

"This is not just any girl," Uncle Sesan interrupts. "This is your niece, regardless of what troubles my father caused by revealing your parentage. She is your sister's daughter!"

"With all due respect, sir, I have known for years—" he stresses the word 'years', "—that Femi was not blood-related, and I didn't take advantage of it."

"So what changed?" Uncle Sesan wants to know. "Is it the will?"

"Yes," he replies. "But I also believe she wasn't ready to hear what I had to say."

I look up and see Toba staring at me from across the table.

"She has always been everything I wanted, and she still is. I love her, and I'm not sure that I should hold back those feelings any longer."

There is an uncomfortable silence around the table, but it's strange how those words warm my heart. I have never had a guy say that to me. That I'm everything he wants.

I hold his gaze for as long as I can stand it. It's warm, and tender, and filled with things I can't even imagine could come from a cousin. And I was brazenly clinging to him at the hotel, burrowing myself into his arms in the privacy of a lonely room at night. What had he been thinking? What had he been feeling? I was drunk. He could have done whatever he wanted to do to me and be done with it and no one would know. But he had shown incredible restraint. Put me to bed and left me to sleep.

I am alarmed at myself. I want to bury my head in my hands in shame, but I'm transported back in time to an incident that occurs when I'm thirteen and he is sixteen. We were standing in the corridor, waiting for my mum to say it was time to go to church. The other children were running around and one of them knocked into me from behind. I fell forwards and smashed against Toba. He put his hands out to try and halt the fall, but tripped backwards over Enitan's tricycle. We both went crashing to the ground, and I landed right on top of him.

For a brief moment, I'd been too stunned and dazed to get up. He was lying flat on his back, holding onto my waist.

"I'm sorry," we both said at the same time, and I scrambled up as fast as I could but not before my cheek brushed his and my nose grazed his mouth.

I felt a tingle that day as I smoothed down my dress but masked my confusion by looking around for the offending culprit. He picked up the fallen tricycle, and we pretended like nothing had happened. After all, we were family, and he was like a brother. It was a moment, awkward, embarrassing, and hastily thrown into the dark recess of my mind where forgotten memories are buried. We were teenagers, on the cusps of understanding the changes that come with growing up. It hadn't meant anything.

This memory has never come to mind in years. I don't know why it's coming up now, or why I'm thinking about it. I don't even know if he remembers it, or if that's the moment when it all began. Twenty years goes back to when I was fifteen, not thirteen, and Toba has been nothing more than family.

"How long has this been going on?" My mother wants to know. She is seated on Toba's left-hand side, opposite me.

Yeah, I want to know, too.

"I asked her to marry me three days ago." Toba stares down at the table. "And she hasn't given me an answer."

"Have you two been ... active?" she looks from Toba to me.

I give my mum a look that questions her right to ask that question—what type of daughter does she think she has raised?

"No," Toba replies.

"What about those girls you've been dating?" my mother asks, and I imagine her wondering what must have happened the day she begged Toba to take me out and about town. Serves her right! I feel like sticking my tongue out at her.

"What about them?" Toba asks with the raise of an eyebrow. "I'm not with any one of them now."

"And Yinca?" my mum asks.

"Was never my girlfriend."

"It's morally wrong!" Uncle Sesan insists. "You are family."

Toba doesn't respond to that.

"It's not really incest," Uncle Deola says, looking around at the other members of the inquisition which thankfully does not contain Uncle Gbenga any longer. "Is it? I mean, they are not really related, are they?"

I see him still struggling to understand what happened to Esosa.

"Technically, they are not," my father says. "They don't share the same blood, or come from the same village, apparently. But it's not ideal. They were raised as siblings. I mean, what would people say?"

"I don't care what people say," Toba's voice thunders.

"You should. You're my wife's brother. What would the invitation card read?"

"The families of Awotunde and Ajayi." Toba stares at him, then sits up and leans onto the table with his forearms.

"I've had years to think about this, sir, and I don't see anything wrong with it, for the following reasons." He starts ticking things off his fingers. "We don't have the same surname; or the same biological father; or the same mother; or a genetic connection between us in any way. We spent time together as children, yes, but for the past twenty years, I've practically been in and out of the country. More out than in, so we've had vastly different experiences in life. I could have slept with her if I wanted to and she wanted to, but I didn't, because I respect my step-sister and this family. This is not a joke to me, and I did not want to jeopardize any good will I have in the Awotunde family by treating Femi as a play thing. We didn't come here with a pregnancy we are trying to hide, so I don't care what anybody thinks. I love your daughter and I want to marry her."

He takes his elbows off the table and sinks back into his chair.

"So Nifemi," he looks at me, "I'll need an answer from you."

I can't resist looking at him and having feelings I am not supposed to be having. Feelings I admit had begun to creep up on me the more time I spent with him.

"We don't even know who your father is."

My father is not giving up, but Toba has an answer.

"I do."

Aunty Ladepe shifts in her seat and looks at him.

"You—you do?" she says.

Toba is not looking at anyone. This seems difficult for him.

"He's in an old people's home in Lagos, alive, but blind. I visit him once or twice a year with foodstuff. He doesn't know that I am his son. I don't think he needs to, because we are strangers and there is nothing that ties us together aside DNA. Pa Awotunde raised me and cared about every single aspect of my life. He taught me to be the person that I am today, and he knew about Nifemi and I. He said it was okay."

Aunty Ladepe bursts out crying, and my father puts an arm around her.

"He needed the truth to come out, so that I could be free to marry her, because he knows how much I love her." Toba looks up at me, "and for how long."

I stare at him with my mouth open, and then get out of my seat.

"Excuse me, please," I say and walk out of the room without looking at anybody.

I find my way to the balcony and stay there with my face in both of my hands. It's clear to me now that my grandfather wanted me to marry Toba. He had no reason to reveal the fact that he wasn't Toba's father. He could have taken that secret to his grave, but he didn't. Revealing it had meant shaming Aunty Ladepe. It also however meant that Toba was free to marry me with no inhibitions. Giving him the farm meant giving it to me, because it would be ours. Giving me the land meant giving us a place of our own to live in.

"Nifemi."

I hear Toba behind me. I take my face out of my hands and fold my arms together across my chest.

"How long?" I ask without turning back. "For how long had Grandpa known?"

"Years."

I hear the shrug in his voice.

"Years." I can't believe what I'm hearing. "Why me?"

"Why not?" he says softly. "You were the first person in the family who was kind to me. You didn't just tolerate me like everyone else aside from my parents. You accepted me. When my mother brought me over to live with your family, you took my hand and led me over to your backyard to introduce me to your sisters. We played with sand. I was ten, well past the age of playing with sand, but I enjoyed it. It was the best moment in the ten short years of my life. The best feeling I've ever had."

I remembered that day. Hushed voices in the parlour, arguments, crying, and Aunty Ladepe had to leave without her son. I recall he was very scared. I was peeping out from behind the long sofa and beckoning to him with a grin that was missing two front teeth, glad to have a new play partner. We played longer than usual in the backyard, and when my mum came out to get us, Toba's mother was gone.

I recall Toba had cried that night and I had sat beside him telling him not to worry because everything was going to be all right. My mum was a great cook, and we would get to play with sand any time that we wanted to.

"It started with just being happy being around you, and looking forward to coming to Lagos. Then it morphed into liking you, and then into thinking about you constantly. You're beautiful, Femi, strong, different. You're not like other women, and I enjoy being with you."

"You didn't give any indication."

"I have now."

I turn around to look at him. He is standing on the balcony, one hand on the railing. I know my father won't accept him, and that Uncle Sesan will tell me that I have to reject his proposal. I know that Uncle Gbenga will protest if he hears that I said yes, and I know that my mother does not really like the whole idea.

"I'm sorry, Toba," I say to him. "But I can't accept your proposal."

There is no sign of the brief regret I saw that day when he was kneeling down in front of me. He is unemotional, like he knew it would end this way. He nods once and looks away from me. "I understand."

I am crushed. Aramide is right. I want more from him. I want Toba to fight. I don't want him to resign to his fate. I want him to walk up to me, pull me into his arms, and beg me to marry him. I want to be sure it's what he really wants because in that moment, I realize that he is what I want.

"I'm sorry I caused you this much embarrassment."

Fight for me, I want to scream. *Tell me not to do this. Tell me again in this private moment, where it's just you and me, that I am the one that you want. Tell me to think about it. Tell me not to give you an answer now. Tell me anything. Don't just give up, Toba, please.*

But I don't say anything, and he doesn't say anything, and I watch him walk away.

Chapter Eighteen

Falling in love is a beautiful thing. It makes one smile, it makes one euphoric, and it makes one vulnerable. It connotes the idea that one is engaging in uncontrollable and risky behaviour. I do not really know how the phrase came about, but we all know what it's come to mean.

When you can't go a minute without thinking about a person, or when your heart stops beating and your breathing ceases on sighting the person, you are falling in love. You want to be with that person all the time and hear their voice and have conversations with them all the time. You don't mind shelving engagements or rearranging schedules or ditching important things in order to be with that person. You would do anything they asked of you without thoughts of how or why, and you would most often be unable to sleep, until you've heard the person tell you they love you, too.

Falling in love is exciting. It leaves butterflies in your stomach and scales over your eyes because you don't see anything wrong with the object of your affection and whatever they say or do. Staying in love, however, requires so much more than all these, and that's the hard part. It's the place where people stumble.

Real love is like a planted seed. It needs time to grow, and develop, and mature, so it can be rich, and full, and fulfilling. You can't take shortcuts with it, and you can't pretend about it. A plant, or a blade of grass, or a flower, cannot last for a long time, but a whole tree—imagine a whole tree with deep roots and green leaves and thick branches. It's robust and durable; it can give shade and protection; and we can eat fruits off of it.

That's how love should be, deep, strong, and functional.

It shouldn't be quick, or wanton. It should be allowed to ferment and mature, like cottage cheese; age, like an old bottle of wine; and grow, like a sturdy old Iroko tree. It should be bottomless and wide and full, like an ocean, able to swallow the little idiosyncrasies that cause clashes between couples. It shouldn't rage, like a wild bush on fire. It should smoulder gently, and imbibe heat, like coal on a hearth.

Esosa and I demanded fruit from a seed that had just begun to sprout. And when we didn't find it, we went searching elsewhere and killed it before it even began. Our shrub didn't have roots, so when winds came, it got swept away in an uncontrollable mayhem of desire and Esosa fell and I couldn't forgive or let go.

I do not know if I started to fall in love with Toba a long time ago like Aramide said, or if I started to fall in love with him the moment he asked me to marry him. His love for me has had over twenty years to deepen and evolve and transform. It has roots so deeply entwined in his heart that they kept him steady, even when he met other girls. I guess because the pressure and excitement of eros love wasn't there for him, or because he had passed that stage the sentiments withered and he had time to think and want and decide that I was the one for him.

On my own part, I have grown to admire and respect him beyond his physical attributes. I have gotten to know his faults and inadequacies, and gotten to like him in spite of them. I've spent time remembering every detail of every moment with him, and my guards are all down. It's been exhausting trying not to like him beyond normal, and I think I have fallen for him, and I might have made a huge mistake.

I sit at work all day, every day, and dream about him. I can't seem to type more than two words on my laptop or read beyond a line in any of the myriads of manuscripts on my desk without remembering something he did, or a conversation we had, or the sound of his voice, and the feel of his arms around me. I am thinking about him a lot. A whole lot more than I have ever done, and he hasn't called me in days. I glance at my phone often, expecting it to ring. I miss his voice, I miss our talks, but I can't bring myself to call him. I recall the ease that comes from being with him, and this desire overwhelms me, the desire to see him and hold him. We don't often appreciate what we have until we lose it.

Marriage might be a huge deal, but Toba means a lot to me.

I stand up from my chair, and Lilian gives me a funny look. She has been watching me be distracted all week, ever since our conversation about Toba being adopted and Toba not being my uncle, and Toba asking me to marry him.

"Where are you going?" She's surprised that I'm packing up at nine in the morning.

"Ibadan," I say as I grab my handbag and throw things in it.

I'm taking a taxi that my mother will throw a fit about. All I know is that I would like to see Toba, the sooner, the better.

"To see your uncle boyfriend abi," Lilian teases. She has not forgiven me for being Toba's choice.

"Lilian, honestly, I had no idea how he felt about me. I would not have encouraged you towards him if I had known."

I think about clinging to him in that hotel bedroom and realize that I would not have done a whole lot of things if I had known.

"I know," she sings. "You would have been all over my ears about how wrong you think the whole idea of you and he is. I know you."

"The thing is, I like him." I hang my bag over my shoulder and stare at her, "a whole lot."

"Go!" She waves a hand in my direction. "Say hi to him for me."

I smile and toss her a kiss as I leave. "I'll be back. Cover for me."

It takes me an hour to get to Ibadan, and another by public transport to get to the gate of the farm. I'm excited and worried. My heart is beating really fast, and even the taxi-driver's grumble that the distance and the fare I gave don't match doesn't rattle me.

I don't know what Toba will say, but I've been distracted and unproductive at work, and I have missed him. I'm willing to give the crazy idea of us a shot.

I walk down the hilly farm and ask the first farmhand I see where I can find Lasisi. After a ten-minute walk to the pig farm, I find him.

"Oga Toba dey for crop area," he says. "Let me take you to him."

We get into this little four-wheel scooter and drive for another ten minutes towards Toba. Each minute that passes changes my excitement to fear. What if it's too late and Toba doesn't love me anymore? What if he's found someone else?

Lasisi hands me a pair of wellington boots. I change into them, and we trudge towards this huge field where Toba is, hard at work in a pair of thick gloves. He is shovelling some mud and making ridges. I stand at the edge of the field and stare at him. He is tall and good-looking; strong and hardworking; kind, caring, and compassionate. He makes me laugh, and he can hold my interest in a conversation. He is honest, he gives good advice, I can trust him, and he loves me for my liver and all of who I am.

Most of all, he cares about me, in a way I've never had any guy care. He had the perfect opportunity to take advantage of me in the hotel room, and he didn't.

"Madam you fit enter field," Lasisi urges me.

I walk in and make my way towards him. When he notices me, he slows to a stop, surprised. He sticks the shovel into the ground, wipes the sweat off his forehead, and pauses to catch his breath. Then he leans an elbow on the handle of the shovel and watches me walk over.

"Hi," I say, stopping about a foot from him. "What are you doing?"

He looks around the field warily. "Creating an irrigation system. We found a way to run water from a river outside the farm area to this portion where we need it, and I don't have too many hands. So I have to pick up the shovel and dig up some dirt."

I nod and search his eyes. I am suddenly shy and tongue-tied. I am never shy and tongue-tied with Toba, but today, not a single word comes to mind.

"How are you doing?" he asks and pulls the shovel out of the mud.

"I'm good."

He turns his back to me and starts shovelling again.

"I came to say hi," I say.

He pushes the shovel into the ground with his foot. "You said it."

I am somewhat hurt by his lack of attention, and all my excitement fizzles away.

"I came here to talk to you."

"About?" He throws the dirt to the side and digs the shovel into the ground again.

"You and I," I look down at my feet. "I'm sorry I rejected your proposal, and I want you to know the reason why."

He sighs. "There is nothing left to say, Femi. I don't think it will make any difference."

"Maybe it will—" I say to him, "—if I understood how it all started."

He glances at me and shrugs. "What's to say I'm still in love with you?"

I'm quiet. I don't even know what to say to that. If he's lost his love for me, I have to help him find it again.

He turns away from me and starts digging again.

"Love like that," I say, watching him. "It doesn't just die."

"We all have to face reality at some point in time, Femi. I have."

"Fight for me," I say softly. "Don't give up. Tell me why you love me. That day was my first time hearing it, and I was caught off-guard, and scared."

Toba keeps digging. He doesn't say anything.

"Look, of all the girls you dated, I think you really liked Bimpe, and she loved you, but the two of you just let it die. You didn't fight for her, Toba. That's why you lost her."

I wouldn't be here if he had fought to keep her. He would have pushed his love for me to the outskirts of his mind, grown out of it and settled down with her.

"She said all those things and told you she was leaving, and you just stood by and let her leave. I'm sure she didn't really want to leave."

He stops digging and looks at me.

"This is not just about giving me a ring and expecting me to accept it. We are going to have to fight for this relationship to even exist. There is going to be a lot of opposition from my dad, and your siblings. I need to know that you can handle it. That you will not give up when it gets tough, or sit back and let it all die if everyone rises up against it. I know that you can care about things and be stubborn and determined enough to push for what you want and make it work. I know that because just looking at this farm, I—"

I stop talking because Toba is looking at me and I have the courage to stare back and face the truth. I've fallen in love with the idea of him and me together, and I can see it happening.

"This place was stagnant, and dying, and you brought it back to life. You didn't give up, so you can't just let this die."

He exhales, and for a moment, I think he is not even going to try.

"Femi, I've loved you for years."

My heart soars, and I let myself soak in the words.

"I was fifteen when I first realised it, sixteen when Dad found out. We were doing holiday homework one evening, you and I, sitting at that big dining table that used to be in the music room. I was stealing glances at you, but you were so focused, you didn't even notice. The light streaming through the window was making you look like some fairy tale princess in my mind. I don't know, I was just spellbound, watching you do your homework." He shrugs. "I had no idea that he had entered the room. I don't know how long he stood there watching me watch you. He took me outside and slapped the living daylights out of the back of my head before he asked me what I was doing staring at my own niece like that. After that, he made sure I got into UI, and that I stayed in UI."

I can't even remember the day he's talking about. I know we did lots of homework in that music room. Toba gained admission into the University of Ibadan after secondary school and disappeared for six years. Grandpa didn't even let him come to Lagos for the holidays.

"He knew what we all didn't know back then, that you and I weren't blood-related, and that even if we were, we could end up doing stuff we weren't meant to be doing. So I stayed in UI, came home just before NYSC to attend Deola and Norma's wedding. And then, I saw you and—" he trails off and throws the mud on his shovel onto the pile behind him.

I recall that the twins and I had been bridesmaids, and we had whispered about how Cousin Toba had grown tall, gawky, and a little on the heavy side. Most of the family members had picked on him, but he'd been nice enough to be good-natured about it.

"I don't remember much of the wedding. Just that the feelings I thought were gone had come back even stronger, and you had grown up. You were this eloquent, beautiful woman, and I was this bumbling idiot. You came up to say hi to me, and I was speechless. I couldn't speak more than a couple of words to you the entire day. You were giving me so much respect and distance, that I slapped myself on the head by myself and took my eyes off you.

"The night before I went for service while looking for my documents, I came across information that made me curious about who my real dad was. So I confronted him, and he told me the truth. That he wasn't my father, and that we needed to keep it hidden from everyone so that my mum could keep her respect and I wouldn't be called a bastard. Then he warned me severely to stay away from you, because he could see that I hadn't lost it, my desire for you."

I nod.

"I knew that any ideas of you and I were still out of the picture, so I sought other women. Your grandpa thought it was over, I thought it was over, but I couldn't settle down with any of them, didn't really want to. Every time I'd come home, I'd see you and we'd talk." He shook his head. "And I'd wonder what I was doing with the girl I was with. I'd give Pa Awotunde advice, and connections, and implement strategies he could use on the farm to make the work easier, and the farm began to improve again. He saw how much I loved it, and decided that the farm needed someone who could tend it, and care for it like he would."

He dug the shovel back into the ground with force and let it stay there. "He saw how much I loved you, and he decided the truth had to come out. That's what he was telling me the night of my mum's birthday party, that he was giving me the farm. That's what we were discussing when you came over. I think he realised that it was futile, and that I couldn't stop loving you."

We stare at each other. He's finished his story, and I am awed that he has loved me for this long.

"In all honesty," he continues. "I didn't think you would say yes, but if I hadn't done it that day, I never would have. I needed to know once and for all if I needed to move on."

Move on? I'm thinking, wide-eyed. "Don't! I don't want you to move on."

He stares at me, and a frown lowers to his forehead.

"I can't stop thinking about you, and I'm worried that I might have made a mistake." I'm avoiding his eyes, but he is still looking at me. "Ever since you asked me to marry you, I haven't been able to stop thinking about you and—"

He takes in a deep breath and then he lets it out.

"I ran, because I was afraid, but I haven't been able to—"

"Stop thinking about me," he finishes as he looks down at his hands and begins to slide the mud-stained gloves off his fingers one after the other. "I heard that. Now what does it mean?"

I shake my head and stare straight at his chest. "I don't know. I want to explore this."

"Explore?" He looks at the gloves in his hands and looks back at me.

"This, us, my feelings, and see where it goes because I like you." I look down at my feet. "More than I care to admit."

My heart is pummelling within my chest at this point in time, and I am beyond terrified. I don't know if he is going to order me to leave or tell me that my rejection of him killed his feelings for me.

Toba takes three steps forward. When he is within inches of me, he lifts my chin up with his thumb and index finger.

"Hey," he booms gently at me. "You broke my heart there for a bit, but I have never stopped thinking about you, and I don't feel any shame about admitting it."

I gaze into his eyes, and he stares down at me with an expression I can read. He wants me, and it's embarrassing to realize that I feel the same way, and that he can tell.

I take my chin out of his hand and stare down at the ground. The gloves drop onto the muddy farm terrain and he puts his hands on my waist and pulls me close. I'm shy, weak in the knees, and battling the strange sweet sensation traversing my form as one of his hands slides from my waist to the middle of my back to pull my chest against his strong, taut, frame.

Suddenly, it's tough to hug him, because it means a lot more now.

"I think the best thing your mum ever did for me was to call me to come get you."

I place my hands on his upper arms and allow my fingers trace them without remorse. "I bet she's regretting it."

He chuckles. "I bet she is. I'm glad it's out, though. I can look at you and not feel guilty."

The strange thing is that I feel safe, like I am right where I'm supposed to be, with someone I trust will do right by me. With Esosa and the others, I was excited about the idea of being in a relationship that people can admire and commend. With Toba, I was already in one; I just didn't know it. There is no pressure to be anything other than who I am.

"I love you," he whispers. "I have always loved you."

He loves me. It's a weird thought, comforting, serene, and entirely sweet.

He's said it so many times now, the words feel like a part of me, but I can't think of a single thing to say to him. So I place my head against his wide chest and revel in the fact that he's mine. He smells of sweat, dirt, and farm animals, the small of hard work. They're not very pleasant smells, but very practical ones.

"The billions of times that I wanted to tell you," he murmurs and lowers his chin onto my head. His arms are wrapped around me, one palm flat between my shoulder blades, solid, strong, and warm all at once, the other holding my waist to his form.

"Why didn't you?"

"I didn't know how you were going to take it, and I didn't want to say it and lose you. I'm so glad you now know how I feel about you."

I pull away from him and look into his eyes. There is affection in them, as well as his trademark look of calm amusement. I want to spend the rest of my life gazing into those eyes and having them stare back at me. Ed Sheeran was right. People truly do fall in love in mysterious ways, and for Toba and me, it's most mysterious.

"What's wrong?"

His deep drawl does things to me that I cannot describe. It always has. I hear his voice, and I'm happy inside. I hear it now and I'm attracted to him, especially with the heat from his hands on my back through the cotton of my dress.

"This feels weird," I whisper. "You're family. I can't get it out of my head."

He chuckles.

"Perhaps it wouldn't feel so weird if you would stop thinking of me as your uncle, or your cousin, or your older brother, because I'm none of those things."

He lifts a hand away from my back and pushes the hair falling across my face behind my left ear. "And perhaps I could help, seeing as it might take you a bit of time to cross that hurdle."

I don't say anything. It's obvious he can read all my conflicting emotions just by looking at me, and the thought causes me to blush all the way down inside. I'm grateful and awed that he loves me. I want him to kiss me, and not like an uncle or a cousin.

"How exactly do you plan to help me?" I ask and steal another look at his face. It's strange how I like him more with each passing moment.

He smiles, lowers his hands to my waist, and heaves me up to eye level. I let out a yelp of surprise at this but he covers my lips with his to halt it.

The kiss is unexpected. Surprising, ardent, and very intent on wiping all thoughts of the affectionate, brotherly love I have for Toba away.

It replaces it with something else though, an unhinged desire that swallows me up and removes the rest of my awkward inhibitions about him. I'm in a trance as I wind my arms around his neck and forget everything I've been afraid off. That awkward line disappears from my mind and my mother's thoughts with it. I connect to Toba in a way that rises in graded intensity and my heart soars with it. The feel is inexpressible.

I am light, but full, grounded yet aware that I'm hanging in the air. His strength supports me. There are no tingling feelings, or tremors, or earth shattering sensations, just peace as our lips find understanding. It's him I want, no one else. He's my friend and confidant, my ever dependable rock.

"I love you," he whispers as he lowers me to the ground, and keeps me matted to his form.

I can't stop blushing, or covering my face with my hands because I can't believe what has just happened.

"Marry me," he says. "Let's cause a hullabaloo."

I lower my hands and stare at him. "I think we already have. Toba—"

I'm worried my next words could ruin this all before it even begins.

"Yes?" he says, "darling?"

"I don't know if I'm the mothering type—" I say, but it doesn't even ruffle him. "I don't know if I want to have babies."

It's the oddest thing for an African woman to say to an African man who has just re-proposed to her. Children are an important must-have, a sign that a marriage is blessed. But there, I've said it. I don't want them, I'm not sure if it'll break both our hearts.

Toba stares at me, quietly considering his next choice of words.

I expect him to tell me that I don't know what I'm saying and that I'll change my mind in the future, but he doesn't say any of that.

"We can just adopt one and give to her to raise." He tilts his head at me, "how about that? I love you regardless."

Relieved, I lean into him. I've been holding my breath.

"I may have to go back to Lagos."

He hugs me tighter.

"Stay," he whispers. "Don't leave just yet."

I don't want to.

"I didn't exactly take an excuse to leave work."

"Call them and let them know you can't make it."

"My Chief Editor will tear her hair out. We have a backlog."

"Beg for a casual leave. We'll wake up early tomorrow morning, and I'll take you wherever you want to go."

I lean back so I can look at him.

"You want me to stay the night," I ask, giddy with a calm sort of fear that thrills me, "with you in the farm lodge?"

"Would that be a problem?"

I stare at him as my mind races with all the possibilities of what could be. "Yes. This is quite early, and still really weird."

He tilts his head. "If you say that one more time, I will kiss you again and make it even weirder."

I grin. "This, is weird—"

Toba's mouth finds mine before I can say another word. It's urgent and breath-taking. It's what I want, what I've always wanted.

He turns me around and we walk away from the field with my arm around his waist and his around my shoulders.

"Where are we going?" I ask, looking up at him as we saunter towards the field's fence.

"To the lodge, I'm hoping I can convince you to stay the night!"

I'm quiet. "Toba, you know we can't—"

He chuckles as he looks down at me.

"I'm just kidding! We are going back to the lodge. I'm going to ask you properly if I can put that ring on your finger, then we are going to call your mum, and my mum, and every other elder to tell them it's going to happen whether they like it or not. After that, I'll take you back to Lagos today, if you still want to go."

I grin as he hugs me closer and plants a kiss atop my forehead.

"Not sure my mum has gotten over the idea of you and me. I bet she's banging her head against a wall for inviting you to have breakfast the other day."

He laughs out loud, and I smile up at him. Though we had been looking for love in all kinds of places, Toba and I, we finally found it, right where we were, where we had always been.

Epilogue

When we twirl around the dance floor on our wedding day months later, I am no longer shy or embarrassed. I love him, and I'm happy, and I'm enjoying dancing with him.

My fish-shaped wedding dress has a low-hanging back that my mother had widened her eyes at—because according to her, there is too much skin showing—and my hair is raked to one side, held down with a jewelled comb and descending down the back of my head in cascading waves. I'm wearing minimal makeup and jewellery, which is a lot more than I usually go with; no point turning myself into what I don't look like every day.

Toba has seen me with and without makeup; at my worst weight ever; with my bad hair days and with sweat all over my face. He loves me in spite of them. Everything is exactly how I'd always dreamed it would be, minus the beach.

When the reverend pronounces us husband and wife, he asks Toba to kiss me. I freeze. There is deathly silence, and I can feel every eye in the church on us. Our family, people who have known us as uncle and niece for years, are here. I can imagine they are still thinking that this isn't exactly right.

Toba has a smile on his face. Amusement! He finds this moment quite funny. We have talked about this, and we have agreed on what we are going to do. I am hoping, though, that my new husband doesn't decide to surprise me. He has a habit of doing the unexpected.

He reaches out an arm to bring me close, and I close my eyes as he places a long, gentle kiss on my forehead. The guests at the church grow wild with disagreement, and I can hear the protest going on around us amidst the clapping. They want the real deal, and we are not giving it to them. I feel Toba's smile on my forehead before he pulls back and looks down at me. Our intimacy is none of anyone's business. We want to spare the family—especially the elders—the *'horror'* of watching us be intimate.

It's a united group of family and friends that witness our marriage. The crowd at the reception includes Yinca, and Bimpe with her husband and three children. Turns out she had another baby that year and is super happy for us. Aramide found Adenrele, and he came, still single. Because it's the same family we both belong to, they all wear the same sky-blue lace and red *Aso Oke*. The sky-blue signifying the sky being the limit concerning hopes, and dreams, and aspirations; the red signifying love.

I don't have any train, just Aiden and his spit bubbles as ring bearer, and the twins as page boy and little bride. Lilian is my lady-in-waiting, and my friends all picked a matching turquoise blue to wear. Like I wanted, there's simplicity in everything.

My mother, and Toba's mother have tears in their eyes for different reasons, Mummy because her first baby is finally getting married, and Aunty Ladepe because she can't believe Toba is finally settling down.

My father is happy. I'm not marrying a doctor, but he can hold Toba to a standard. Uncle Gbenga can't say anything anymore because nobody cares to listen to him. Also, the lawyer came for the wedding and played us a video at the start of the reception. It's Grandpa, addressing Toba as my husband and blessing our wedding with his approval. Toba and I are not surprised, but most of the family members are. The lawyer tells me later that Grandpa had made two videos. One to Toba as the groom on my wedding day, and another to the random stranger I might have married, in case I hadn't said yes to him. Or in case Toba hadn't gathered the courage to ask.

In it, he says he is happy that the family didn't turn us down. He tells me to take care of Toba and give him that affection that he knows I have been saving up because he is no longer around to receive it.

Then he tells us to have lots of babies—Yikes! I look at Toba. He raises his eyebrows at me. I know it means we will cross that bridge when we get there.

At the end, Toba whirls me around the dance floor in circles until I roll into his arms. He is the perfect gentleman, and I feel like a princess in a fairy tale. He does not take his eyes off me as we take our first dance as a couple in public, and I don't see anyone except him. We have danced to this song a thousand times in the privacy of the farm lodge, so our movements come off as synchronized and well-executed. The youngsters scream and clap with delight when it ends—and my family can scream. They shout for an encore.

When we both can't dance anymore, we hold each other. We are too emotional. The song reminds us of my grandfather, his father. It is *'Thinking out loud,'* the last song he ever danced to before he passed away. It's spilling our thoughts out loud to the whole world. We plan to love each other 'til we are seventy and more, and over.

As usual, the family all find ways to join in the dance, and we don't mind. It's a huge celebration for me because, eventually, love happened.

I am thirty-six years and a couple months old when I marry my husband, Toba. And on the morning of the day after our wedding, I have a new epiphany.

I think I might be forced to like babies, because I realise I want Toba's baby.

And when I do, I know that love will happen.

Eventually.

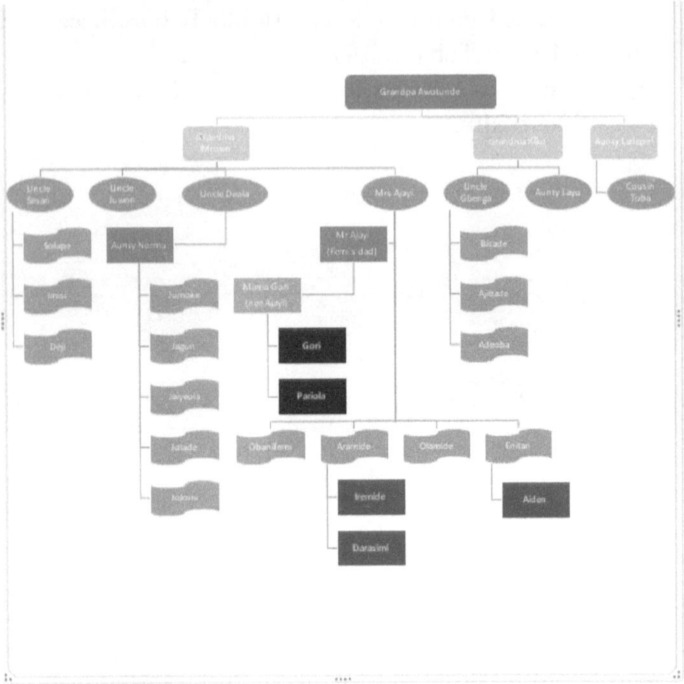

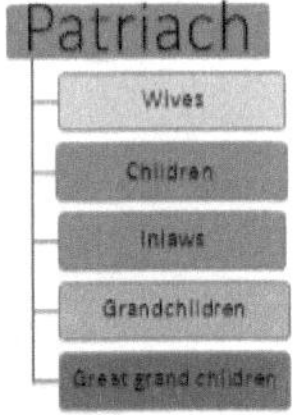

Grandpa Awotunde
Grandma Mosun
Grandma Kike
Aunty Latigan
Uncle Smart
Uncle Juwon
Uncle Deola
Mrs Ajayi
Uncle Gbenga
Aunty Layo
Cousin Toba
Solape
Aunty Neema
Mr Ajayi (Femi's dad)
Bisade
Ayitade
Adeoba
Imisi
Morris Gori (Uncle Ajayi)
Deji
Funmike
Jagun
Jayeola
Juliade
Jolomi
Gori
Pariola
Obanifemi
Aramide
Olamide
Enitan
Iremide
Darasimi
Aiden
Patriach
Wives
Children
Inlaws
Grandchildren
Great grand children

From the author:

Thank you for reading Love Happens Eventually. Please leave a review on the site of purchase.

Olufunmilola Adeniran writes as Feyi Aina and is the self-published author of Saving Onome and Love's Indenture.

She is the winner of the RWOWA Author of the year Award 2019 and enjoys reading historical novels, cooking and travelling. Most of her poems, short stories and novels can be found on Naijastories, Okadabooks, TCLibrary, and Smashwords. She lives in Lagos with her family.

CONNECT WITH FEYI
Blog: www.dfunpen.wordpress.com
Facebook: https://www.facebook.com/dfunpen
Twitter: https://twitter.com/funminiran
Instagram: https://www.instagram.com/feyi_aina/

OTHER BOOKS BY LOVE AFRICA PRESS

A Place Called Happiness by Diana Anyango
One More Night by Rosemary Okafor
Scars, Secrets and Scores: The Ben & Selina Trilogy by Kiru Taye
Fine Scotch by Emem Bassey

CONNECT WITH US
Facebook.com/LoveAfricaPress
Twitter.com/LoveAfricaPress
Instagram.com/LoveAfricaPress

SIGN UP TO OUR NEWSLETTER
https://www.loveafricapress.com/newsletter